THE GUARDIANS OF
ROCK HILL

BRET ALLEN

Copyright © 2025 by Bret Allen

ISBN: 978-1-966343-16-5 hard cover
       978-1-966343-17-2 soft cover

Allen. Bret
The Guardians of Rock Hill.

Edited by: Erika Nein

Published by Warren Publishing
Charlotte, NC
www.warrenpublishing.net
Printed in the United States

To Jade, Emily, and Michael

CHAPTER 1

ABIGAIL

The New York Diner wasn't in New York but in York County, South Carolina. It was supposed to be a play on words, the *New* York Diner. At first, Abigail worried the name wouldn't be well received in Rock Hill—after all, it was the Deep South. She imagined the locals asking, "What do New Yorkers know about grits?" Perhaps a good point, but Abbey was traveled enough to know that New Yorkers loved a good diner. In fact, one of her favorite restaurants was a diner just outside of Tarrytown. From 5 a.m. till midnight, you could order anything from Belgian waffles with fresh-made syrup to rack of lamb with mint jelly—and everything was good. Better than good. It would leave your tastebuds begging for more. It would make a food memory, a flavorful experience that lingered forever and compelled you to go back for another taste.

Well, it didn't matter that Abbey's diner wasn't in New York; her grits were exceptional—creamy and just sweet enough, but not overly so—and the New York Diner quickly became the premier go-to breakfast spot in Rock Hill.

Brunch every weekend saw every table filled straight through 2 p.m. Abbey was elated by the diner's success but driven to introduce Rock Hill to her dinner menu. She was currently working up a new dinner recipe: grain-fed lamb shanks with a port wine reduction fused with her fabulous grits. She could practically taste the lamb as she drove into town that morning.

Just past the piano shop on Dave Lyle Boulevard, the sun's rays reflected in her eyes and danced from every window of every building. To someone else, it might have been the same as any other sunrise, but Abbey felt, in the moment, like she was part of it. She pulled to the roadside, next to the train tracks, and sat on the hood of her car, letting the sunrise and more memories wash over her.

Abigail had always loved dining, be it for breakfast, lunch, or dinner, although breakfast fare might be her favorite. It was warm and satiating, inviting thoughts of hot beverages, golden pancakes dripping with butter, fresh biscuits, and savory, crunchy bacon. She found the dining experience to be captivating and often orchestrated her vacation time around trying new restaurants. Last year she traveled to the White Horse Tavern in Rhode Island. While her hostess entertained her with stories about "America's oldest tavern," Abigail eyed the colonial building with awe and wondered how many food memories were made within those walls.

Locally, Abigail had been to every restaurant in Rock Hill. She knew every eatery, from the time-honored Red's Grill— the oldest, and still going strong—to the newer, swanky Pump House on the other side of the town.

It's too big now to really be called a town, but Rock Hill, South Carolina, had always been Abigail's home. Named after a bothersome hill made of flint and steel that caused construction slowdowns when the railroad was being built in the mid-1800s, Rock Hill lies just south of Charlotte, North Carolina, nestled on the Catawba River. Through its burgeoning growth, Rock Hill never relinquished its town-like feeling. An open-air farmers' market popped up next to the bank every Saturday morning, while Sundays remained slow and quiet.

Abigail grew up just down the street from Winthrop University, which grew up with Rock Hill. The college was founded in 1866 as a training school for teachers and built from the labor of state convicts. The historic Tillman Hall retains the iron shackles that held convicts in the stone walls of its basement. The namesake for the building was a US senator, governor, and an avowed proponent of racial injustice. They say Tillman Hall is haunted, and why shouldn't it be? Everything is haunted by the past.

Abigail had loved her time at Winthrop. Although many of her high school classmates couldn't wait to spread their wings because of Rock Hill's small-town feel, Abbey never shared that sentiment. As a teenager, she wandered Winthrop's campus, meandering down the oak-shaded paths and occasionally stopping in front of the older architecture that was somehow just as majestic as the oaks themselves.

Even as a child, Abigail dreamed of going to Winthrop because it reminded her of a school for wizards. In fact, she called it Hogwarts. Every day from kindergarten through twelfth grade, Abbey rode past the university on bus 57, imagining wizards were inside learning magic. She would stare at the college students and wonder what spells or incantations they were reciting in their heads.

Abbey still flirted with magical thoughts, because for her, there was magic in cooking something wonderful—in blending a culinary potion with onions, garlic, and butter, and just gathering in the aroma. Abbey sighed happily. She absolutely loved her job. She loved watching as people waited longingly for her presentation, then as they paused and smiled widely with their first taste of her fare.

That image made Abbey smile, and she stretched her legs under the sun's warm rays. Her smile was a true reflection of her affection. Simple things meant a lot to Abigail Stewart. A one-line email from a friend could make her sparkle and shine. She was an optimist by nature, a woman who woke up singing and set her alarm an hour early each day so she would have enough time to fill the bird feeders in her yard. Her optimism did not dissociate her from the day-to-day struggles in life though. Abbey could write a book filled with her disappointments, but they did not define her. When she was angry, there was hell to pay; but mostly she was the kind of person who sat on the hood of a car with the traffic passing, smiling at the sun.

A bellowing horn from a distant, approaching train startled Abbey. Glancing at her phone, she realized it was time to get going. She got back into her car and drove to the corner of Main Street, with her new recipe in mind and feeling warmed and energized. She laughed out loud, imagining she was like a sunflower or a solar panel.

CHAPTER 2

OLIVIA

She remembered reading somewhere that the lethal height for a fall is fifty feet. The tallest building in Charlotte is the Bank of America Corporate Center at sixty stories, 871 feet. *That should do it*, she thought.

Suicidal thoughts were like a comfortable old sweater Olivia kept in her closet but no longer wore: neatly tucked away, but she still held on to it. Today would be like every other day. Another cold morning, another empty day. With an unhappy sigh, Olivia locked the door to her apartment— her pitiful apartment that was a constant reminder of her failures—and headed to her car. As she walked through the parking deck, the heel of her shoe broke when it caught in a drain grate. They had been a gift from her mother.

They're just shoes, she thought.

Sitting in her car, she took out a leatherbound journal from her purse and scribbled an entry: *Is everything about being broken? Aren't we more than the scar tissue that we feel and the numbness or pain we project?* She began to close the journal, then reopened it and added: *Fix shoe and avoid that grate in the future.*

Some people cope by slipping through the seams unnoticed, but Olivia always felt noticeably unnoticeable. Many nights in her childhood, she had listened to her mother crying from her bedroom next door. For a long time, Olivia felt nothing, then anger, and then nothing again. After her mom was gone, she still could hear her crying, indistinguishable from her own tears. It was a pain memory, a phantom limb.

Olivia stopped at a light and thought, *Not today.* She was determined that today would not be a pain day. For starters, there was coffee, a drink from the Aztec gods. She wasn't sure if that was true, but if not, it ought to be. She continued toward the diner, and soon enough she threw on her signal and pulled onto the curb.

Olivia entered the restaurant, and Abbey held a steaming pot up in question.

"Yes. Black, black, black," she said in response, peeking through eyelids half closed, hardly revealing her emerald eyes. She sat down as Abbey turned over two cups and poured coffee for both of them. Olivia took a deep breath, taking in the aroma. It was the rich and warm to her poor and cold.

"Are you sure you don't want a little sugar?" Abbey asked with a smile.

"Sugar is for idiots," Olivia snapped back.

"I'll give you this," Abbey said, sitting down in the open chair opposite Olivia. She tipped over the sugar container—one of those tall glass containers with a metal cap and spout—and filled a teaspoon, letting the sugar overflow into her cup. "I love the stuff; it's a weakness."

Olivia watched, shaking her head. "How do you stay so thin?" she asked.

Abbey shrugged, holding her hands up. "Genetics," she said. "But I'll admit, my dentist loves me."

"We have the same genes, Abigail," Olivia said with a smiley pout, drawing her lower lip and jaw forward in an oddly shaped pucker that Abbey called her "fish face."

They did share many of the same genes and, for that matter, often shared the same jeans. They had a favorite pair of jeans that each claimed as their own. Olivia had them in her closet at the moment, but they constantly played "capture the jeans," covertly locating and extricating the denim from one another.

Born a mere eleven months apart, the sisters were the exact same age for brief stints each year, which delighted and annoyed them in equal measure. But they had always been close and never needed spoken words to communicate. Often, a single glance would send them into girly giggles or convey their need to be left the hell alone. They instinctually knew when the other needed support and tenderness.

Olivia was at the diner for coffee every day at 7 a.m. Sometimes, if she was in a hurry, she'd take her coffee to go, but seldom did she not show up to see her sister.

"Busy morning?" Olivia asked.

"Just another manic Monday. Did you catch that sunrise?"

Olivia looked up from her coffee and raised an eyebrow. She knew Abigail was a sunrise sort of person. *How can we be so alike and so different?* "Um, there was a sunrise this morning?" she teased.

Abbey refilled her cup and smiled. "How's the coffee?"

Olivia took a sip. Abbey's coffee was hot and bold, but never bitter.

"Perfect as always," said Olivia. "Whatever they pay you, it should be doubled."

They both knew that wasn't going to happen, because Abbey owned the diner and Olivia had scrapped together all of her earthly belongings to invest as her silent partner.

They chatted for a few minutes, and after another pour of coffee, Olivia shuffled through her purse for her keys. "I gotta get going. I'm late again," Olivia said. "Are we still on for the weekend?"

Olivia had written dozens of one-act plays, and finally, one was being produced. It opened on Friday, a comedy about a girl who stops to help her friend change a flat tire. After her good deed, she drives away, and her car runs out of gas. Olivia was sure it would be her first and only production.

"I don't know. Are we?" Abbey asked with a glimmer in her eyes.

"You better be there," Olivia said. Abbey helped her feel grounded. "I'll see you in the morning."

Abbey had already moved on to fill another customer's cup. Olivia looked down into her own. It was still warm in her hands. She knew Abbey would be there. After all, she was a cup filler.

CHAPTER 3

RACHAEL

"Chalie, where's Crystal?" Rachael asked as she touched him gently on his left shoulder.

He was still asleep.

"Honey, something's wrong," she said, nudging him a little harder.

Slowly, Chalie opened his eyes. "What's the matter?" he whispered, rolling onto his back. He took a deep breath and could smell Rachael. She smelled like lavender. He loved waking up next to her in the morning. Too many mornings, he woke in the hospital physician's call room. This morning, the lavender gave way to her concerned voice, an intonation that sparked his immediate attention.

He had learned to trust Rachael's intuition years ago. Sometimes it was annoying, but it was most often accurate. He remembered the first time she told him she "had a feeling" about something. They were on a date at a movie theater watching a superhero flick when two men walked by her in the aisle. She told Chalie that something "wasn't right" about them. She felt it so strongly that she could not enjoy the movie and asked to leave. He politely downplayed her fear, but before the radioactive event triggered the hero's superpowers, Rachael pointed toward the men. They were throwing popcorn on a young man who was trying to watch the movie with his date. A fight started, the police were called, and Chalie learned his first lesson about Rachael's intuition.

Lately, her intuition was related to concern about their relationship. They seemed to be arguing more—not fighting, just disagreeing, often about trivial things. But they'd been together a long time now. They'd met twelve years ago as freshmen at Winthrop. And the truth is, it was easy for them not to have meaningful conversation for days on end. There was work, cooking, cleaning, homework, dance, soccer, and TV, but not much time dedicated to their relationship. When time did avail itself, they would have these pop-up arguments.

Chalie sat up in bed, rubbing his eyes, and looked around the room.

Crystal, their cat, was like an alarm clock. Each morning, she would go to both of the children's rooms, first vocalizing her intention for them to wake up, with a sharp, chirping "meow." Then, if they didn't respond, she would hop onto their beds and sit on their chests until they submitted. She had them well trained.

They discovered her on Christmas Eve when their daughter, C.J., was five and Simon was still in diapers. Rachael heard her tiny peeping voice in their backyard. She was small and helpless and could fit in the palm of Rachael's hand. They fed her with an eyedropper. The bond between Crystal and the kids was strong because she had imprinted upon them from such an early age. House cats are usually solitary, but she was extremely social ... well, when she wanted to be. She never seemed to lose her inner kitten.

Chalie had a sinking feeling in his chest. Nobody wants to, but most people start thinking about the worst possible outcomes, in those quiet places where fear resides. That's the way the brain works when it knows there's something wrong. Then, once sobering reality sets in, it is followed by an intellectual fog, like a circuit that's overloaded.

They got up and searched quietly through the house, in all of Crystal's usual hiding places, until Chalie spotted her unmoving body on the roadside. The kids were just getting up, still sleepy eyed, when Rachael brought them into the primary bedroom and sat them on the edge of the bed. C.J. and Simon could tell that Rachael was upset, holding back her tears.

"Daddy found Crystal outside. She was hit by a car," Rachael said. She said the words tenderly but knew their weight.

The kids began to cry immediately. Simon asked if they could hold her, so Chalie brought her in, wrapped in the blanket she had slept on since she was a kitten. They buried her in Rachael's rose garden that morning in a misty rain.

Later, Rachael found C.J. on her bed, holding Crystal's blanket and sobbing. She held her daughter close.

"Is Crystal in heaven?" she asked, wrestling with the concept of death.

"Yes, sweetheart. She's in heaven with God," said Rachael.

C.J. looked confused. "But I loved her," she said, and Rachael understood her meaning completely. Why would God take something she loved so dearly?

Rachael sat quietly on the bedside and hugged her heartbroken daughter. Her own heart was breaking too.

This world can be a scary place. How can you protect anyone if you can't protect your cat?

CHAPTER 4

ALIYAH

Every so often, Aliyah would return to the house where she grew up because it reminded her not so much of where she came from but where she was going. Now it was being torn down.

Frankly, it should have been bulldozed a long time ago. When her family lived there, the floors had been scraps of carpet over cardboard, over dirt. There was no air-conditioner or heater. In the summer, they used box fans when they had electricity. In the winter, they kept the oven on to stay warm, when they had gas.

Back then, Aliyah didn't know they were poor. It's not the way children think. She had food to eat, most of the time. Aliyah learned the basic rules of survival at her supper table. She had three brothers, and they would snatch the food off her plate if she let them. All these years later, her family would remind her how she had poked her brother's hand with her fork when he reached for her biscuit one Saturday morning when she was four years old.

As a small child, it didn't occur to her that her momma rarely ate meat. When she was in the fourth grade, Aliyah learned what a vegetarian was. She remembered coming home from school and asking her momma if she was a vegetarian.

"Why no, honey. I love meat," Momma told her.

As she grew, she realized her momma saved the meat for her children.

Thinking back, Aliyah knew they didn't have much money, but she wouldn't change a thing. Her momma taught her about love and sacrifice.

Moving forward is the goal. Keep moving or get off the highway. Holding on to the past was not her way, but success in the here and now is a balance of what has happened and what's going to happen. Hard work and vision. That's what brings things together. That, and sometimes a little luck, which is, in essence, the unpredictable quality of circumstance.

Success is seldom a random occurrence, and Aliyah had just the right combination of intellectual curiosity and willingness to take a risk. Perhaps more important is timing, and hers seemed impeccable. Aliyah remembered hearing somewhere—was it Roosevelt? No, it was Tony Soprano—that a bad decision was better than indecision. Her business model started with an idea: bringing people together who have common interests. That's what marketing does in its purest sense. These people want red basketball shoes, and these people make red basketball shoes. Seeing a need people have and matching it to a solution—that was her gift. In her mind, her approach was simple, like a road map.

Six o'clock in the morning was brainstorming time, and she'd built it into her daily schedule, part of her personal road map. She'd also found that ideas could come into her consciousness at almost any time of the night or day. Sometimes she would wake up at two in the morning after stirring in her sleep, and an idea would hit her. She kept an iPad on her nightstand for just such occasions. Sometimes it could be in the shower, or while driving, or after sex. Even during sex. The first time she'd grabbed her iPad after an orgasm, Jonas was hurt, but after a long discussion about it, he'd understood that he had to frame things differently: He didn't bore her; their sex inspired her.

"I'm sorry," she had told him that night. "I'm a little hypomanic."

"You think?" he said with a smile before leaning over to kiss her.

Tonight, she fidgeted on their bed and sighed deeply as she tapped out her ideas on the keyboard.

Putting his book down and taking his glasses off, Jonas turned to her. "What's on your mind?"

She sighed again and closed her eyes momentarily. "I've been thinking about something …."

Jonas nodded encouragingly. He loved listening to her voice, especially when she was confiding in him. He had worked hard to earn her trust, knowing she didn't spill her heart to many people.

"Thinking about … a baby?" he asked playfully. They had been talking about starting their family.

She touched him gently on his chest, brushing the pads of her fingertips on his skin. "Yes," she said slowly, "but that's not what I was thinking just now."

He sat up a little and kissed her shoulder. "What's up?"

"I've been thinking about putting together an offer on the mill."

S&S Mill had been vacant for years, occupying a large swath of space adjacent to downtown. The property belonged to Abbey and Olivia, and they had received numerous offers from real estate developers who wanted to turn the factory into condos. Aliyah knew Abbey and Olivia weren't interested in any of the offers.

"It's just business," Aliyah had suggested to them once.

"It's more than that to us," Abbey told her.

As a result, Aliyah hesitated in taking an active role in the development of the mill. She knew business and friendship could be like oil and water, or sometimes like fire and gasoline. Emotions can cloud judgment, and she loved her friends dearly.

"And you're worried about Olivia and Abbey?" asked Jonas.

"Mostly Abbey," she said.

Although Abbey and Olivia came from a family that had been affluent, that was before everything happened and a string of bad decisions lost them their inheritance.

"I don't know. She and Olivia have talked about developing the property or selling it outright, but I think holding on to it is important to Abbey. Maybe I shouldn't mix friends and business."

"Maybe you're right, but if you can't do business with friends, then who will you do business with?" he asked, raising an eyebrow cutely. "Your enemies?"

"Hey, I don't have any enemies," she said, poking his stomach playfully. She finished typing her thoughts, then closed the tablet. "Okay, now I'm all yours," she said.

He leaned in for a kiss, and she happily obliged.

CHAPTER 5

NEIL AND AMY

"Look over there." He pointed at the horizon, and their eyes followed his finger. "You can't see it, but our car is right there." He was so calm. The girls looked into his eyes, checking to make sure he wasn't afraid.

They were having a vacation before Neil's deployment to Afghanistan. All four of them loved to travel, and the North Carolina mountains were easy driving distance from Rock Hill.

When they'd begun their excursion that morning, everyone had been excited. They each had a leather canteen, bought at the Trading Post, a souvenir shop in Boone. It was the kind of shop that sold just about everything. There were mountains of gemstones that could be put into pouches and bought by weight. There were trinkets, toys, T-shirts, and leather jackets. Each of the girls left with porcelain Native American dolls. The dolls were identical, but the girls quickly found small differences in the workmanship, which identified each doll as their own.

Abbey loved the excitement of traveling and woke with excited energy. Amy would get them buckled up and tucked in with comfy blankets. She loved playing I Spy, finding imaginary animals from puffy clouds, and singing songs together as they drove. They avoided fast food chains, instead stopping for breakfast at small local restaurants. Olivia would say she preferred staying home, but she would gaze out of the window while they drove on Skyline Drive, looking for unicorns among the hardwoods and evergreens.

Before starting their hike, Amy had questioned Neil about the difficulty level of the trail.

She was keenly studying a guidebook that contained maps of the best backpacking locations in the Appalachians. They were in the parking area, getting ready to set out.

"Are you sure about this, Neil?" She looked at the map, then at the mountain in front of them. "This says it's a challenging hike."

She handed him the guidebook, and he studied it for a few moments. He looked around to get his bearings, tilting his head back to see the top of the towering mountain.

"We're not climbing the mountain," he said with a grin as he opened the pages and flattened the book out on the hood of their Jeep. "Look. We're going to take this trail. It leads through the forest and to this waterfall. It's only a mile."

They packed up and set out. The girls were five and six. Abbey was a few inches taller, but otherwise, people frequently thought they were identical. Their jeans were cuffed and rolled above their little hiking boots that Amy had bought for this occasion.

Amy looked nervous. "I read a story last week about a cougar spotted in Blowing Rock," she said.

"Hmm," Neil rubbed the stubble on his chin. "Okay, Amy, you take the lead, then the girls, and I'll walk behind." He knew that attacks by cougars were rare, but he felt safer with the girls between them.

They took a trail that led them between a couple of cabins, then through an empty campsite, where the path became indistinct.

"I'm not sure which way to go," Amy said, looking into the mountain forest.

There were two paths. The one to the left seemed a bit more overgrown.

"Let's go left," Neil said.

"Are you sure?" asked Amy. "The trail to the right seems more … um—"

"Traveled?" he asked, smiling. "Two roads diverged in a yellow wood …"

The girls smiled at the real-life adaptation of a poem they knew by heart, Robert Frost's "The Road Not Taken." Amy and Neil loved poetry and read to the girls every night. They all liked to recite the poems they had memorized, taking turns while alternating verses.

"And sorry I could not travel both," Amy continued.

"And be one traveler, long I stood," said Abigail.

Olivia was the youngest, but also knew every line. "And looked down one as far as I could," she said.

Neil loved listening to their voices.

"To where it bent in the undergrowth," they all said together.

They voted for the trail that was less cultivated and walked for an hour through the forest, winding through maple and birch trees, past fields of yellow wildflowers, watching for deer, unicorns, and dinosaurs until Amy stopped abruptly.

"Can you hear that?" she asked the girls. They listened, hearing the indistinct rolling and trickling sound of a mountain stream.

Neil took out his guidebook. "The waterfall is just a little west of here," he said, pointing. "Do you see where the trail veers off to the left?"

Amy peered into the forest at what looked like an animal trail and was not convinced.

"I'm not sure that's a trail, Neil," she said.

The girls looked, too, but said nothing.

"Let's just try to follow the trail for a little bit," he said.

Amy didn't want to argue. This was a special trip; they wouldn't see Neil again for at least six months.

"I don't want us to get lost," she said nervously.

They stopped for a moment, and Neil took out his compass and map. Amy surveyed the terrain. She had a very visual memory and related to distinct landmarks better than maps. She noticed the direction of the sun in the west.

"I think we're here," said Neil, pointing with his index finger at a point on the map.

She was reassured and took out her camera, capturing images of the girls gathering wildflowers in the primeval forest.

They set off again and were soon on the trail to the waterfall.

"Anyone can get a little lost," Neil told the girls. "The important thing is, when you get off track, stay calm."

CHAPTER 6

BEFORE AND AFTER

The weather in Rock Hill is as near to ideal as weather can be. Summertime is warm, but not unbearable. It's the kind of warm where, on most days, a nice shady tree can still provide a cool place for a person to rest. Winter is cold, but a sweater and jacket are usually enough to keep comfortable.

Abbey loved the sun, but Olivia loved the rain. "It washes everything," she liked to say. In the Carolinas, the rain can come down soft and easy or hard and torrential. It might be a storm blowing over from the Gulf or a front moving down from the north.

The girls were playing outside when the rain started that day. It was a springtime rain that started as a sprinkle of big droplets and soon changed into a downpour. Their mother was letting them play outside because there was no lightning. Their shoes and socks were on the porch, and they were splashing through the puddles in their six-year-old bare feet.

A loud clap of thunder prompted Amy to call out to them from the porch where she sat watching them. "Okay, girls, it's time to play inside." The girls dried their feet and ran past her as she smiled.

She had been working on a letter to her husband, which she folded delicately and placed on the table. She ran her hand through her blond hair, cut in a fashionable bob just off her shoulders, and sighed. His deployment had been hard on the girls. On the day Neil had left, Abbey had hugged his neck tightly, breathing in the smell of his cologne. "You're my favorite smell," she told him. As he held her, she tore the Velcro patch from his arm, the unit crest for the 101st, an eagle, and held it in her little hand. He closed her hand around his patch and kissed her forehead.

She carried his patch with her almost everywhere.

Olivia had hidden on the morning he left, having a hard time navigating the emotions of saying goodbye. Neil found her in her favorite hiding spot in the turret. She got her hug, and he brushed the hair from her eyes, kissed her cheek, and left for the airport in a taxicab.

Twelve months can seem forever. Amy tried not to let her mind get stuck on her fear, but every time the news was on, her ears were tuned to reports of casualties.

After the girls were dry, they had a snack of chocolate chip cookies, then ran upstairs. They had set up an elaborate dollhouse in the turret of the Victorian mansion.

The raindrops on the metal roof had a cadence and rhythm, like a mountain stream rustling over stones, but with a metallic echo. Distant thunder drummed an intermittent stereo bass solo.

The girls were playing in the window of the turret when a dark sedan pulled into the driveway. A soldier in dress blues walked to the door. For a brief moment, Olivia's heart raced with joy, but peering through the rain, she realized the man was not her father. He wasn't as tall, and he didn't walk the way her dad walked, like he couldn't wait to get in the door to see her. She heard the door open and a glass shatter on the floor. The girls looked at each other, and Abbey reached out and held her sister's hand. In that second, she knew her dad was never coming home.

Combat deployment includes several unavoidable truths, and the girls had questions that Neil and Amy had tried to answer gently. Even at their tender ages, the girls had a basic understanding that there were risks associated with going to war. The risk was implied in saying "going to war." They understood that Daddy wasn't simply going to work.

"Are you going to fight bad guys?" Olivia had asked.

He and Amy had tried to explain the concept of war in terms of good and bad, because that is how small children think. The gray areas of morality develop as children move toward adolescence.

"I don't think of the enemy soldiers as bad, sweetheart," Neil said. "But they are doing bad things, and I have to help stop them and protect our country."

"Are you going to die?" asked Abbey.

Both of the girls and Amy fixed their eyes intently upon him.

"No, darling," he said. He didn't know at the time, but it had been the right moment for a tender lie.

Before he'd left, they'd made a chain out of construction paper with 365 links, one link for each day he would be gone. On each link, Neil wrote something to Amy and the girls. The first link said, "I will always love you." Every day, the girls would remove one link and watch the chain grow shorter.

The last 170 links would never be removed.

For the first days and weeks after Neil was killed, they were very busy. Sometimes Amy felt like a spectator and sometimes like a reluctant celebrity. She focused on Abbey and Olivia, but at night, after the girls were sleeping, she felt alone. They flew to Dover and met the president as Neil's casket, draped by the American flag, was carried off the airplane. They called it an Angel Flight. Their picture was on the national news. Amy was in black, the two girls in pristine white dresses. Amy looked young, beautiful, and heartbroken.

Amy was an only child: her father died in an accident when she was young, and her mother developed breast cancer in her thirties, dying shortly after Abbey was born. So outside of the girls, Amy felt she was drifting on a life raft in the ocean, lost with no end in sight.

Grief and depression share common symptoms. Both have elusive end points that people struggle to find. Keeping her home beautiful had always brought Amy joy, but now she didn't even bother to make her bed in the morning. One day she walked into her bedroom, and Abbey was straightening her pillows and sheets while Olivia was trying to spread out her quilt.

"It's gonna be okay, Mommy," said Abbey.

They both looked up at her, and Amy felt the sharp intensity coming from Abbey's big blue eyes. There's nothing in any parenting manual on how to proceed when you lose the person who seems to hold your world together, but that was the end point Amy needed. In that moment, she could see Neil in them, and herself in them, and them in her. She realized that some things can be complicated and simple at the same time. She needed to try returning to some semblance of normalcy, and it started by simply making her bed. She hugged her girls and helped them finish the bed, determined to find her path through.

The girls went back to school the following Monday, and Amy began cleaning the house. She couldn't bring herself to give away Neil's clothing, so she stored everything in a large cedar wardrobe in the turret. Touching his military gear brought memories of his last day at home and a fresh wave of grief.

On the morning he left, Neil had three duffel bags, each big enough for her to fit inside, and a huge rucksack with all sorts of military gear attached. There were clips holding ammunition and medical supplies. Even the pen in this breast pocket was designed to be a weapon if necessary.

Most people didn't know that side of Neil, but Amy had. He had a quiet intensity that she loved. His energy wove into the matrix of her life. Then just like that, it was gone, leaving her in a fog, almost like being drugged or being caught in a dimension that was not fully in the present. The effect was overwhelming.

There was an empty space in the universe, like a black hole drawing everything into its center. She thought about something she learned in college, the first law of thermodynamics: Energy cannot be created or destroyed. If that's true, then what happened to Neil's energy? Maybe his energy went to heaven, and maybe some of his energy lives in the girls. That thought gave her comfort.

Amy kept pushing herself forward. She focused on the girls, who started dance class, piano, and soccer, and she started scouting locations on East Main, with an eye to finally opening a photography studio.

Bit by bit, tomorrows became yesterdays.

The holidays were approaching. Rock Hill transformed into a Carolina winter wonderland for Christmas. There were twinkling red and green lights in the store windows, and every year an outdoor ice-skating rink was set up downtown in Fountain Park.

Christmas had been Neil's favorite holiday, and he would start playing their Christmas CDs as soon as the temperature dropped below fifty degrees at night, usually in late October. The first Christmas without Neil was filled with their memories. Amy initially considered a scaled-down holiday, then she thought of going overboard with extravagant gifts. She decided to stick to traditions.

Neil had always taken the family shopping for a Christmas tree. The selection process was part of the tradition and was not to be rushed. Neil would stand the tree up, and they would examine it from all sides, looking for empty spaces, and check to be sure the trunk was straight and true. The real test for the tree was a more visceral, inexplicable, emotional attachment. It had to feel like their tree.

The three girls had an unspoken agreement that this year's Christmas tree shopping was going to be more subdued. Amy felt that they needed to try and keep the holiday festive, but wondered what parts would stay the same and what parts would be lost in loss.

When heartache inevitably smacked her in the face, Amy reminded herself that she was born a McAlister. She had always liked the idea of being Scottish, coming from a people who had been enslaved, then cast away from their homeland. "They were people who *overcame*," she emphasized to the girls as they tromped around the tree lot.

They chose a blue spruce. The salesman got the tree onto the car, but getting the tree into their house and then finally level in the tree stand was challenging. It took all three of them to drag the tree inside. Then Abbey and Olivia held the tree steady while Amy tightened the bolts.

"Ohh," said Abbey, looking at the tree's backside. "It has a bare spot."

They all stood and stared at the back of the tree.

"It looks like a butt," said Olivia, matter-of-factly.

Indeed, the bare spot was shaped like rounded buttocks.

Amy clasped her hand over her mouth, then suddenly ran off to the bathroom. The girls were afraid she was crying, but their mom came back with a roll of toilet paper and hung it next to the tree's butt.

They all started to laugh. It started a new tradition, and every year to follow, they looked for an imperfect tree, a Christmas tree with a butt.

Poinsettias lined the wraparound porch and steps at the entrance to their house. There were candles in the windows and brightly wrapped presents under the tree. Gift wrapping was Amy's specialty. She selected every wrapping paper and ribbon with care. Neil used to unwrap her gifts slowly and always marveled at the attention she gave to something people would tear to pieces. She didn't mind. She loved watching people open their gifts. It reminded her of the girls, something marvelous under something beautiful.

On Christmas Eve, the girls went to bed after watching *Frosty the Snowman*. They had been sleeping with Amy since Neil died, but tonight they went to their own beds. Their bedroom was across the hall from Amy's. Each had an adorable twin canopy bed. She tucked them in but knew that within minutes, Olivia would scramble over to Abbey and settle in for the night, sleeping next to her sister.

Last Christmas Eve, they stayed awake as long as they could, waiting for Santa. This year felt different, and it didn't take too long for them to fall asleep.

Abbey awoke suddenly to the sound of Olivia's crying.

"No, no, no!" she cried with her little hands stretched desperately out in front of her, frantic but deep in sleep.

Abbey shook her sister gently until she awoke. Olivia opened her eyes, then lunged forward and held tightly to her sister, sobbing.

"It's okay, Olivia," said Abbey, looking frightened as she rubbed her sister's back. "Daddy is in heaven."

Olivia shook her head, trying to get her words out.

"No," she said, crying large crystal tears. "It was you."

"What was me?" Abbey asked, consoling her.

"You were falling, and I couldn't reach you."

Abbey continued to rock her sister softly in her arms.

"I'm right here," said Abbey, "and I'll never leave you."

CHAPTER 7

AN UNLIKELY START

Aliyah didn't think of people in terms of how much money they had until she was in the fifth grade. It was the first time someone made fun of her for the clothes she was wearing. Most of her possessions were hand-me-downs, and she thought nothing of it. Like the floor of her house, it was normal to her. She loved when her momma would bring clothes home from church. They would be in paper grocery bags. She and her momma would go through the bags and choose clothes for her and her brothers.

It was the second week of a new school year, at a new school, on a new bus, and she had new shoes. They were pretty blue tennis shoes her momma bought for her. Aliyah didn't get many new things, and that was her favorite part of August: new things. She liked the notebooks, pencils, and binders, all fresh and shiny.

Walking onto the school bus can be anxiety provoking, like stepping onto a stage, all eyes examining the new kid at the front of the bus. There was a cute boy, AJ, that she noticed looking at her each morning.

A.J. played quarterback for the Panthers in the Rock Hill Youth Sports League. Rock Hill proclaimed itself to be Football City, USA, because of the number of professional football players who came from the South Carolina town.

That morning, Aliyah scanned the bus for him as usual. He wasn't hard to spot, talking about last night's football game to his school-bus entourage. She slowly approached his seat and noticed his eyes meeting hers, then scanning over her. She didn't find that offensive; for that matter, she liked checking him out too. Although they had never spoken, she was developing a little crush. He looked at her face again, and she was excited because he was about to talk to her.

"I saw them shoes at the dollar store," he said, pointing down at her new shoes.

At first, the insult didn't register. She liked her new shoes. When the other kids began to laugh, she suddenly felt very small. She didn't think he was cute anymore.

"Leave her alone, Avery," said a girl in the seat in front of his.

She was very pretty, about Aliyah's age, and she was not laughing like the others. Seated next to her was a girl who had to be her sister, just as pretty, maybe a little younger. She looked scared, and she pulled on her sister's arm, trying to keep her from getting involved.

"Or else what?" A.J. replied, irritated that she had used his first name. Everyone stopped laughing. They all knew A.J. and Abbey had been going together over the summer and had broken up before school started.

Abbey stood up next to his seat. "Just because you have a dick doesn't mean you have to be one," she said to him quietly. "Do you really want to be known as a guy who picks on girls?"

"Come on, Abigail, I was just joking around," he said.

Abbey's sister had remained silent and unnoticed, not moving in her seat through the incident, but she watched every move A.J. made. Tightly in her hand she held a pointed steel compass that she had removed from her pencil bag. Nobody was going to hurt her sister.

Abbey turned her back to him and looked at Aliyah.

"I'm Abbey," she said.

Aliyah was hurt but also angry.

"Yeah, well, fuck him," she said, glaring at A.J. "And I can fight my own fights," she said to Abbey, then walked confidently down the aisle without another word. *Keep moving forward*, she told herself.

The bus driver looked up through the huge mirror on top of his sun visor.

"Hey, you kids need to sit down back there," he said.

Near the back of the bus, she saw most of the seats were full. There was an open one next to another new girl, a White girl, who was watching her carefully.

Aliyah sat down, and the girl quickly looked down at the book bag in her lap. Aliyah grabbed the girl's left hand and then rubbed her own wrist hard against the girl's forearm. "I'm Black, but it don't rub off," she said.

The girl sat quietly, looking at Aliyah. "I know," she said, holding her arm, which burned a little from the friction. "My name is Rachael. We just moved here."

Aliyah tilted her head to the side and sighed heavily. "I'm sorry," she mumbled as a single tear slowly moved down her cheek. Rachael reached out and touched Aliyah's hand; their friendship was born.

CHAPTER 8

STEWART HOUSE

Oakland Avenue is Rock Hill's small-town equivalent of New Orleans's St. Charles Avenue or Charleston's East Bay Street. It's a four-lane boulevard with wrought-iron streetlamps and sprawling oak trees that runs from historic downtown through the university. Some of the old mansions have been converted to attorneys' offices. Two Presbyterian churches, established in the 1700s, stand next to a coffee shop nestled in an old Amoco service station with antique gas pumps out front. Old and new side by side, a reminder of how a city is alive, always changing, but ever the same.

Olivia and Abbey grew up in the Stewart House, a striking Victorian mansion on Oakland Avenue. Their father, Neil, was the heir to the cotton mill, once the largest in the state. All that remained of his textile empire was an empty, monolithic brick building that flirted with decay. Its towering smokestacks emitted their last smoke many years ago.

Textile mills in South Carolina were a vibrant staple of the economy for a hundred years. The Stewart and Sherrill Mill Co. was formed in 1901, and in its prime, S&S Mill

Co. provided jobs for Rock Hill and thirteen other bustling towns in the Carolinas. Today, these mill towns are more like ghost towns. Their storefronts are empty. They have railroads, but the trains don't stop. They only rattle through town, slowing at the intersections, breaking the silence with the horns on their locomotives. The streets are lined with weathered houses. Some are small single-gabled, plank-board homes with couches on their porches. Others are elegant colonial estates or ornate Victorian minimansions. They are all quietly fading but hold generations of memories. On the outside, they are sun-bleached, with chipping paint and broken shutters. Inside, they have pictures of soldiers on their living room walls and echoes of children's laughter, with the aroma of pumpkin pie and Thanksgiving turkey embedded in the plaster walls. Souvenirs in time.

The Stewart house had a large tower with a wraparound porch and looked very much like a castle. Inside the house were two tremendous brick fireplaces. From the outside, a passerby would think the house contained beautiful furnishings, but in reality, many of the rooms were empty.

It was late summer, and Olivia and Abbey were playing with their friends upstairs, pretending to make a music video. They had written out scripts for each of them and made a storyboard and then acted it out with their Barbie dolls.

Amy tapped on their door, then peeked her head in. She smiled a tired smile. "You girls sound like you're having fun." They giggled. They were in that magical age where girls live between make believe and makeup, unicorns and preteen crushes. "Hmm, looks like someone has been in their mom's closet."

Olivia was dressed in Amy's clothes and had quite the fashion sense. "I'm Miley Cyrus," she said.

Amy held in her desire to laugh. "I think you should have asked my permission to wear my clothes," she tried to say sternly, but her smile broke through.

"Mom, will you help us make a music video?" asked Abbey. She looked over their set.

"This is pretty good," she said. "Why don't you all get dressed for the video, and then we'll do makeup."

She helped them choose clothes, then put on makeup. They all liked a lot of glitter. Amy set up her camera and tripod, and they shot a video of them singing songs from *High School Musical.*

As the girls watched their video, Amy checked the time on her phone. "I have to get to my studio," she told them, referring to the small office space downtown that she had rented to launch her photography business.

Amy blew kisses through the air as she left, and the girls decided they were bored.

"Let's play in the tower," Aliyah suggested.

The mood of the girls seemed to change. Abbey stopped playing and was motionless, but her eyes looked up toward the dark staircase. Olivia looked at Abbey nervously and shook her head so slightly that only Abbey noticed.

"I don't want to play in the tower," Olivia said. She had moved closer to Abbey and their fingers interlaced.

Rachael could see that Olivia was frightened. In truth, she didn't like playing in the tower either, but Aliyah was already on her way up the winding staircase.

The door to the tower was made from thick oak boards, rounded at the top and bound with straps of iron. It looked like the door to a dungeon.

Aliyah pushed open the latch, turning the antique glass doorknob. The door was heavy, and she pushed hard, opening the door just wide enough to allow the entrance of a ten-year-old girl. "It's not scary," she said. "See?"

Inside, the turret was much larger than someone might imagine. It was two stories of open space with century-old joists overhead in the pointed tower. The tall windows were covered with dark-gray curtains, which emitted little light, so the contents of the room were hidden in muted sepia shadows. The girls watched Aliyah squeeze through the opening and reach for a vintage gilded floor lamp.

Hide-and-seek was once the Stewart girls' favorite game. They would ask Neil to play every day, and when it was his turn to hide, he usually hid in the turret. They would know he was there because he would leave the door slightly ajar. After he died, Olivia hoped and prayed that he wasn't really gone, that he was just hiding in the turret. In reality, Olivia wasn't afraid of the turret. She loved the turret. It was the darkness she feared.

CHAPTER 9

THE CIVITAS

Four bronze sculptures stand like sentinels on the corners of Dave Lyle and Gateway Boulevard. The Civitas, as they are known, are ten feet tall, on ten-foot pedestals, and extend their arms above their heads, offering their gifts to the growing city. They face every direction of the compass. In the day, they blaze like fire; at night, they watch from the shadows. Like guardians, they never sleep.

The statues were commissioned in 1988 and positioned at the Gateway intersection at the entrance to the historic district. Each holds a disc symbolizing essential components for success: the flame of knowledge, stars of creativity, energy of lightning, and gears of industry.

At the foot of the Lightning Civita is the Tech Park Trailhead. It's a linear park, a nature trail, winding through rolling hills and woods in the Lakeshore area. The girls rode their bikes on the trail every day, and every day they would play in the shadow of the statues. Before long, each had adopted a statue's identity as their own. Rachael was the flame, Abbey the lightning, Olivia the star, and Aliyah the gears. All four statues were beautiful. The same, but different, like a four-part harmony in a song.

Rachael was home sick with a stomach virus and lying on the sofa, still sleepy eyed, when a story on the morning news captured her attention.

"Controversy is swirling over the statues on Dave Lyle Boulevard," the news anchor said. "A group of local religious leaders issued a statement condemning the statues as obscene."

It seemed that the nipples on the breasts of the Civitas were *too* nippily, and the group was advancing a plan to sand down the nipples to make the statues less sensual. Rachael sat up on the sofa, fixated on the television. The statues belonged to her and her friends. They belonged to everyone.

"Mom? What's wrong with the statues?"

Her mother, who was cleaning the kitchen while listening to the news, had not realized Rachael was paying such close attention.

"Those pastors think the statues are ..." she struggled to find the right word, "inappropriate."

"Why?"

This is the million-dollar question that gives ammunition to every inquisitive child. Of course, the anti-question "because" could be offered in response, but that was not how Rachael's mother parented. For that matter, she was also a "why" person. A questioner, or seeker of answers.

"I'm not sure," her mom answered truthfully. "Some people find the statues offensive because of their breasts."

"But I like them," Rachael answered.

Her mom looked at her quizzically. "The breasts or the statues?"

Rachael began to giggle.

She knew her mother believed homosexuality was sinful, but her mom also was open-minded and raising Rachael to welcome people of all persuasions.

"The statues, Mom," she said, although truthfully, she also liked breasts and, at eleven, was hoping for a little more rapid development of her own.

"Just because we like something doesn't make it right. What if someone likes to steal?"

That was a good point. Rachael understood the logic, but still could not see anything wrong with the statues.

"It's not exactly the same," Rachael argued respectfully.

"No, it's not," her mother agreed. "Now how about watching *Lizzie McGuire*?"

Rachael's eyes lit up as her mother changed the channel. Like most kids, Rachael loved TV, especially comedies about kids her age navigating the dilemmas that accompany adolescence. Eventually, she dozed off while watching her favorite program. Later in the morning, as lunchtime was nearing, she woke with a gentle growl in her stomach. She could hear her parents talking in the kitchen and could tell from their tone that it was not a pleasant conversation. They were arguing about the statues. She didn't like it when her parents quarreled. She knew they loved each other, but when they argued, she felt frightened and alone. Usually, she would sit in silence, praying for it to be over, but this time, she had something she wanted to say.

"Calling it art does not justify the sin," she heard her father say. He was so definite and convincing. She felt confused. She didn't want to be sinful.

Topics of faith and morality came up a lot around the dinner table. They were a very religious family. In fact, her dad was the pastor of Lakeshore Baptist Church, and her mother worked in alternating roles as a mom, church secretary, music leader, and protagonist of all church activities.

"What sin?" Rachael heard her mother ask. "And whose sin are we talking about here? Are you saying men can't drive by without lusting at the sight of the breasts on a statue?"

Her father paused in thought at the strength of her argument.

"Daddy?"

Her father and mother both stopped and turned to Rachael. They had been unaware of her presence. She walked into the kitchen, still in her pajamas, and looked up at him. "What's wrong with the statues?"

"Some of the church pastors think the statues are too revealing."

"Do you think they are?" she asked.

It was an honest question from the mind of a child. The truth was, not once in the two years they'd been living in Rock Hill had he ever found the statues offensive. He hesitated, trying to form his response.

"Am I bad if I think the statues are beautiful?" Rachael asked her father.

He looked at his wife and daughter. His argument was gone, dissolved by their blue eyes. He took his daughter's hand.

"My sweet girl," he said. At this point, Rachael was nearly crying. "You are not bad." He drew her close, and she hugged his neck tightly. "Honestly, I think the statues are beautiful too."

The next day, Rachael headed back to school, eager to tell her friends about the statues. Her mother decided to drive her, and Abbey, Olivia, and Aliyah were waiting for her at their favorite table near the stage. The school cafeteria also doubled as the school theater and had a full stage with a purple curtain in the front. Typically, when the girls arrived each morning, they bounced with excitement and laughter as if they had not seen each other in years.

"Did you hear what they want to do with the Civitas?" Rachael asked dramatically.

"No," the girls said simultaneously.

Rachael lowered her voice to a whisper. "They want to sand away their nipples."

"What?" Aliyah said in a loud voice. "Sand their nipples?"

This attracted the attention of a nearby teacher, who shot Aliyah a disapproving glance.

"I know, right? I saw it on the news yesterday," Rachael said, then told them the complete story.

"No woman should ever have her nipples shaved off!" Abbey said emphatically, unconsciously folding her arms to cover her chest. She had been the first of the four to get her period and begin breast development.

"Well, I have an idea," said Aliyah.

The girls met at Rachael's house after school and made signs from poster boards. On Saturday morning, Rachael's parents drove the girls to the Civitas. The girls set up a table and the poster signs. Aliyah waved a petition. Things went smoothly, and they had a lot of signatures by the time Abbey and Olivia's mom arrived with breakfast sandwiches. But by midmorning, the opposition showed up, and then the newspaper and television reporters came.

It was a big surprise when the girls were on page one of the Sunday morning paper. The photograph showed the four girls and their signs of protest standing under the Lightning Civita with the caption, *Guardians of Rock Hill Statues*.

CHAPTER 10

ALIYAH

After junior high, A.J. and Aliyah attended separate high schools, only to meet again on their fall semester break, freshman year of college. He was home for the weekend, and they both happened to be at a Halloween party. He had come as Batman, and she was Harley Quinn, so it appeared destined that they would at least meet for introductions and polite hero-versus-villain conversation.

"Hey," he said. "I know you."

He took off his mask, and she looked at his face.

"Yeah, well, you should," she said.

"Aliyah, right?" He looked at her feet. She was wearing white high-heeled boots, which were part of the costume but had been hard to find. "Those are pretty shoes," he said.

She thought about that long-ago morning on the school bus and how it had started bad but became a good memory. It was the day she met the girls.

"Avery Jonas! You were such a prick."

Aliyah remembered how she hoped he was going to talk with her that day when they were kids.

"Okay now, don't hold back your feelings," he said with a grin. "It's long overdue, but I owe you an apology."

"Yes, I believe you do," she said, serious but playful.

"I'm sorry," he said.

"We're good," she said and added, "but you know we can never be friends."

He looked disappointed.

"I'm Harley Quinn, and you're Batman. It would never work," she said. "What would your superhero friends say?"

He looked at her with a sly expression.

"That we are complicated, morally gray characters in a media-driven culture that insists on perpetuating a black-and-white narrative."

"I can't argue with that," she said, laughing. "In that case, let's get a drink."

They both selected local, dark, foamy craft beers, which were served in tall frosted glasses. After finding some comfy seats, they began to talk, and the night seemed to fly by.

They talked about college life.

Basketball, not football, turned out to be Avery's sport, but he didn't have the height to focus on the NBA.

"I like to say I'm six one, but I'm really just shy of six feet," he confessed to her with an embarrassed laugh. "Tall, but not NBA tall."

He was an art major at Clemson and the starting point guard on their basketball team. He told her it was the art of the game that he loved, and boasted playfully about being such a talented ball handler and shooter.

"I don't know a whole lot about basketball," she said with a laugh.

He smiled and sipped his beer. "Are you in school?" he asked.

She told him about her academic scholarship at Winthrop and her full-time job in the business development center. "My plan is to finish college without a dime of debt," she said.

They talked about career goals.

He was planning to teach high school art and coach basketball.

She wanted to start her own brand in business consulting, real estate, and marketing. She told him how she loved the concept of marketing because she wanted to bring people together and to make old things new.

"I'm going to make a name for myself in business, but it's hard to make money without money," she said. "That's the wrinkle in the starting plan of everyone who starts without a big bankroll."

"Yeah, but aren't the best things made from scratch?" he asked. Then he scrolled through his phone and showed her pictures of some of his artwork: portraits done in acrylic on doors and windows. The paintings were contrasts of things that are the same but very different—things we see every day but never notice. Most of them were places she noticed from Rock Hill, like one of the bank on Main Street with a child holding a tattered rag doll on the sidewalk. He told her he chose doors and windows for his surfaces because they were part of the vision, things people can open or close, that bring people together or keep them apart.

"Are you painting anything now?" she asked.

"I'm working on a portrait of the old S&S Mill," Avery said.

"I know the owners of that property," Aliyah said.

"Abbey and Olivia?"

"They're my best friends," she said. "Weren't you and Abbey, like, dating when we were all ten?"

"Hey! I was almost eleven," he said, laughing.

Aliyah moved closer and snapped a quick selfie of them. She sent it to Abbey, who responded almost immediately.

"Look," she said, showing Abbey's response—a big smiley face with the message, *Say hi for me*.

"So how are the Stewart sisters doing?" he asked.

Aliyah wasn't sure how to answer, so she just responded honestly. "They have been having a hard time. Their mom is sick."

"I'm sorry to hear that," he said.

Aliyah looked at the text from Abbey and sighed. "You know, since that day on the bus, they've been a big part of my life."

On the dance floor, people were lining up for the Cupid Shuffle.

"Do you know this dance?" he asked, holding out his hand to lead her to the dance floor. Aliyah smiled and nodded.

They danced and talked for the rest of the party. Before the night ended, they both knew that after all the years and a bad start, they liked each other. Even though they were very different—he liked hip-hop, and she was more into rock and old Motown; he liked comedies, and she liked horror—they had a lot more in common than not.

She held up her glass.

"To second chances, Jonas," she said.

Nobody else called him Jonas, he said. He liked it.

They touched their glasses together.

CHAPTER 11

SILVER SPRING

It was Easter Sunday in Washington, DC, and Abbey and Olivia were with their mother, who was being treated at Walter Reed Army Medical Center. The girls went out to look for something other than hospital food for breakfast when they happened upon the Dining Car Cafe, which was originally established in a repurposed Union Pacific Railroad dining car that had been planted on an empty lot in Silver Spring, Maryland. That lot was now considered prime beltway real estate.

In real estate, the mantra is location, location, location. That's not exactly what Abbey believed. She understood the importance of a good location but also that an address is not the final factor in a winning restaurant. She had finished her first summer internship at a French restaurant fifty miles outside of New Orleans. Although it was in the middle of swampy pine forest, far from the French Quarter or the Central Business District, it was widely considered one of the best restaurants in the city. So it's not just location, she often told people, it's visibility: "The real trick is in making something a good location, *making* what was invisible, visible."

The old dining car now served as the entrance area, silver and shiny, with a cash register and a hostess station. The hostess greeted them with a warm smile and brought them to a two-top next to the window.

"How's this?" she asked as she handed them menus.

"It's perfect," said Abbey, looking around the dining room while Olivia looked out the large rectangular window.

An auburn-haired waitress popped over shortly after they sat. "My name's Estelle," she said, with a hint of Southern accent. She appeared to be in her early fifties and was in good shape, probably because she was always in motion.

A loud burst of laughter from a large group of men turned the ladies' attention to the adjacent table. The men were nicely dressed, mostly middle aged, and unquestionably enjoying their family-style breakfast. Plates were passed back and forth filled with biscuits and gravy, and bacon and eggs.

Nobody will leave that table hungry, Abbey thought.

"Welcome to our Last Supper breakfast, ladies," the man in the middle said. His voice was a blend of rich, raspy baritone. His skin was brown and his jawline square with a closely trimmed beard that had the slightest touch of silver. "These are the twelve apostles," he motioned with his hands around the table, "but no, I am not Jesus," he said grinning. "My name is John." He had a distinguished look with just enough edginess to be very sexy. His eyes were brown, rimmed with green. He had the body of an athlete, not big and bulky, more like an MMA fighter than a body builder.

"John tha Baptist," one of the other men added with a preacher's cadence.

John's eyes twinkled, and the men laughed. Abbey counted. There were twelve men gathered around that table, and for all the world, they looked like the image that may have inspired da Vinci.

"The twelve apostles have been meeting at the diner on the first Sunday of each month for ten years," said Estelle.

"It's been eleven years," said John, as he buttered a biscuit. "And Estelle has been our waitress for every breakfast."

As the ladies looked on, each of the men introduced themselves in turn. "There will be a quiz after breakfast," joked one of the men.

They learned that John was an attorney. He ran a legal clinic called Last Chance and worked with homeless people.

This year, the first Sunday of the month fell on Easter, and here they were, praying while they ate and eating while they prayed. Their words were comical and touching, not a pious pseudo conversation but more as if God were at the table with them, passing them the syrup.

"This is our last Last Supper with Estelle. She is retiring next week," John said, as the apostles began to clap.

"I've been waiting tables for twenty-five years," Estelle said, gently sighing. There was pride and a hint of sadness in her sigh.

"Twenty-five years," Abbey repeated. "That's wonderful!"

"I can't imagine doing anything for twenty-five years," Olivia said flatly.

Estelle took no offense. Through her decades of experience, she had developed a knack for reading people's emotions, and she could see Olivia was carrying a hurt. "Well," she said, "I started waitressing when I moved here with my husband.

He was in the army. We met in my hometown, Columbia, South Carolina."

"Olivia and I are from Rock Hill!" said Abbey. She was going to say that their dad had been in the army, but she didn't want to go there. She was already feeling too emotional.

"And here I am now, twenty-five years later. I didn't plan it this way. It just kind of happened," said Estelle.

"Well praise the Lord. Nobody does it better!" one of the apostles said. "God almighty, please bless Estelle!" Then he filled his mouth with a bite of pancake, not bothering to wipe the butter from his mustache until he was done.

"Okay now, what would you like for breakfast?" asked Estelle.

"Just coffee for me," said Olivia.

Estelle looked over her pink rhinestone-covered reading glasses. "Are you sure? The breakfast here is very good."

"I'm sure," she said.

"Well, I want your blueberry pancakes and two eggs over medium," said Abbey.

"Now you talkin'," said one of the apostles.

Estelle gently put her hand over Olivia's as she picked up the menus. "I'll make sure there's extra on your sister's plate so you two can share."

"It's like she knows us," Olivia said after the waitress left. Since adolescence, Olivia would decline food but nibble off her sister's plate. It was part of their interconnection. Abbey thought it was a way of being sure her sister ate, and Olivia thought she was helping Abbey avoid too many extra calories.

The pancakes were perfect: toasted golden brown, soft, and moist. Estelle brought two forks for the pancakes, and as predicted, the girls shared. They were subdued—consumed with thoughts of their mom—especially compared to the men next to them, who were quite the spectacle for the unsuspecting pair of women that misty morning, loosening their belts and loudly putting the finishing touches on their breakfast.

"The apostles paid for your breakfast," Estelle said when Abbey flagged her for the check.

Abbey turned to thank the apostles, but John began praying, so she waited. She noticed Olivia had her eyes closed tightly and her hands folded on her lap.

CHAPTER 12

THIS IS NOW—MILL TOWN GIRL

Saturday mornings are the pinnacle of breakfast. The New York Diner cracked more eggs, flipped more pancakes, and ladled more hollandaise on Saturday than on any other day.

Abbey enjoyed making hollandaise, carefully whisking the eggs in a double boiler, adding the melted butter slowly to create the emulsified sauce. It's all about the temperature of the ingredients. If you're not careful, the hollandaise separates, and you have to start over. Her hollandaise always held together nicely.

She took a clean spoon and dabbed it into the bowl. "Just a bit more paprika," she said and sprinkled a pinch of sweet vibrant red powder into the yellow sauce.

Abbey rarely missed a day at the diner. She was confident in her team but knew that the restaurant's success depended upon her. She viewed her employees like members of a family. The diner began as an idea, a recipe. Tables, ovens, walk-in refrigerators, and stainless-steel counters are things in a restaurant, but they are not *the* restaurant. The restaurant is its people.

Aliyah was Abbey's business manager. She advised Abbey *not* to view employees as family members. They disagreed on this management philosophy, but she understood Aliyah's point. If they were a family, Abbey had to be the mom, not a sister.

At 7 a.m., Olivia pulled onto the curb and parked. Abbey shook her head cheerfully. They had been through the "you can't park on the curb" discussion more than a few times, to no avail. Olivia parked on the curb both from a sense of entitlement and from pride in the diner's success. So much of Olivia's life was a struggle, and she liked to be associated with success. Today's parking was different. Yesterday, Abbey had made a sign, Olivia's Parking Spot, and placed it on a metal pole in front of the curb.

Her sister walked in with a big smile. It wasn't the smile Olivia used in her beauty shots. That smile was artificial, more like a mask she learned to wear a long time ago. Abbey remembered how nice it was to see her real smile. Her sister had two perfect dimples, and her eyes could light up like fireflies. Her cheekbones were perfectly high, and her face a gently curved oval.

Today, Olivia wore their *capture-the-jeans* jeans, faded to light blue, soft as silk, and a little frayed at the cuffs. They were tight and looked as if they could have been painted on. They fit perfectly on both women, and Olivia had recently stolen them back from her sister's closet.

"Nice pants," Abbey said wryly.

Olivia chuckled, sat at her favorite table, and turned over her cup.

"Oh, I'm sorry. We ran out of coffee," Abbey kidded.

"No coffee at the New York Diner? There will be pandemonium in the streets of Rock Hill, starting with me." Her voice sounded funny.

Abbey filled her cup and eyed her closely.

Nobody else would have picked up on it, because Olivia had learned to hide her fear behind her disarming allure. She stopped biting her fingernails when she began competing in pageants, but Abbey still recognized her sister's anxiety and the various expressions of it. The timbre of Olivia's voice shifted ever so slightly; she became more introspective, a little edgy; her face and shoulders tense and her gait stiff.

Abbey put the coffeepot down on the table, then kissed the top of her sister's head. Her hair smelled just as it did when they were tweens covered in Coppertone at the pool. It smelled like the sun.

Heart of a Mill Town Girl was written, and she was meeting her agent and publisher today to work on moving toward production. Olivia's first production, a one-act play, had been a success. The audiences liked it, and the reviews were mostly positive. *Mill Town Girl* was new ground, full length, and a musical. It was her heart poured out onto the pages, and now everyone would see it play out at curtain time. Writing the script had been cathartic, like a high school commencement, but also cleansing like a baptism.

Olivia could hardly believe the play was actually going to open. She began flirting with the idea so long ago. When she started writing, she knew the story had always been there. For her, writing was a release, but the business end of publishing and moving to production was the opposite. It left her feeling bottled up.

She told Abbey about her story at the onset. The main character was based on Olivia's interpretation of her sister, and she had let her read the first draft. Abbey felt humbled and couldn't see herself the way Olivia saw her, but she thought it was a good story.

"It's so well written," she told Olivia. Some of the scenes were painful because they hit so close to home.

Olivia's next pitch had been to Aliyah. She knew Aliyah would be honest from a dollars-and-cents perspective, and she told herself she wouldn't take rejection personally, but how could she not?

Aliyah listened to the synopsis without making a comment.

"Is it terrible?" asked Olivia.

"No. It's good, but that's not really the issue. The question is, can we sell it?" She agreed to read the script and think it over.

A week later, they met again for coffee at the diner. It was just after the morning rush, and when Olivia walked in, she saw Abbey, Aliyah, and Rachael sitting at a table in the center of the restaurant.

After Aliyah read the script, she secretly asked Rachael if she would write a song for *Mill Town Girl*. Rachael, who had majored in music education, then got her master's in music therapy, agreed immediately, because the songs were already written on the pages of her life. The play may have centered on Abbey as *the* Mill Town Girl, but it was really about all of them. Olivia had changed their names, but not their characters. It was, essentially, a story about love.

Aliyah put the script on the table, and Rachael laid out a few pages of sheet music next to it.

"I wrote this for the first scene," Rachael said, smiling. "What do you think?"

Olivia picked up the pages. "Sunrise in Carolina," she read the song title out loud. "Well, let's hear it."

Rachael was always ready to sing, as if music lived in her, just waiting to bubble over and escape through her lips in song. She stood up quietly and let it go. It took the diners in the restaurant by surprise, but when she finished, there was loud applause.

Olivia looked at her three best friends and held the sheet music close to her chest. "Wow."

CHAPTER 13

ELEVENTH-GRADE SUMMER

Abbey started her first job in the summer after eleventh grade, waiting tables at a restaurant. On her days off, she would hang out with the girls or kayak on the Catawba. That same summer, Olivia won the Miss York County beauty pageant. The pageant scene was work too. Every day, Olivia practiced for four hours and spent another hour in the gym.

Rachael spent her summer days in acting camp and track practice.

Aliyah had worked at the Harris Teeter supermarket every summer since she was fifteen. She was determined to stick to her financial plan to get through college.

The Stewart family owned lakeside property with a cabin and boathouse on Lake Wylie, on the north side of Rock Hill. The Fourth of July was always a busy weekend at the lake. Abbey was excited because all four of them were planning a girls' weekend at the cabin. It would be their first weekend at the lake unchaperoned. Amy had been reluctant at first to agree and nervous about the girls going there alone, but Abbey argued her case well. She was almost seventeen and starting the twelfth grade in a few weeks. The girls had been going to the cabin their entire lives and knew all of the neighbors. The cabin was just fifteen miles away, and they had spent nights at home alone.

Amy agreed, but with a few ground rules. They would not swim alone, which was a basic rule that applied to swimming in general. No boys in the house, which seemed a reasonable concession, and they had to check in every morning, noon, and bedtime, while also keeping Amy in the loop with any plans away from the cabin.

As the weekend approached, things didn't work out as planned. Olivia had to cancel after being invited to attend a Miss South Carolina preparatory weekend at Myrtle Beach. The current and past Miss South Carolinas were hosting the event for next year's hopeful contestants.

Aliyah ended up having to cover shifts at the grocery. She was sad to miss the weekend but glad to make overtime pay.

At first thought, Abbey was going to cancel the weekend plans, but she knew she and Rachael were bound to have fun, so they held to their plan of action. They would leave Friday afternoon when Abbey got off work.

Rachael's mom dropped her off at around 4 p.m., and when Abbey ran out to their car to say hello, she thought it looked like they had both been crying. Rachael usually told Abbey just about everything, so she figured they'd talk about it later, but Abbey worried about her friend sometimes. On the surface, Rachael seemed to have everything together, but Abbey knew Rachael struggled. She seemed to push against all the boundaries, and Abbey wondered how hard it was to grow up as a preacher's daughter. At other times, Abbey envied her; after all, she had two parents who loved each other and her.

"Have fun, girls," Rachael's mom said, then kissed Rachael on the cheek and said quietly, "I'm sorry."

"Me too, Mom," whispered Rachael.

Rachael's mom left, and the girls went upstairs to get Abbey's clothes.

"What swimsuit should I bring?" Abbey asked to lighten the mood a little. Her bathing suits were in a small pile on her bed. "I like this one," she held up a red, white, and blue one-piece she had selected for the holiday.

Rachael sat on the bed and began picking through the bathing suits one by one, appearing to look at them, but her mind was clearly somewhere else.

"I got into an argument with my mom," she said. "I told her I might want to go to New York after high school."

Rachael loved acting, and Abbey knew she had secretly sent in applications to some of the best acting schools in New York.

"What about your track scholarship?" asked Abbey. She knew that Rachael had already been contacted by college recruiters from Clemson and the University of South Carolina.

"Now you sound like my mom."

"I didn't mean it like that," said Abbey, turning to face her friend. "You know I want you to follow your dreams. I just know how hard you've worked for a scholarship and how fast you run."

Rachael drew in a sigh. She loved running and was one of the best sprinters in the state. "I was accepted to the New York Academy of Fine Arts," she said, sounding both happy and sad.

Abbey sat on the bed next to her. She thought that if anyone could make it in the music industry, it would be Rachael. Music had been part of Rachael's life from infancy. Her mom was filled with pride when she told people that Rachael was singing before her first birthday, and she loved busting out the old VHS video tape of her daughter singing along with *The Lion King* as a toddler. Songs were somehow bottled up inside of Rachael, and when they came out, people were compelled to listen.

Still, Abbey knew Rachael's tendency to jump into things headfirst, and in spite of all this, she was still shy in many ways.

"What are you going to do?" Abbey asked.

"I don't know. The scholarship is a big deal, and ... I'll miss you."

"Don't forget me when you're a big star," Abbey said, adding some wavy jazz hands for emphasis.

"I could never forget you," said Rachael. "No matter how hard I try."

They both laughed, then Rachael picked out a small two-piece swimsuit. "Here, this one's perfect," she handed it to Abbey.

While Abbey considered the bathing suit, Rachael went to the mirror above the bureau. Abbey's makeup was arranged neatly on top. She took a ruby red lipstick and put it on her lips, then pressed her lips together and smoothed it with her tongue.

"I like this color," she said. "What do you think?"

"It's lovely," said Abbey. She walked up behind Rachael and held the swimsuit top against her chest while looking in the mirror. "I think this would look sexy."

Rachael flushed.

"So what does your mom think about New York?" asked Abbey.

Rachael put down the lipstick, flustered by the question.

"My mom thinks acting is a hobby, and she thinks *you're* perfect." The last part came out unexpectedly.

"Wait. What? Where did that come from?" asked Abbey.

"I don't know. I guess I'm jealous. You do seem perfect."

Both girls were beautiful, but Rachael struggled with acne in early high school and didn't get as much attention from boys. She was the last of the four girls to develop her curves and stop padding her bra. Adolescence can be a cruel stage that magnifies the wrong things when girls are most vulnerable. Now, at almost seventeen, Rachael was very pretty but sometimes had difficulty realizing who she was.

"Perfect?"

"Yes," Rachael said flatly. "You're always the prettiest and the smartest."

"Look, I don't deserve guilt from you. You know how hard I study for my grades, and believe me, I have monsters in my own attic."

Rachael knew that was true and that she was wrong for casting any blame toward Abbey.

"I'm sorry, Abbey. I can be such a bitch."

Abbey didn't like to hold on to negative feelings. She liked to imagine them flying out of her soul like a freed bird.

"You're not a bitch, and I am certainly not perfect," Abbey said.

"Well, I'm a perfect bitch then," Rachael said, smiling again.

"Hey, you're in a win-win situation. College athlete or actress; either way, you're going to make your parents proud."

She drew in a big breath and nodded. Abbey was right. Her mom and dad loved her and would ultimately support her decision.

"And besides, you *are* the second-prettiest girl in school," Abbey teased.

"And the prettiest is …?"

"Olivia," they agreed simultaneously.

"Let's go have some fun," said Rachael, scooping up the two bathing suits and heading for the door.

They arrived at the lake later than expected. Abbey unlocked the front door, and they went in together. Amy had taught her to be cautiously aware when entering an empty house. Her eyes scanned the interior, and all was secure. Then she called her mom to check in while Rachael brought her suitcase into a bedroom.

The cabin was a three-bedroom rustic lodge with an exposed log interior. Amy and Neil had decorated it with dark leather furniture. The living room had a white oak cathedral ceiling and a stone wood-burning fireplace with a large window that looked out over the lake. Amy had updated the living room a few years ago with a home theater system. Abbey loved the kitchen, which was well designed and professional, built for hosting parties.

Rachael came out of the bedroom with a small brown paper bag that looked like it held a sandwich and sat on the large sofa. From the sandwich bag, she took out a small plastic bag and some rolling papers.

Abbey knew Rachael had been experimenting with marijuana but had not anticipated her bringing it to the cabin.

Abbey didn't smoke herself, but she was nonjudgmental. "What are you doing?" she asked.

Rachael was sprinkling dried cannabis onto the paper.

"Is it okay?" she said, looking up at Abbey. "I should have asked first."

Abbey didn't answer. She was positive that this would not be okay with her mom, and Rachael could see she was tentative.

"Never mind," said Rachael. "It was my mistake." She put the bag down and out of sight. "Let's go for a swim."

They quickly changed into their bathing suits and walked to the pier in the backyard. The sun had set, and a huge full moon was shining above the pines. The water was perfect, just deep enough, warm at the top and cool at the bottom, and they were the only two people in the water. On the other side of the lake, a family was grilling and shooting colorful fireworks.

After their swim, they lay out to dry on the deck, looking up at the stars.

"My dad taught me the constellations when I was a little girl," Abbey said.

Whenever Abbey or Olivia talked about their father, Rachael felt a weight upon her, solemn and kind of spiritual, like being in church.

"See that bright star?" she pointed at the dark horizon. "Well, it's not a star. It's Jupiter."

Rachael stared at the bright white dot intently.

"Look left from there," she said, pointing out five stars and tracing a W in the air with her finger. "That's Cassiopeia." They looked at the constellation that lit up the heavens.

61

"Cassiopeia was banished to the stars by Zeus because she was too beautiful for Earth."

The sky was so big and expansive. There wasn't a cloud in sight, and the stars reflected off the smooth water on the lake.

"Where is the North Star?" Rachael asked.

Abbey looked, then pointed with her finger into the northern sky.

"Do you see those stars there? That's Ursa Major."

She leaned over and behind Rachael, with her arm pointed skyward, and pressed her cheek against hers so she could follow her finger and identify the Big Dipper. Rachael could smell Abbey's hair. It smelled like coconut.

"Now look just right from there."

"That little blue star?" asked Rachael.

"Yes, that's it! Now you can always find your way."

They lay back down and enjoyed a few minutes of comfortable silence.

"I want to try it," Abbey said quietly.

"Try what?"

"Marijuana."

Rachael now felt oddly protective. "I don't know, Abbey. Are you sure?"

"Just a little, to see what it's like."

Rachael went inside and came back with the joint she had rolled earlier. Abbey had moved onto a large wicker swing built for two. It was her favorite place to nap on a warm summer day at the lake.

Rachael lit the reefer and showed Abbey how to inhale and hold the smoke before she exhaled. Abbey was already a little dizzy from the secondhand smoke, but she took a drag, then coughed a little.

"Are you okay?" Rachael asked.

"Yes, but I feel lightheaded," Abbey said, then she started to giggle.

They smoked for a few minutes while gently rocking on the chair. Rachael stopped smoking, and the chair stopped rocking.

"I think I love you," she told Abbey.

They were both a little high, and Abbey didn't get the meaning, or she pretended not to.

"Well, I love you too, silly," she said to Rachael. She suddenly felt flushed and excited. Her lips were dry, and her heart was beating quickly.

Rachael leaned forward and kissed her gently. Abbey was surprised, and she touched her fingers to her lips, as if registering what had just happened.

"I'm sorry," said Rachael, pulling away. Her own heart felt like it was going to burst out of her chest, and though she didn't want to stop, she also felt that it was wrong.

Then Abbey leaned forward and kissed her back. She could hardly believe what was happening. Rachael's lips were so soft.

"But ... we both like boys," Abbey said when they came up for air.

"I know," said Rachael, trying to will herself to stop, but she felt almost outside of her own body, as her hand touched Abbey's breast.

The next morning, Abbey was up early as always. She was prepping a spinach quiche for breakfast. The Mexican ceramic-tile floor felt cool on her bare feet.

"Perfect," she said to herself as she sprinkled a mixture of sharp cheddar and shaved Parmesan cheese on top. As she put the quiche into the convection oven, her mind was elsewhere, and she burned the back of her hand on the oven top, almost causing her to drop the pie dish.

"Ouch!" she said and turned immediately to the sink to run cold water over the burn.

The reflex arc that causes the body to react to a burn requires no input from the brain. It causes action before pain is even perceived, with involuntary contraction and withdrawal from the hot object.

There was a red line on the back of her hand.

It's not too bad, no blister, she thought. *It's just part of cooking.*

While that was true, it still burned.

She heard Rachael stirring in the bedroom and realized she had never been nervous about seeing Rachael before. Her heart was beating a little fast, wondering what she should say.

Rachael had actually been up for a while, lying in her bed thinking and feeling nervous. Dichotomous thoughts filtered through her mind. She wished it hadn't happened, but she was glad it did. It felt wrong, but it felt right. She felt bad, but she felt good.

She felt hungover from the weed and in a mild fog. Weed hangovers are real. She put her hand over her mouth and breathed. "Ugh," she groaned. She didn't like weed breath either. She got out of bed and hurried to the bathroom to brush her teeth.

"What happened?" Rachael asked when she saw Abbey sitting at the kitchen table with ice on her hand.

"I burned my hand putting the quiche into the oven."

"Can I see?" Rachael asked.

"It's not bad …."

Rachael sat next to her and gently took Abbey's hand, looking at the thin red line.

They looked at each other, then gazed down at their entwined hands. They both had things they wanted to say, but like an emotional reflex, they pulled back.

"Does it hurt?" Rachael asked as she picked up the ice and gently rubbed it on Abbey's burn.

It did hurt, but Abbey shook her head, then took a deep breath. "So about last night …"

Just then, they heard a key unlocking the front door.

"Surprise!" Olivia said, walking in with Aliyah.

Late summer has a different feel than early summer, as the long days become shorter and the mornings a little cooler. The Carolina cornfields brim over with stalks ten feet high. The squirrels that populate the oaks at Winthrop become plump and begin burying acorns in preparation for the winter. Summer vacation always passes too quickly, and this one was no exception. And as it drew to a close, Abbey and Rachael still had never talked about what happened.

At first, they felt awkward, both wanting to talk but neither knowing how to start. Then they both thought the other must not want to talk, so neither brought it up.

Abbey and Olivia were spending the morning at the SouthPark Mall in Charlotte, shopping for clothes to start the school year. Olivia, a top contender for Miss South Carolina, could make any type of clothing look good. Abbey was the kind of person who didn't seem to notice how pretty she was, but she looked good in everything too.

They went to Nordstrom, and Olivia bought a pair of jet-black designer jeans and high-heeled pumps. Abbey found some jeans at American Eagle. And then they checked out the latest phones at the Apple Store.

"Look at this one," said Abbey, as she selected a deep-red phone that she knew would be Olivia's favorite.

"I think I like this one," said Olivia. She picked up a lavender phone with a smile, knowing it was her sister's favorite.

After looking at the new phones, they were thirsty, so they took a break from shopping and found a cafe in the food court, where they each got a bubble tea. This was a treat for Olivia, who rarely drank anything with sugar, but she couldn't resist the way the raspberry bubbles popped in her mouth.

They both got a text and checked their phones. It was their mom, just sending a heart emoji—her way of checking in with them.

Abbey sent a return heart, then looked through her messages for a moment. "Have you talked with Aliyah and Rachael this week?" she asked.

There was rarely a day, much less a week, that the girls were not together, but Rachael had been on a family vacation in Florida, and Aliyah was visiting her grandparents in Augusta.

Olivia had noticed a subtle change in the dynamic between Abbey and Rachael and was waiting for Abbey to confide in her, but she was running out of patience. They rarely kept secrets from each other; in fact, it was difficult for them to surprise each other, even with birthday gifts.

Olivia tapped her fingers on the table, then blurted out, "What's going on between you and Rachael?"

Abbey wasn't sure how to answer. She wanted to talk with her sister but didn't want to betray Rachael's confidence. She scoffed, trying to play it cool. "What do you mean?"

"Come on, Abbey," said Olivia tenderly. "I can tell when you're upset. It's my superpower."

"Sometimes, I swear you know me better than I know myself," Abbey said, then she hesitated briefly, letting her head catch up with her heart.

Olivia sipped her tea and waited quietly for Abbey to continue.

"So ... remember the Fourth of July, when I was with Rachael at the lake? I did something I've never done before."

Olivia thought back to that morning when she and Aliyah both had last-minute changes in their plans and decided to go up to the cabin.

"What did you do?" Olivia asked, remembering how Abbey and Rachael seemed a little uncomfortable with the intrusion.

"I ... um," started Abbey. She wanted to tell her sister what happened with Rachael but chickened out at the last moment. "I got high ... I smoked a joint."

"Oh," Olivia said, a little surprised. "I knew something was up that morning."

Abbey nodded. She and Olivia had promised each other that if they ever tried marijuana, they would do it together.

"I know I promised that I wouldn't try it without you," said Abbey. "I'm sorry."

Olivia was annoyed, a little angry, but also curious. They had made their pact when they were thirteen, and Olivia had turned down invitations to try marijuana multiple times, in spite of her temptation to give it a try, because of their promise. She stared at her sister. "Well, what was it like?"

"I felt light-headed, like I wasn't totally there, like I was floating. But it made me cough, and it burned my throat."

"Maybe I'll try it this weekend," Olivia said, with a crispness that revealed her underlying emotion.

"I didn't really like it," Abbey said sheepishly.

"So that makes it okay?"

"No, but …" Abbey's voice trailed off. She wanted to tell Olivia everything that had happened at the lake and how she and Rachael had not discussed it. How she couldn't discuss it with anyone.

"Things have been tense between me and Rachael," she said quietly.

"Hey," Olivia said softly when she realized Abbey was holding back tears. "What's really wrong?"

Abbey's head was spinning, afraid she had screwed up her friendship with Rachael forever. She felt utterly confused and all alone. She gulped back a sob, then shook her head. "Nothing," she said finally. "Are we … okay?"

Olivia hesitated. She really wanted to push her sister to tell her what was going on. Instead, she grasped her hand and smiled warmly. "We'll always be okay."

Abbey knew something was wrong when Ms. Bradley came into the class. It's not that it was particularly unusual for the school principal to visit classrooms. It was known to be her favorite part of the job, but today she seemed more business-like and less cheerful. She whispered briefly to Ms. Martinez, the American lit teacher, then approached Abbey's desk, quietly asking her to come with her to the office.

They did not speak as they walked through the hall. Abbey had no idea what could be wrong, but she was scared. Was there some kind of emergency? It reminded her of the feeling she had when the soldier came to the door.

As they approached the office, she saw the school resource officer—Lauren McAllen, who was a family friend and hardly older than Abbey—waiting with another police officer. Through the etched-glass door, Abbey saw Rachael sitting in the office. She looked like she'd been crying.

"What's wrong, Lauren?" asked Abbey desperately.

"Please refer to her as Officer McAllen," said Ms. Bradley. Her tone was stern, and this confused Abbey, who never had an honest moment of tension with the principal. "Let's go into my office."

Abbey's fear turned from panic that something bad had happened to apprehension that she was somehow in trouble.

"Please sit down," Ms. Bradley said.

Abbey sat nervously on the end of a chair.

Lauren looked concerned. As she started to speak, the other officer interrupted her.

"Abigail Stewart," said the police officer, "I am Officer Williams with the drug enforcement unit. I'm here because drugs were found in your locker this morning."

Her mind raced. *But I only smoked one joint in my whole life.*

"Drugs ... in my locker?" Abbey repeated. She and Rachael shared their school locker.

"Abbey," began Lauren, "Is there anything you want to tell us?"

Abbey had no knowledge of any drugs in her locker, but she had a certainty about how they got there. She thought of Rachael crying in the other room. A drug-related charge would cost Rachael her scholarship and push her further away from her parents.

"I'm sorry," she said. "The drugs are mine."

Ms. Bradley shook her head in disbelief.

Officer Williams put a hand on Abbey's shoulders and reached for her handcuffs.

Abbey swallowed hard, scared. "Can I call my mom?"

CHAPTER 14

AMY

Amy had opened her portrait studio next to the big bank downtown. She was the city's most requested wedding photographer, but her passion, what she really loved, was to capture different images or common images from different viewpoints. It could be almost anything, like the last leaf on a tree in autumn. She had a unique way of looking at people and things and would imagine her eyes as the camera. She looked *at* things but also through, under, and above them. She viewed the world as her canvas, and light was her paint. She knew lighting could change a landscape and alter a mood, make a house seem warm and inviting or dark and haunted. But there was not enough light in the world to hide the dark shadows on the afternoon she found out about her cancer.

Her cancer is exactly how she thought of it. Of course, she knew about cancer and had known people with cancer, but this was *hers*. Her own body had made it. *Dammit. Don't women already have enough pain worrying about their bodies?*

After two weeks of sleepless nights, hours upon hours of research, and begging God for a miracle, Amy decided that there just was no right time to deliver the news. She asked the girls if they would come by that Sunday for dinner.

They had all been through so much already, and Amy dreaded the very idea of what her death might do to the girls. They had all dealt with Neil's death differently. For Amy, Neil was killed—*that sounds so harsh*, she thought, *but it's what happened*. It wasn't an accident, and it wasn't an illness; he was killed; a hot piece of lead cutting through a frigid, dark, Afghanistan night. After the shock, Amy's initial anger had been overwhelming, almost to the point of hatred, but then she wondered how many Afghan women had lost their husbands the same way.

Abbey, on the other hand, hid her pain deep inside. Amy knew she would probably arrive early to help with dinner. Abbey gave and gave—it was who she was, but it was also her way of coping. Sometimes, she would get overwhelmed and come near to breaking.

Olivia had fostered a self-destructive sort of defense. She would arrive with news of her latest borderline boyfriend, a bottle of wine, and a couple of joints for dessert. She might eat a little dinner, then would politely excuse herself to vomit quietly in the bathroom. She was always fighting back against the darkness.

Olivia told her mom she'd pick up Abbey, who was living in a dorm at Winthrop, no more than a half mile from their house on Oakland Avenue. Abbey's college start had been delayed by the drug charges from her senior year. Olivia knew how grateful her sister was for the full college experience of living on campus, even though Abbey admitted it was an unnecessary expense. Olivia, on the other hand, was living in Charlotte after winning the Miss South Carolina pageant the year before. The prize for the pageant had included a college scholarship, but Olivia decided to take some time off to work on her modeling career.

Abbey was waiting outside the dorm when Olivia pulled up. The girls chatted about their mom's oddly formal invitation to dinner on the three-minute drive to the house.

"Do you think she wants to sell the mill?" Olivia asked.

Olivia felt an odd attachment to the mill. There was something about the old building she had always been connected to.

"I don't think so," said Abbey. "Maybe she met somebody."

That thought occupied them as they pulled into the driveway. Amy didn't date for ten years after their dad died. It's not that men didn't ask; they asked often. And a lot of people encouraged her to "get out there again," but she was focused on the girls. When they graduated high school, though, Amy admitted she was lonely and finally agreed to go out on a date last year. The man seemed nice and handsome, but Amy broke it off after a couple of dates.

"I guess we'll find out," Olivia said, turning off the car.

They walked up to the front door, both feeling a sense of trepidation, somehow knowing that this dinner wasn't *nothing*.

Amy was waiting for them in the foyer, and the girls hugged, kissed, and complimented her.

"You look as pretty as ever," Abbey said.

Olivia nodded. "Did you go blonder?" Then, forgoing the conventional rules of engagement, Olivia abruptly added, "So what's going on? Do you have a new boyfriend?"

This was Olivia's personality. She put it all out there on the table.

"Boyfriend?" asked Amy. This was not the direction she wanted or intended this conversation to go.

"Girlfriend then?" said Olivia.

Amy sighed.

"Olivia Grace," she said with a smile, "come in and sit down before starting your inquisition."

"I was just teasing, sort of," said Olivia sweetly. "Abbey and I worry about you a little."

"Now hold on there, sis," said Abbey. "Don't drag me into this. Ouch!"

Olivia had pinched Abbey, and they laughed as they walked toward the kitchen, feeling relaxed and at home.

"I smell spaghetti!" said Abbey with excitement. "Did you make meatballs?"

As children, the girls would argue about the better protein: meatballs or meat sauce.

"I made both," Amy said.

Olivia stuck her tongue out at her sister. In reality, the girls almost never fought or fussed but had fun teasing each other about silly things like meatballs.

Amy set the table elegantly with her blue-and-white china. Abbey poured sweet tea for her mom and herself and ice water for Olivia.

During dinner, they talked about Abbey's classes and Olivia's new apartment in Charlotte.

"It's different," said Olivia. "Small but comfy. It seems like I'm hardly ever there though. I have photoshoots every day. Tomorrow I'll be in Charleston and Wednesday in Clemson."

"It sounds exciting," said Abbey.

"It was at first. Now it's more like work."

Olivia grew accustomed to the bright lights and celebrity status. She had always liked being on the stage, but Abbey knew her deeper side, her loneliness.

"I miss you," Abbey told her.

"Well, I'm a quick drive up I-77."

"I'm a poor college girl, not a famous Miss South Carolina," Abbey joked.

Olivia held out her hand like a queen.

"You may kiss my ring now," she said, and they laughed.

Amy loved to watch her girls talk together, and hearing their laughter was her favorite sound in the world. She didn't want to start the next conversation. She thought about putting it off until another day but then cleared her voice and straightened down the front of her dress.

"Is that a new dress, Mom?" asked Abbey.

Amy didn't answer. "I have ovarian cancer," she blurted out.

She had rehearsed how she might conduct the conversation but realized she just had to get it out. And so there it was, like a bloody tumor upon her china on their beautiful oak table.

The girls said nothing. Denial. It was a shock, and Amy knew it would be. It seemed unfair, but hiding her news wasn't fair either. The girls wondered if she had a new boyfriend. Well, this was their introduction to her new "boyfriend." She knew he would consume her attention and energy and be the topic of her daily conversations. They would spend all of their time together, and finally, he would break her heart—all of their hearts.

The silence of their denial was brief, but it led to the necessary questions.

"Are they sure it's cancer?"

"Yes."

"Have you gotten a second opinion?"

"Yes."

She explained how she had a little bit of irregular bleeding and went to her doctor, who did an ultrasound and immediately recommended she see a specialist at Walter Reed Army Medical Center, a gynecologic oncologist.

"I knew something was wrong because I had an appointment with the specialist within two weeks. I'd never even heard of a GYN oncologist before."

"When was this, Mom?" asked Abbey.

"Last month, when I went to DC," she said. She had told the girls she was visiting friends in northern Virginia. "Dr. Song ordered a CAT scan of my abdomen and pelvis. The next day, she called and asked me to come in." She was quiet for a moment while the gravity of her words settled in.

"Is it bad?" asked Olivia.

Amy reached out across the table for their hands. "Yes," she said. "Dr. Song said they can't be sure until the surgery, but it looks like stage three."

"What does that mean exactly?" asked Abbey.

"It means … well, I have a battle ahead of me … but we need to prepare ourselves—" Amy choked up and heaved in a shuddering breath.

All three women had been trying to keep their emotions in check, but when Amy looked into her daughters' frightened eyes, she started to cry.

Attachment in humans plays out differently than in other animals. Humans attach longer and stronger. By the time a Carolina wren hatchling is two weeks old, it's on its own, flying independently away from the nest. The brevity of the new bird's attachment is essential for its survival. On the other hand, prolonged attachment is necessary for the human child.

Object permanence is the ability of a child to establish a permanent construct of objects, with the understanding that just because an object is not seen does not mean the object is gone. This develops in the first year of life, when a child is four to eight months old. Prior to this ability, if a ball rolls under a chair, the child thinks the object is gone.

When Neil died, the girls' six-year-old lives imploded, and the fabric of their experience and understanding collapsed in on them. That first year, Abbey and Olivia didn't want Amy out of their line of sight. It was as if their object permanence had regressed. They clung to her as if their lives depended on it. Amy became their lifeline, and they became hers. At first, they didn't want to allow anything or anyone new into their world. Amy worked hard to help foster their independence.

When Aliyah and Rachael entered their lives, they learned to love somebody new, and Amy knew they were healing.

She did not know how to help them heal now.

Death has a way of making people think that what matters most in life is life. But if there is anything to take away from the empty spaces and quietness that follows a terminal diagnosis, it's that what matters most is love. Sometimes, love can fall between the cracks and get lost in the appointments, chemotherapy, fear, and grief.

After Amy's diagnosis, the unspoken plan was that life would go on as though nothing had changed, but everything in life had changed.

Amy's surgery had been extensive, with the removal of her uterus, ovaries, and fallopian tubes. And her prognosis was even worse; the cancer had spread to her intestines. It was consuming her.

Even though Amy asked her not to, Abbey had flown to DC to be there for her after the surgery.

"How is school going?" Amy asked from her hospital bed, hoping to prompt a distraction from their nightmare.

Abbey was hesitant to reply, knowing her mother would not like the answer. "I withdrew from my classes," she said. "I just can't concentrate on them right now."

Amy looked away from her and toward the window. She could see the massive flagpoles on the lawn of the army hospital. It was autumn in Bethesda, Maryland, and leaves were blowing in the wind. "Please don't quit college because of me," she pleaded quietly.

Everyone shared in the denial. For Amy's part, she knew she was very sick, but she wanted to feel some sense of control, as though her cancer could not exert itself into her children's lives.

Abbey had rehearsed this conversation. She stared out of the hospital window and watched the leaves swirling in a little vortex of wind; reds and yellows coming together, then spreading out to find their place and land lightly on the ground. Abbey loved the fall. Some people thought of it as the death of summer, but for her, it was living and vibrant, like the coolness of harvest or the first frost.

"Mom, it's not like that. I just need a little break. That's all."

Amy didn't reply. What could she say? She knew she needed Abbey right now.

Abbey tried to reassure her. "I'll be fine," she said, although that's not how she felt.

Amy could see the sadness in her eyes. "Sometimes," she began thoughtfully, "things don't fit into the package the way we intend. In the end, it's still a beautiful gift."

Abbey smiled and nodded.

"Have you talked with Rachael and Aliyah?" asked Amy.

"They call me every day. Rachael said she is coming next weekend to see you."

Amy reflected on this for a moment.

"You know, she really loves you," Amy said.

"I know, Mom," said Abbey, deflecting. "We've been friends since we were ten."

"That's not what I meant," said Amy, laying her hand gently on her daughter's arm. "Do you love her?"

Abbey closed her eyes and thought of Rachael.

"Yes," she said, looking down, her voice choked with emotion. "But there are so many moving parts in our lives. I just can't go there right now."

"You know something," started Amy, gently brushing the long hair from Abbey's face, tucking it behind her ear, "Ever since you were a little girl, you've always made the most out of every moment."

Time was their enemy. They both knew it, and neither wanted to talk about it, so Amy changed the subject.

"How is Olivia?"

Her sister would be there later that day. Olivia's way of coping was to focus on her goals. After she won the state pageant, she moved on to the national scene, where she was the clear favorite to be the next Miss America. In public appearances, Olivia was poised and glamorous. To look at her, she seemed to exude confidence and grace; in secret, Abbey knew she was struggling to hold it together.

"She'll be here tonight," said Abbey.

"But you didn't answer my question. How is she?"

Amy knew her girls. It amazed her how they were so alike yet so different. They could simultaneously be both inseparable and immiscible, identical and divergent. Each exceptionally individual but also as if they shared the same heart and mind.

"I don't know," said Abbey, unable to look into her mother's eyes because she did know. She knew that her mom was dying and that her sister was falling apart and dying in her own way, another casualty of carcinoma.

Amy sat up and, although it hurt, bent forward, removing the pneumatic compression devices that squeezed her legs.

"Come here, sweetheart," she said.

Abbey embraced her, holding her tight. She buried her face in her mother's hospital gown as she cried her heart out.

Alarms sounded from the infusion pump on Amy's IV, and a nurse came to the room. She checked the IV, quietly turned off the alarm, and let them share their sorrow in peace.

CHAPTER 15

AFTER AMY

Miss America, Olivia Stewart!

She heard the words, and she played the part. Like everything she did on stage, it was well rehearsed. Her hand covered her mouth, and tears filled her emerald eyes. She had worked hard for this title and won in a field of talented and amazing young women. While standing on the stage, she thought about her mom, who was dying in a hospital bed in Bethesda. Amy had tried chemotherapy, but nothing seemed to stop her cancer. It had been a year filled with pain and disappointment. Now, standing under bright lights, Olivia began to feel like she was in a dark tunnel, as if her own light was also fading, flickering in the darkness.

She hugged the runner up and walked forward. The last thing she remembered was the tiara being placed on her head. The crowd started to sway, and the flashes from the cameras became dim. When she woke up, she was in a hospital bed with Rachael and Aliyah at her bedside.

"Olivia?"

Olivia could hear Aliyah's voice. It seemed distant at first, then gradually came closer. She looked around.

"Where am I?" she asked.

"You're at the medical center in Atlantic City," Rachael said, leaning over and putting a hand softly on her shoulder. "You passed out, and they couldn't wake you up."

"My head hurts," she said.

"You hit your head pretty hard, but the doctor said you are going to be fine," said Aliyah. "You won. You're Miss America."

Olivia's memory began to come back. She did not have a clear memory of the end of the pageant. She looked at Aliyah and Rachael, who were both flushed, their faces stained from tears mixed with makeup.

"What is it? What's wrong?" Olivia asked, but she already knew.

"Abbey's on the phone," said Aliyah, and she held the phone out tentatively toward Olivia.

"Olivia," she heard her sister's voice through the cell phone. Her mind felt paralyzed; words seemed distant, like listening to someone talk from another room. Her hand trembled as she took the phone.

"I'm here," she said.

There was a pause, an emptiness, a void.

"It's bad, sis," came Abbey's voice, choked with emotion. "Mom just died."

Olivia took a deep, shaky breath and looked around. Aliyah and Rachael stood on each side of her, and nurses gathered outside the glass trauma-room door. There were television crews in the parking lot and pageant officials in the waiting room.

Her evening gown had been set aside on a plastic chair in the corner of the room. It looked out of place. Her tiara, the crown for Miss America, lay on the ground, under the chair where it had fallen.

Amy had made all of the arrangements for her cremation soon after she started her final round of chemotherapy. Abbey told Olivia she didn't have to come to Maryland, because "they" would be home tomorrow, but there was no "they," only a lonely, quiet plane ride back to Charlotte.

Olivia was waiting at the bottom of the escalator in arrivals, where all departing passengers were funneled. She wanted to be unnoticed, wearing yoga pants and a Carolina Panthers sweatshirt, but the video of her crowning and then losing consciousness had gone viral.

Abbey had been alone since her mother died, and as she stepped off the escalator, she saw Olivia. She stopped walking and started crying. Olivia ran up to her and they wept together, dividing the stream of arriving passengers.

People began to recognize Olivia, and some started to take pictures, until a TSA officer came to disperse the crowd and escort the sisters toward the baggage carrousels, where Rachael and Aliyah were waiting. The four girls reached out, joining hands for a moment, forming a circle. When the four of them were together, there was always a special energy, even in their sorrow.

"How was your flight?" asked Aliyah.

"It was okay," said Abbey. Her carry-on was slung on her tired shoulder, and it slipped onto the ground. She just let it fall, exhausted physically and emotionally. Rachael stepped forward to pick it up, and Abbey reached out to embrace her.

"Hey girl, I've got you," said Rachael.

Abbey hugged her tightly.

"They've hardly left my side since I went to the hospital," said Olivia. "Where are Mom's—"

Ashes. She couldn't bring herself to say it.

Abbey nodded in the direction of the baggage conveyor, where the scores of arriving passengers all anxiously awaited the appearance of their suitcases. She wondered if anyone else was picking up the ashes of somebody they loved.

Baggage claim brings out interesting human qualities, like an airport feeding frenzy. Travelers stand at attention, anxiously waiting to be reunited with their luggage, watching for their baggage, and grabbing it as soon as it passes through the black plastic-strip curtains into the lobby.

The conveyor started, and the crowd inched forward in anticipation. The girls stood at the back of the crowd, keeping an eye out for Abbey's suitcase. It was vintage, or antique—Olivia wasn't sure what the difference was, but it was old. Its weathered leather case was covered by travel stamps from the past century, collected from hotels, airlines, railways, and national parks.

Luggage rolled past them, then rolled past again and again. The crowd dispersed as passengers grabbed their bags, but Abbey's suitcase never appeared. The conveyor stopped.

Aliyah walked to the airline's baggage desk and returned with a middle-aged woman dressed in an airline uniform.

"I just arrived from Dulles, and my suitcase is missing," Abbey said dully. Her exhaustion was clear for all to see. She pulled a ticket from her jacket and handed it over.

The agent took a quick look at the baggage claim. "I'm sorry for the inconvenience," she said sincerely, then handed a form to Abbey. "Please list the contents as accurately as possible. Was there anything of value in the baggage?"

"Our mother's ashes," Olivia said sharply. She was visibly upset.

"Oh," the agent said. She recognized Olivia as soon as she peered at her. "I'm so sorry."

"So am I," said Olivia, biting down on her lip and closing her eyes.

The agent told them honestly that she was not sure where the suitcase was but that almost all lost luggage was eventually recovered. She said she would call personally as soon as Abbey's suitcase was located.

That was that. It was over. Their mom was gone, and they didn't even have her ashes.

As they walked out through the sliding glass doors, a woman was standing with her back to them, waiting for a shuttle. They couldn't see her face, but she had golden blond hair and, for all the world, resembled Amy. All four girls stopped in their tracks.

"Mom?" said Olivia.

The woman turned. She did favor Amy, with soft, beautiful features. Olivia stopped, trembling, and for a moment just looked into the woman's eyes.

Olivia's lip quivered. "I thought," she took a deep, heavy breath, "you were my mom."

"I'm sorry," the woman said tenderly.

Everybody was sorry, but that didn't change anything.

Abbey had moved back into the house with her mom the previous year. Amy was upset when she withdrew from Winthrop, but Abbey insisted and, in the end, was thankful for the time she was able to spend with her mom.

When she had gotten home the night before, it was dark, and she was so tired. In the light of day, she saw that the kitchen, and the house in general, reflected the headspace she was in: scattered and out of order. The coffee in the pot was weeks old. She washed and scrubbed it and the filter basket, which was moldy, then started a fresh pot.

Olivia had spent the night there, and they'd slept in the twin beds in their old bedroom. She came downstairs and sat with Abbey as she watched the coffee brewing.

"The agent from the airport called," said Abbey. She walked to the counter and got the coffee. "They found my suitcase."

"Thank goodness," said Olivia. "Where is it?"

"Get this—it ended up in Glasgow."

"Scotland?" asked Olivia curiously.

"Yeah, right. How crazy is that?"

They sat at the table, and Abbey poured the coffee into Amy's porcelain coffee cups. She looked at the beautiful cups, which depicted an Italian countryside, and realized they belonged to her and Olivia now. Amy taught them that coffee tasted best in porcelain. Abbey sipped her coffee and had to agree.

"Mom always wanted to go to Scotland," said Olivia.

Abbey nodded sadly. She remembered how their mother had become interested in their ancestry and bought the girls memberships to an online genealogy tracing site. They discovered that their ancestors had been expelled from Scotland in the 1700s and the name Stewart was derived from the old English word for *guardian*.

In the moment, there was a blurred line between happy and sad memories.

"I have to pick up the suitcase this afternoon," said Abbey, trying to refocus. "What are your plans for the day?" She was hoping they could spend the day together.

"I can come to the airport, but first I have to get back to my apartment. I'm supposed to go to New York to be on *The Tonight Show*."

"That sounds exciting," said Abbey.

"I guess so." Olivia tapped her fingernails on the porcelain coffee cup. "The Miss America organization has been very supportive, and I'll meet Jimmy Fallon …."

Olivia sounded tentative, like she was trying to convince herself of something. Abbey knew how hard her sister had worked for this.

"But?" asked Abbey.

"I wasn't there when Mom died," she said, shaking her head slightly as she stared into the black coffee, as if it held all the answers. "Now I'm supposed to jet off like nothing happened? I feel like it's exploiting Mom, you know, because it makes a good news story: 'Miss America's mother dies as new Miss America collapses on stage.'"

There was no denying it was a good story.

"Hey," said Abbey, reaching out and touching Olivia's hand across the table. "Mom wanted you to be on that stage. She was so proud of you. None of us knew when this was going to happen."

Olivia thought of her earliest memories, when there were four Stewarts, Amy tucking them in, and Neil softly playing his guitar as she and Abbey fell asleep. Then she thought of the last time she saw Amy, lying in a hospital bed. Some might say she had already been gone, in and out of consciousness.

"Tell me about that last night," asked Olivia.

"She just drifted off to sleep," said Abbey, which wasn't true. She watched as her mom began to draw in deep, gasping breaths, like she was hungry for air. She watched every one of her mother's last breaths. In the end, they slowed, to only a few breaths a minute. She couldn't tell her sister that.

"I should have been there," said Olivia.

"You were there. You were on the TV in her room, and after you won, it was like she knew it was her time."

They were pretty much out of tears, cried out of emotions from the previous day, but felt the connection they'd shared since infancy, when they'd formed their first thoughts and words.

They finished the pot of coffee together, then cleaned the kitchen, and Olivia left for her apartment. It felt lonely in the house, quiet.

Abbey looked out the window at her car, which was fairly well covered with leaves. It was chilly, but she went outside, brushed off the leaves, and hosed down the windshield and rear window. Her fingers were cold and numb when she was finished. When she tried to start the car, the battery was dead. Abbey had tried so hard to hold herself together, but this was like the feather that lands on the cartoon character as they try to hold on to the edge of a cliff. She felt like her car, broken down, and put her head on the steering wheel, trying not to cry.

A tapping on the driver's side window startled her, and she jumped in her seat.

"I didn't mean to scare you. Are you okay?"

It was Rachael.

Abbey closed her eyes and nodded, then opened the car door.

"My car won't start," she said. "I think the battery is dead."

"Don't worry," she said sweetly, "my car is your car." She held her hand out to Abbey.

She took Rachael's hand, which felt so warm.

"Mom's ashes are on their way to the airport," said Abbey.

Rachael didn't know what to say. She was heartbroken for Abbey and Olivia.

"Can I borrow your car this afternoon to pick up my suitcase?"

"We can go together," said Rachael.

They walked inside, and Abbey asked if she wanted breakfast. Rachael had already eaten. Abbey asked if she minded coming with her upstairs, so Rachael followed her to Amy's room. They stood outside the door. Her mother's belongings were all very neatly arranged, as if they were waiting for her to return.

"I'm not sure where to start," Abbey said as they stepped inside, looking at a lifetime of things.

Amy's clothing was very nice, and they agreed it could be donated. The personal items—her photographs, letters, and even poetry—would be harder to deal with. Amy had written journals for years. Reading any of them at the moment was more than Abbey could bear, so together they decided to tackle Amy's dresser and chest of drawers. They worked for about an hour, fighting the feeling that they were trespassing, doing something wrong, looking at things that didn't belong to them.

The airline called again to let Abbey know her luggage would be delivered to the house. By then it was almost noon. Abbey texted Olivia with the update, and then she and Rachael walked into town for lunch. It was chilly, and they both wore sweaters. They ordered and ate salmon salad on toasted brioche at their favorite cafe on Main Street. The sky was overcast, and it was going to be a cold walk back in the rain, so they finished quickly and started back to the house. They were a block away when the rain started, and they came inside dripping wet.

They went upstairs to Abbey's room and took off their heavy, wet sweaters. Abbey got towels for both of them. They were shivering, and she started to undress. Yesterday's airport travel was still on her skin, and she wanted to shower. She loved standing in the shower and imagining the day's stress being washed away by the water.

"Would you like a hot shower?" said Abbey, with a slight tilt of her head.

Rachael was trembling all over, but it wasn't only from the winter rain. She took the towel, which was a perfect Abbey towel, soft and warm, and dried off her face and hair. She was unsure how to interpret Abbey. The question, while direct, contained an unspoken ambiguity. An image of standing under hot water while holding Abbey flashed in her mind.

Abbey had not consciously intended to be ambiguous, but now the question was out there. She thought about what her mother said in the hospital, about Rachael loving her, and in the moment realized that she wanted Rachael to hold her but didn't want to risk their friendship, which she valued more than any love affair.

They both stood for a moment, uncertain what to say, censoring their emotions.

Abbey stepped forward and unfastened the top button on Rachael's blouse. Rachael moved in closer, and Abbey held on to her for a moment. It was the first time in a month Abbey felt anything other than sorrow.

Rachael moved back a half step and began to unbutton her blouse. Abbey helped her undrape it from her shoulders. At the moment, she wanted so much to let this go where it was going.

They fell back onto Abbey's bed, and Abbey began to kiss her and moved down toward her stomach. Rachael had a naval piercing, which Abbey found very sexy. Her hands began to unfasten the metal clasp on Rachael's jeans.

Rachael's hand moved on top of Abbey's.

"Wait, Abbey," she said.

Abbey immediately stopped, wondering if she had misinterpreted something.

"Did I do something wrong?"

They both sat on the bed, facing each other.

"There's nothing I want more at this moment than to feel you next to me," said Rachael.

Abbey didn't say anything, but her eyes told Rachael that she felt the same.

"It's been a crazy couple of months with you gone, and your mom, and Olivia."

Abbey nodded in understanding, but Rachael wasn't saying something.

"What's wrong?" Abbey asked.

"I have a kind of serious boyfriend," Rachael said. She let out a deep breath she had been holding in. "His name is Chalie."

Abbey's long hair fell into her eyes, and she pushed it back with her fingers.

"Really? I'm so sorry. I mean, I didn't know," she said.

"I know," said Rachael. "I met him in theater class. We both have lead roles in the fall production of *Phantom of the Opera*."

At a different time, she would have told Rachael how happy she was for her, but right now, Abbey felt confused. She leaned forward and kissed Rachael's forehead.

"I love you too," Abbey said.

Rachael smiled, though part of her wanted to cry.

"But I didn't say I loved you," she said playfully to her closest friend.

"You didn't have to," said Abbey. "The question is, do you love him?"

"I think so," said Rachael tentatively.

"Then I know I will too," said Abbey.

The doorbell rang.

Abbey looked at her phone. It was almost 3 p.m.

Two agents from the airline stood at the door, which seemed a bit much for Abbey's single suitcase. She recognized the woman from the airport. The other agent introduced himself as the operations control officer of passenger services, which certainly sounded important. He explained that there had been a problem in Scotland with her baggage. The "remains"—he called her mom's ashes "the remains"—were identified on X-ray as needing direct inspection. This was not unusual, he explained, because the X-ray appearance of the remains are indistinct, and this had been identified as a potential risk—a way a terrorist could bring explosives onto an aircraft.

Abbey didn't understand the connection until he told her that while conducting the inspection, the remains were accidentally dropped, and the container broke open. This would not have resulted in any significant damage, except that at the exact moment the package spilled, the electronic door behind the security area opened and an uncommonly strong burst of wind scattered the remains throughout the airport.

Abbey couldn't focus on all the words. She felt outside of herself but did hear the part about her mom's ashes and a strong gust of Scottish wind.

Rachael had come to her side as the agent handed her a very small purple urn, which the airline had purchased, containing what remained of the remains.

"So my mom's ashes are blowing through the Scottish moors?" asked Abbey.

It was more of a rhetorical question, and the agents could only offer sympathetic expressions.

Rachael put her arm around Abbey's back.

"Are you okay?" she asked.

"Yes, actually," Abbey said reflectively. "I think my mom would like that."

After the agents left, Abbey wondered how she would tell Olivia. As it turned out, she didn't have to. Her phone rang.

"Abbey? Two airline agents just left my apartment. They gave me this tiny urn with Mom's ashes. What kind of bullshit is this?"

Her voice wasn't slurred but was a little rapid, with a subtle change in intonation. Abbey could tell she had been drinking.

"I know. They came here too," said Abbey.

Olivia was furious.

"I mean, what the fuck? This is like some miniature bottle of booze you get on the plane. Is it supposed to be a consolation? A parting gift?"

Abbey drew in a big breath.

"Honestly, Olivia, I was upset at first, but to tell the truth, I wasn't sure what I was going to do with the ashes anyway."

"Well now they're blowing in the wind," said Olivia, which struck them both as funny, although unintended.

"Mom liked that song," said Abbey.

"Blowing in the Wind" was a song they remembered Amy singing from their childhoods.

Olivia was still angry.

"I'm going to call the news networks for a press conference," she said.

Abbey put her head into her hand. She wanted this day to be over.

"Is that a good idea, with you being Miss America?"

Actually, calling a news conference would be expressly forbidden by the Miss America organization.

"No, you're right," said Olivia. "I'll just stay home tonight."

Olivia sounded calm now, and Abbey thought that was the best she could hope for.

After the call with Olivia, Abbey spent the afternoon with Rachael. They bought a new battery for Abbey's car and came up with a plan to install it with help from Rachael's boyfriend. Chalie enjoyed working on cars and offered to show them how. Abbey thought he was handsome and sweet. He was a premed major and wanted to be a gynecologist. She told herself he was a perfect match for Rachael. They both stood back and watched as he picked up the heavy battery. It was cold, but he was wearing only a Winthrop T-shirt, and his muscular arms flexed. He turned his head and winked at the girls.

CHAPTER 16

PICKING UP PIECES

As obligations come with most professions, certain rules and requirements govern Miss America's social life. These rules are deemed important to the organization because Miss America is the very image of their brand and is expected to portray a wholesome, healthy, and beautiful appearance at all times. Olivia was all of those things, but in reality, there was more.

Abbey knew the dimensions of her sister's personality. The most beautiful things in the world can also be the most dangerous. The purple nightshade or the pristine lilly of the valley, two flowers both alluring and lovely, both also deadly. The Outer Banks are spectacular, but the rip currents are treacherous. Tiger cubs are adorable, but they become perfect predators. Life is filled with examples.

Olivia was not a poison or a predator. There was a hidden danger in her, and her bite could be terrible if provoked, but her true perils were mostly to herself. She was an all-or-nothing kind of person, which gave her both the intense dedication needed to become Miss America and the inherent risk to lose herself in darkness or addiction.

Intense emotions can have indistinct boundaries. Anger can spill into places it doesn't belong. Sorrow can discolor an entire landscape. Boundaries are key. Don't put poisonous flowers in your mouth, or swim in the riptide, or turn your back on a tiger.

Alcohol consumption is a strict no-go for Miss America, and public intoxication results in disqualification. Olivia was very careful to do her drinking in secret, and for her, alcohol was an elixir of self-destruction. When she started drinking, she told herself that alcohol helped her to relax, but that wasn't true. Intoxication lowered her inhibitions but did not help her anxiety in any meaningful way.

The insidious essence of addiction, with the gradual loss of control, under the illusion of relaxation, is a vicious cycle. It can be a feedback loop that leads to death.

Initially, Abbey was caught in the web of enabling. She went to the ABC store and bought alcohol and hid the bottles inconspicuously in grocery bags with produce from Harris Teeter, telling herself that a woman should be able to drink responsibly and still be a contender for Miss America. She knew that was bullshit. Olivia did not drink responsibly.

The week after their mom died, Olivia asked her if she would mind bringing "some vodka" to her apartment.

"How much?" asked Abbey.

"Could you bring three bottles?"

She couldn't stand by and watch as the person she loved most in the world fell and shattered into pieces.

"I don't know," said Abbey.

"I'll pay you back as soon as you get here," said Olivia.

Amy's cancer had left them in a financial mess, and there were so many bills to pay. Abbey was trying to be careful with money.

"I'll be over in about an hour," said Abbey.

She picked up the vodka, disguised it in a grocery bag, and drove to Olivia's apartment in Charlotte.

Olivia answered her door, looking anxious. She had not showered and was in the same clothes she had worn to the airport. Abbey looked around the apartment. She saw a bottle of Xanax on the counter.

"Thank you," Olivia said flatly, not looking Abbey directly in the eyes as she held out two twenty-dollar bills.

"What's going on?" asked Abbey, not taking the money.

"Take the money, but no lectures please," said Olivia.

"I don't care about the money," said Abbey. "I'm worried about you."

"Yeah, well don't." Olivia said as she snatched the bag of vodka from her sister's hands and dropped the money at Abbey's feet.

Abbey was sincerely worried, but the natural course of an intervention often leads to anger.

"This isn't you. It's the drugs and alcohol," she said.

"What if this is me, Abbey?" she said bluntly. "Maybe it's time to see me as I really am."

Abbey did see her clearly. She saw her sister, who was another part of herself, beautiful and wounded and now powerless to stop her self-destruction.

"Do you think I don't know you?" said Abbey. "We can get through this together."

"You're not my mom," Olivia said.

Abbey looked at her sister, then at the money on the floor.

"How can you say that to me?" Abbey asked. She turned for the door, tears in her eyes.

Olivia's telepathy had been dulled by the alcohol and Xanax, but now she felt it and was terribly frightened at the thought of losing her sister. She reached out and touched Abbey's shoulder.

"God, what's happening to me?" She fell to her knees. "I'm sorry, Abbey."

She went home to Rock Hill with Abbey and checked into a rehab hospital the next day.

Two weeks later, she announced her resignation as Miss America.

Olivia liked to go fast. She kept a season pass at Carowinds, the amusement park north of Rock Hill and just south of Charlotte, because in a paradoxical way, roller coasters helped her relax. The park's 325-foot super-coaster, the tallest in the country, could be seen from her high-rise apartment.

In contrast, Abbey liked going slow, especially around curves. She didn't want to miss a thing. While driving, she liked to see the hawks in the trees and could spot a deer at the edge of her headlights. Olivia would speed into the curves, outrunning her headlights. Like acoustic and electric guitars, they played the same music, same melody, same six strings, but had their own distinct sounds.

Life was a struggle for the first few months after their mom died. Olivia completed her rehab and came to terms with her addiction. These were her terms: Alcohol was destroying her, and her relationship with alcohol had to end, like a divorce.

Abbey worked on settling the estate. She thought of selling the house, but in her mind, the house was not just a memory box, it was like a living thing, and she couldn't part with it. During Amy's illness, the big house had fallen into a state of disrepair, so Abbey poured her heart into its restoration.

Rachael would spend weekends with Abbey at the house, stripping floors and painting. She and Chalie got engaged. He had started medical school in Greenville but came back on weekends to see Rachael. The three of them spent many Saturdays with paint splattered on their hands and faces, and eventually they completed painting the entire interior. It was a sort of therapy for Abbey, stripping away the old and painting it with something new. She and Rachael had an unspoken understanding that they would be best friends, but not lovers. She enjoyed her time with Rachael and getting to know Chalie. She thought that he was going to make a good doctor. He was sweet, handsome, and outgoing, but not conceited. He loved talking to people, but not about himself. Like Abbey, he had a genuine interest in people. She could see why Rachael had fallen in love with him.

Olivia helped Abbey at the house as often as she could. For the prior two years, her life had been consumed with her mom's cancer and her pursuit of the Miss America crown, and now they were both gone. She needed a new life plan, so she called for backup.

"What were your original plans?" Aliyah asked when they all met for lunch. "You were only going to be Miss America for a year, right?"

Aliyah was the most business minded, and she had a way of looking at things and developing solutions that her friends had come to respect. She was also a planner. Her need to make clearly actionable plans was a behavior she had learned in order to manage attention-deficit/hyperactivity disorder. She found that the energy provided by ADHD was nice, but the attention deficit part left her scattered. Medicine helped a lot, but she still used written plans to stay on track. She had plans for the day, month, and year. She even had a five-year projection for her long-range goals. For now, she was working hard on her marketing degree at Winthrop, but she was working just as hard on a business project called the Catawba River Park.

Olivia shrugged and tilted her head back, "Clearly, I didn't give it enough thought."

Abbey tilted her chair toward Olivia to give her a supportive side hug, "You're a good writer," she suggested.

"My problem with writing is the delayed gratification," Olivia said glumly.

Everything was very here and now for Olivia. It's hard to accomplish difficult tasks without being present in the present. Her talent in song and dance required hours of daily practice. While Aliyah was always thinking ahead, Olivia seldom thought beyond the next contest. This helped her to stay focused in the first stage of her sobriety, which was a day-to-day commitment. Now, a month out, she had to think about her future.

"What if you started modeling again?" asked Rachael.

Olivia took a deep, resolved breath. "Yeah, I think that's the right decision."

She had been a successful model before Miss America.

"You need an agent," said Aliyah. "This is the right time to be assertive."

"Oh, I'm good at being assertive," said Olivia, as she signaled to their server to refresh her coffee.

All four of them laughed.

"I know," said Aliyah, as she typed Olivia's name into the search engine on her phone. "Right now, your image is still fresh in the mind of America." She held up her phone with Olivia's picture and headlines in bold letters on the search page. "People want to hear your story."

As Olivia and Aliyah worked on a plan to find a modeling agent, Abbey and Rachael noticed two women at the table adjacent to theirs who had just finished their meals and were talking over dessert. They were dressed elegantly and seemed, upon observation, to be close friends. Abbey was amused at the thought that the women could be her and Rachael in thirty years. They could easily hear the ladies, who were engaged in polite conversation, when one of the women leaned forward and said to her friend, "Claire, you have a booger."

The word seemed out of place coming from the dignified lady.

Her friend initially did not seem to understand her meaning, but then was taken aback. She flushed and wiped her nose with her napkin, then discreetly looked down at the booger, folded the napkin, and placed it on her dessert dish.

"Well," said the offended woman, "you have bad breath." And with that, she stood and exited the dining room in a huff, leaving her friend somewhat perplexed.

The lady looked over to Rachael and Abbey and shrugged her shoulders. "I suppose I should have let her keep the booger," she said.

There's no other word for a booger, and no easy way to tell somebody they have one.

After lunch, Abbey and Olivia went back to the house. Olivia checked the mailbox and came in with a stack of mail.

"Look," said Olivia, holding up a letter. She dropped the rest of the mail on the table while examining the name and address. "It's from Estelle, the waitress at the diner in Silver Spring."

It was a sympathy card. Apparently, Estelle had seen Olivia's Miss America video and resignation story on the news and looked up their address online.

"She is officially retired and lives nearby, just outside Columbia," said Abbey. "We should invite her over."

She put the card down, and two identical envelopes caught her attention. They were on stationery from Walter Reed Army Medical Center. One was addressed to her and one to Olivia. They were from their mother's gynecologist. Both of them had developed relationships with their mom's doctor over the course of her treatment. The doctor had even called to check on Olivia after she resigned from Miss America.

Both letters were brief, asking Abbey and Olivia to contact her directly and giving her cell number.

"I wonder what this is about?" asked Abbey, rereading the words in the letter as if looking for missing information.

Olivia took out her phone. "Let's just find out," she said, calling the number and putting her phone on speaker.

"Dr. Song, this is Olivia Stewart," she said, placing her phone on the table between her and Abbey. "You're on speaker with me and Abbey."

"Well hello then, Olivia and Abbey." There was a slight pause before she spoke again. "How have you two been?"

Abbey was quiet. She had not heard the doctor's voice since her mom died.

"We're fine," said Olivia politely.

Another pause.

"Okay," said Dr. Song, "but how are you really?"

The girls looked at each other, then at the phone.

"It's been hard," said Abbey.

"You know, many people think of grief as a destination," Dr. Song said thoughtfully. "I think of it less as a place to be and more as a journey, or a story that's being written."

"Mom's story was beautiful but also so sad," Olivia said, almost more to herself.

"Beautiful things can also be sad," said Dr. Song.

The girls reflected quietly on their thoughts for a second.

"So Dr. Song," said Abbey, leaning closer to the phone. "Why did you need to talk to us?"

"It was about your mother's cancer," she said. "Amy was BRCA positive."

The girls looked at each other and shook their heads.

"We don't understand what that means," said Abbey.

"BRCA is an abbreviation for genes that prevent breast and ovarian cancer," she told them. She explained that Amy's ovarian cancer was associated with a genetic mutation in these genes, which made her more likely to develop cancer.

"I apologize, Dr. Song, but I still don't understand," said Olivia, with some concern in her voice.

"Your mother had a mutation in this protective gene that made her more susceptible to cancer. That mutation is hereditary."

"So," said Abbey as the message slowly sank in, "Olivia and I could be at increased risk for cancer."

"Yes, Abbey," said the doctor. "That is correct. You should both consider being tested."

For the next few minutes, Dr. Song discussed options for testing, then answered some of their questions before telling them to call or text her any time.

After they hung up, Olivia took her phone and looked up BRCA, reading aloud what she discovered. "Women with BRCA mutations have a 50–70 percent risk of having cancer—"

Abbey interrupted her almost immediately. "We should be tested," she said.

"Why?"

"Because if we're positive, we could get cancer like Mom."

"Yeah, and then what?" Olivia asked. "Can the test stop it from happening?"

"I don't think so," Abbey said.

Their mother's cancer battle was still painstakingly vivid in their memories—the surgeries and chemotherapy, her body wasting away while the cancer monster grew. In the end, she died because the cancer invaded her intestines, causing bowel obstruction and starvation. She had no energy and could hardly talk. The pain eventually led to her being on high doses of morphine night and day. Finally, on that last night, she went to sleep and never woke up.

"Then I don't want to know," Olivia said. She could hear the uncertainty in her own voice. She thought of how the cancer stole their mother's voice.

"I think I do," Abbey said tentatively.

Olivia looked at her for a long moment before glancing back at her phone. "The screening," she read, "could save women's lives by catching the cancer early, because, unfortunately, most women get diagnosed in the advanced stages."

She put down the phone. "Okay then, let's get tested."

Olivia liked to drive fast, but she did wear a seatbelt.

CHAPTER 17

A NEW START

Within a few weeks, Olivia had signed with a highly recommended agent in New York, Brianna, and was back on the calendar for *The Tonight Show*. She flew up to New York with Abbey.

The Tonight Show studio set was smaller and more intimate than they both expected. Jimmy Fallon was marvelous, equally able to make the audience roar in laughter with his standup or cover a song with his band that would sound as good as the original.

Olivia had a small dressing room, where they waited with Brianna. Olivia had been undecided about what to wear, and her outfit had to be approved by the producers. She decided on a short black and red dress with high heels. Her hair was down, long and wavy.

Staffers brought Olivia to a waiting area behind the curtain.

"You're Miss America, right?" asked another young woman, who was also waiting to go on stage. Olivia looked up and realized she was talking to her favorite actress.

"I was," said Olivia, looking wide eyed at the stage.

"I saw you win. You're beautiful," she said.

"Thank you," said Olivia with a slight blush. "And you, I can't believe it. You're even more beautiful in person."

The actress smiled. "Why did you step down?"

Olivia was masterful at answering questions, a skill honed through her years of competition, but this answer was simply from the heart. "Being Miss America was my life's ambition, but I got lost when my mom died. Then alcohol got bigger, and I got smaller."

They were interrupted by one of the show's producers. "Olivia, you're on in sixty seconds," he said.

Olivia took a deep breath.

"Are you nervous?" the actress asked.

"I am, a little bit," said Olivia.

"Just tell your story to him, like you did to me," she said, "and everyone will love you."

The interview was fantastic. Jimmy Fallon made her feel important and special. Olivia knew there would be questions about her family, but when he showed a picture of her and Abbey with their dad just before he left for Afghanistan, she began to cry. Jimmy came from behind his desk and hugged her, then they went to commercial break.

"Are you okay?" he asked warmly. She was touched by how real he was.

She said she would be okay, then he talked about losing his mother until the break was over. Back on air, they discussed her Miss America win and resignation and, finally, alcoholism and her rehab.

The interview lasted eight minutes. Then, to her surprise, he announced a special guest and brought out Abbey. The three of them discussed Amy and ovarian cancer. When he asked if anyone in the audience had lost a family member to ovarian cancer, three people raised their hands. They, too, were brought on stage. The audience gave them all a standing ovation.

Olivia's agent was elated. By that night, she had booked Olivia on all the New York City morning talk shows and had a full week of talk shows booked on the West Coast.

Olivia walked to the dressing room feeling optimistic about her career. It had been a long time since she felt that positive. While she took off her makeup and changed, Brianna and Abbey waited outside. Brianna fairly aggressively tried to persuade Abbey to join them in California and audition for some cooking shows. But Abbey had no interest in that idea. "I don't want to be a cook on TV. I want to cook," Abbey told her.

Abbey *was* momentarily tempted by the top-notch restaurant scene in Los Angeles, but ultimately told Brianna that it just was not where her heart was. "Besides, I'm starting a new position at a French restaurant in Charlotte," she said, "and I cannot wait to get back to the Carolinas."

"You're really not interested in being rich and famous?" Brianna cajoled.

"I guess not," Abbey said. "But I know someone who is—Olivia."

The dressing room door opened, and Olivia stepped out. "I heard my name …."

"We were just talking about how you are going to make it big in Hollywood," Abbey said with a smile.

"And I was trying to talk Abbey into coming to California," said Brianna. "You two could cut costs by living together."

Abbey's face froze for a few seconds. "You're *moving* to California?"

Olivia touched her fingers to her lips, realization dawning. "I thought you understood," Olivia said honestly, "that if I'm serious about this career, I have to be in LA."

Abbey looked at her sister and tried to smile but said nothing.

"You should come," said Olivia sincerely.

Abbey gave it another moment's thought and reached out both hands to her sister. "You know you're my whole world," she said tenderly. "But I have to get back home."

"I know," said Olivia, hugging her tight.

CHAPTER 18

TINSEL TOWN

Los Angeles is where dreams are born or where they die. Olivia spent her first two weeks at a hotel, then moved into an apartment Brianna found. It was sparsely furnished with inexpensive items, but it was a place to sleep. She was very busy on the talk shows, getting her story out and making an image for herself, establishing her brand. Her days were filled with acting classes, memorizing lines, and auditioning. In the evening, she went to the gym, then to dance class.

Olivia had the Hollywood look. The kind of look where people noticed when she entered the room. But LA was filled with beautiful people trying to make it, and she knew she was fortunate. She had a good agent and some level of fame, or maybe infamy, and was able to generate income from her brief flash of media attention in the spotlight.

Good things were happening. She was working hard day and night and meeting amazing people. She read for dozens of commercials, and then got cast for a cosmetics line. Additionally, the viral clips of her Miss America freefall gave her the inspiration and motivation to start streaming her experiences. This turned out to be a very creative and time-consuming job. She worked every night for hours to create her content, but it paid off. People were noticing her, and her followers grew. She found she enjoyed writing so much that she began a new project, writing her first play.

At first, her jet-paced, all-or-nothing lifestyle seemed suited to her personality, until that first drink and then the next drink. She hid her relapse behind her successful celebrity. And like other addicts, she lied to herself. She built a facade, telling herself that she could have a drink now, because this time, she had control. It was just polite social drinking, and the nightlife was necessary for her career. Besides, she felt good when she was drinking. But soon, she *only* felt good when she was drinking. In the mornings after drinking, she felt the weight of guilt, which she began to cover up with a little morning cannabis.

Early one morning, she opened her eyes and felt confused. She looked around the room, but it wasn't her room, and she had no memory of how she had gotten there. There was an empty bottle of vodka next to her cell phone on the nightstand.

This wasn't the first time she had felt confusion the morning after drinking, but this blackout was an entirely new depth, and it was unsettling. She was in a fairly nice hotel judging by the bedding and decor. She was naked but could see her clothes on the floor next to the bed. The shower was on in the bathroom.

She quietly slipped out of bed and quickly put on her clothes. Although she was inquisitive, she wanted to be gone before whoever was in the bathroom got out of the shower. She checked her wallet, but nothing was stolen. She took her phone and hurried for the door. As she passed the bathroom, the door swung open.

The man was a little bit older than her, wearing only the white hotel towel. He was trim, tan, and good looking, like most men in Hollywood. She had no memory of who he was.

"Olivia?" he asked, surprised. "Where are you going?"

She didn't answer but rapidly unbolted the door and rushed out of the room.

She went to her apartment and showered, but she still felt dirty. She was rocking back and forth, holding her arms around herself, when the hot water ran out and she heard her phone ring. She finally got out of the shower, dressed, and then called her sister back.

"Hi, sis," Abbey said cheerfully. "I know it's early out there. Are you busy?"

Olivia thought about how to answer, and her pause was enough to tell Abbey that something was wrong.

"Are you okay?" asked Abbey.

"I … well, I don't think so," said Olivia. "I've been drinking."

Abbey was silent for a moment. "I'm coming out there."

"No," said Olivia. "Don't bother. I'm coming home."

Within a week, Olivia was back in Charlotte and in rehab.

Within a few weeks, her agent tried to persuade her to keep her LA apartment. "Very few people will ever have an opportunity like this," Brianna said. "It's one in a million."

She tried several different logical arguments, even telling Olivia that she could be an example for other girls and help them to stay healthy. She could be their spokeswoman, their advocate. She was very persuasive, but Olivia was adamant.

"I'm not going back to LA," she said, and she knew what this meant for her career.

"Just tell me you will think about it," Brianna persisted.

"I will," said Olivia, but she knew her final answer. If she went back, vodka was going to kill her, or more honestly, she was going to kill herself. Rock Hill held painful memories of loss but also the best things in her life. The Carolinas were where she had come from, where she loved, and where she would heal.

CHAPTER 19

ALIYAH

Old money is a term used to describe generational wealth for people who have the fortune to have a fortune. Gold is gold, whether it's shiny and new or old and buried. In terms of ownership, when you've got it, you've got it; but when it's gone, it's gone, whether lost in a stock market crash or stolen from a vault.

Aliyah made her first dollar when she was ten. Actually, it was five dollars, which she earned by working all Saturday with her grandmother cleaning offices in Columbia. She had never had five dollars before. After admiring it, she rubbed her fingers over it, then held it to her nose. She learned that new money had a distinct, sweet smell.

She took her crisp five-dollar bill and put it into her right front pocket. When she got home, she ran inside to show her mother, who was in the kitchen, cooking cornbread and cabbage.

"Look, Momma!" she said with a wide grin, reaching into her pocket. She stood still for a moment, feeling nothing in her pocket but some lint, then frantic, pushing deeper, felt her fingers push through a hole. Her pocket was empty.

She brought up her pocket, inside out, understanding now that her money was lost. Aliyah was not a child who cried, but her mother knew from the bewildered and angry expression on her daughter's face that Aliyah had lost something.

"I had five dollars. I put it in my pocket," she said, trying hard not to cry.

Her mother turned down the flame under the cast-iron pot of simmering cabbage, put the lid on, and then walked to Aliyah. "I'm sorry, Aliyah. I know you worked all day for that money."

Her heart ached for her daughter's loss and because she knew there was not another five-dollar bill in the house at that moment. She reached into an old tin coffee container on a shelf above the counter. She took a small change purse out of it, the kind with a metal clasp that clicks when it's opened or closed. There was a dollar bill, two quarters, and three dimes inside. She gave the dollar to Aliyah.

"No, Momma," Aliyah said, giving her mother back the crumpled dollar. "It's okay."

Her mother looked at her thoughtfully, put the money back into the coffee tin, and gave Aliyah the change purse. "Well, I'm proud of you, working like you did. You keep the coin purse for your money."

Aliyah took the purse and smiled.

Throughout her life, she would remember her mother telling her, "If the only problem you have is money problems, then you got no problems."

Even as a child, she knew what her mother meant. Everybody wants money, but there are more important things in life, like family, health, and love. Still, when the pocket is empty, it sure is empty, and there's no cabbage for the pot.

Aliyah kept the coin purse and never lost another dollar to an empty hole.

CHAPTER 20

NEW BUSINESS

For years, old money had provided insulation against the reality of monetary need for the Stewart girls. They were not raised in luxury but were raised without feeling the weight of financial burdens. They knew wealthy people, because their family had once been rich, but now there was a degree of separation.

The Stewart family was wealthy two generations ago, when the Carolina textile mills were still in full operation, before the outsourcing and mergers. In the 1980s, everything could be milled cheaper in other countries. Eventually, the Carolina manufacturing world was boarded up and closed.

Fortunes from past generations didn't factor into the consciousness of two small children. From their perspective, they lived in a castle. In reality, the girls were raised in a fairly well-situated, middle-class environment, surrounded with remnants of past wealth, such as their Victorian house and the abandoned mill off Main Street that bore their family name. They grew up having everything they needed, and most of what they wanted, but with no awareness that their ancestral fortune was dwindling.

Everything was different now, and they had a financial crisis.

Olivia's Hollywood apartment was very expensive, and she had six months remaining on her lease. Drug rehab required payment up front, and she had no insurance.

Abbey had dropped out of college to help Amy and had not worked for a year. Although she was working now, she had nothing saved in her account as she played catch-up with all the bills.

Creditors and collection agencies were calling. They became familiar with the collection agent disclaimer: "This is an attempt to collect a debt. Any information collected will be used for that purpose." They spent every dollar trying to pay down debt.

Though there was very little money in either of their bank accounts, all hope was not lost. Olivia had a new agent and was modeling, mostly in the Carolinas. She got an apartment in downtown Charlotte. In recovery, every month is a reason for reflection and remotivation. She kept her AA sobriety chip with her constantly. She liked to feel it in her fingers. It helped to keep her grounded.

Abbey was still working as a chef in Charlotte and had developed a great reputation and a strong following. The media gave her the moniker "The Most Beautiful Chef in Charlotte." She didn't care for it at first, but it brought publicity and exposure to her cooking, which was her art.

Food is big business, and as with any business, there are opportunities for success and risks of failure. Even knowing the high risk of failure in new restaurants, Abbey wanted a chance at her own eatery. She had fresh ideas, optimism, and energy.

There were several well-established restaurant corridors in Rock Hill. In the east was the Dave Lyle and Red River district, brimming with traffic and shopping centers. There was the Cherry Road to Winthrop area, which was rebranding itself with trendy shops and cafés. The hospital district, with its affiliate outpatient clinics, eateries, and nice neighborhoods, extended north of Cherry Street. Abbey loved all the different parts of her town, but the old downtown business district was her favorite spot. It reached from the bell tower of Winthrop south to Saluda Street. It was where she grew up, in the old heart of the city.

Abbey often spoke with Aliyah—who was becoming a key mover in the Rock Hill business-development arena—about aspiring to own a restaurant. One day Aliyah asked Abbey to meet her for coffee at a café across from the bank building downtown, on the corner of Main and Dave Lyle. It was the kind of café where customers would place their orders at the register. Abbey got a bagel with cream cheese. Aliyah ordered a bowl of dry granola with raisins, with a separate empty bowl, and a glass of milk.

Aliyah had a special way of eating her cereal. Abbey smiled every time she watched and thought of how it summed up Aliyah's personality. She took the empty bowl and put in a few spoonfuls of cereal, then splashed some milk onto the granola and ate it. She repeated this until she was done, a spoonful and a splash at a time. She wanted every bite to be crisp and fresh. Every bite was intentional.

Abbey sipped her black coffee, then removed the plastic lid, opened a large handful of sugar packets, and added them to her coffee along with a generous amount of cream. She took another sip and smiled.

"How's your bagel?" Aliyah asked between bites.

Abbey was not a complainer, but she was honest about food as it was her profession. "It's a little stale," she said. Always the optimist, she added, "But it's okay dunked in coffee."

"My shoes would taste okay dunked in that coffee," said Aliyah, "which is a good segue as to why we're here."

"Your shoes in my coffee is a good segue?" asked Abbey.

Aliyah nodded with an insightful grin, "This café and the adjacent space are being listed next week … and I think you could get it for a good price."

Abbey looked around, slowly taking in the layout and mentally calculating how to make the most of the space. The location was perfect. It was across the street from the public parking lot, had excellent visibility, and was in the historic downtown. She could definitely envision herself opening a restaurant here. She sighed and shook her head to dismiss the idea. "I can't," she said. "I'm in no financial position to buy property, much less start a restaurant."

Aliyah would not have presented the idea, though, if it was not well thought through. "You can do it," she said. "You have assets."

It's true. She and Olivia owned valuable property.

"I can't risk the house or the mill," said Abbey. She could not and would not. She felt like the house was part of her, and the mill was the Stewart landmark in Rock Hill.

"You have the lake house," Aliyah quietly suggested.

Abbey paused, surprised she had not thought about the lake house. She had not spent much time there since the weekend before senior year. The memory brought a smile.

"I'll talk to Olivia," she said.

Aliyah nodded. "We need to move fast. This is going to be a good thing, Abbey."

Aliyah's choice of words did not escape Abbey's notice. She knew she had the right stuff as a chef, and this *was* a perfect location. She needed a good business plan, but that, of course, was Aliyah's specialty.

CHAPTER 21

AN EVENING OUT

Rock Hill is the kind of place where it's easy to see someone you know when you're out and about. There are twenty grocery stores, but only one shopping center, which is located off Dave Lyle Boulevard on the eastern edge of town.

The four girls each had a framed photograph of their footprints, side by side in the sand, that Amy had taken years before and then given them at their high school graduation.

The summer after the girls met, Amy had taken them all to Myrtle Beach. They spent the week buttered up in sunblock, walking on the boardwalk, and making castles in the sand. Each morning, Amy took her camera, and they would walk the beach together as the sun rose on the cool seashore, combing for seashells. The four girls would walk ahead of her, like fairies dancing on the sand. She took a picture of their footprints, eight perfect silhouettes, separate but together, walking toward the sunrise and leaving a trail on the beach.

People make trails for themselves and follow the trails without wide deviations, at least five days a week. The trails intersect at meeting places, homes, schools, parks, and businesses.

If the four girls' steps left indelible footprints, their footprints would be seen side by side, together, on the streets of Rock Hill from Mt. Gallant Road to Saluda.

On Friday nights, their footprints often led to their favorite dining spot, the Pump House. It was the finest example of reclamation a building can offer. In its previous life, the Pump House had been the water pumping station for the Celanese Celriver Plant, an enormous chemical company on the outer rim of the town. Celanese was the name of the first synthetic fiber, called "artificial silk," which led to the creation of plastics and textiles from cellulose acetate. It was world changing, and at its inception, the Celanese Celriver Plant was heralded as a marvel of modern technology. Chemical plant operations ended after a fire in 1964, but the chemical spill contamination had to be addressed. It was designated by the EPA as a Superfund site for cleanup, and a massive effort helped to restore and recover the beautiful riverfront property.

Aliyah had a talent for seeing the potential in people, places, and ideas. The thousand-acre development began while she was an intern at the business development center. As a grad student completing her MBA, she was chosen to assist in marketing the restaurant. She watched it grow from the idea phase of undeveloped space to highly valued real estate, an overwhelming success.

Now the Pump House and the adjoining land were marvelously repurposed, with the huge pumps and pipes as part of its unique decor. The restaurant opened in 2016 as the anchor of the Riverwalk development, located at the base of the River Walk Trail. It was the kind of restaurant where people could meet for romance, family fun, or business proposals, while being equally in step and style. For the past few years, hardly a weekend passed that didn't include the girls meeting there for food or drinks.

Their first time there had been at the grand opening. Abbey and Aliyah were drinking wine while Olivia was sticking to sparkling water. They were seated at a window table on the fourth floor, overlooking the river, when Rachael arrived with Chalie.

"Well, look who's here," said Abbey.

"I know, right?" said Rachael.

It was a rare weekend when Chalie wasn't at the hospital. He was a first-year ob-gyn resident, working day and night.

"Isn't there somewhere else you might want to be, like a quiet hotel room?" asked Aliyah with a smile.

"Are you kidding?" Chalie replied. "Do you see any other guy here surrounded by four beautiful women?"

"Well, not to worry. He's coming home with me," Rachael said, tugging on his tie, pulling him closer and kissing him. It was a passionate kiss, with a quick touch of their tongues, but not something that drew attention. Olivia and Aliyah diverted their glances politely for a quick second.

Abbey watched as they kissed, then said, "He must be comfortable in this setting. After all, he spends all day with women."

"Maybe so," he said, pulling out the chair for Rachael, "but trust me, there's a difference between being an ob-gyn and being an expert on women."

"You don't have to tell me," Rachael said playfully. Everyone laughed.

"Now I don't think I'm as comfortable as I thought I was," said Chalie softly but grinning, feigning shyness.

"In all fairness," said Abbey, coming to the rescue, "we think we're experts on men, but are we really?"

The four women were quiet for a moment.

"I don't know," said Olivia with a seductive tone. She picked up a hot breadstick from the basket on the table and dabbed her finger on the pat of butter on her plate. "I think I have men figured out," she said, gently rubbing a dollop of creamy butter on the breadstick, then licking the butter off her fingertip. "Women think all men want is sex, but that's not true."

"Then what do they want?" asked Chalie.

"More sex," she said with a sexy, throaty whisper.

"Guilty," he said, raising his hands in surrender.

"Excuse me," said Rachael, signaling to a server walking next to their table. "Can we get some ice water to our table ASAP please?"

They laughed, and Abbey changed the subject.

"Aliyah, this place is extraordinary! I can't believe this used to be the old pump house."

They all looked out the huge floor-to-ceiling windows to watch the fading sun reflecting on the Catawba River.

"I know—it's insane. It's exactly how I imagined it," said Aliyah. "You should check out the dining room on the fifth floor. There's a terrace."

"That's a special thing about you, Aliyah," said Abbey. "I love the way your mind works. Nothing is better than what you can imagine."

Aliyah stopped, her eyes were a little glassy from wine and the excitement over the restaurant's success. She looked into Abbey's eyes. "I think that's the nicest thing anyone has ever said to me." She stood up. "Come on," she said, leading Abbey by the hand to the kitchen.

A busy kitchen is an orchestrated frenzy, calmed by the compelling presence of the chef. They were greeted by Andre. He was handsome, medium height with dark hair and a dark mustache. He was dressed for the occasion in his bleached white chef's coat and tall white hat. Like all chefs, he projected an air of confidence with an expectation of respect in his domain.

"Who is this you are bringing into my kitchen?" he said with a smile, the lines around his brown eyes crinkling.

"Andre Lenoir!" Abbey said with excitement before Aliyah could introduce them.

"Abbey!" he said. He was French and pronounced her name Ah-Bey. "How have you been?"

She ran up to him, hugged his neck, and kissed his cheek, and he blushed.

Aliyah's eyes widened with surprise, "It looks like you two already know each other".

"We met at Commander's Palace," Abbey explained.

The network of executive chefs is a rather tightly woven community, and Commander's Palace in New Orleans was a highly prized position in the world of food artists.

"So where are you cooking now?" he asked Abbey.

She hesitated before answering. Everything was in the works for her restaurant—she and Olivia had sold the lake house and made an offer for the café on Main Street—but she wasn't making any announcements yet.

"I've been working in Charlotte," she said, then added, "But I'm not sure what the future holds."

At first, Andre appeared puzzled. He knew her passion for cooking. Then his eyes widened, and he smiled slyly. "So you are thinking of a new job?" he said. "Hmm ... I am in need of a sous chef ...."

"Really?" she asked excitedly and looked over the kitchen. It was beautiful and brand new. She leaned in toward Aliyah. "*Sous chef* literally means 'under chef,'" she whispered. "They are second in command of the kitchen."

Aliyah nodded politely. She had been working to put Abbey's own restaurant dream into play.

Andre watched Abbey as she gave his kitchen a once-over. "Yes, my sous chef did not work out so well. What do you think? It's a nice kitchen, yes?"

"It's beautiful," she said out loud while thinking, *I'd have to be crazy not to jump at this opportunity*, but answered, "But I have something else in the works."

Aliyah looked relieved.

"Of course you do. You have a great talent," he said as he turned to give instructions to a prep cook. "If you change your mind, give me a call." He gave a slight bow, then went back to the main line.

Aliyah looked at her proudly. "Girl, you are in high demand, opening new restaurants and getting offers from celebrity chefs." She brushed something from the front of Abbey's dress.

Abbey looked down. She was wearing a very pretty black cocktail dress, cut just above the knees, with a slit on the left side to mid-thigh.

"Oh. It's just some flour from Andre's coat," said Abbey.

"It's crazy that he offered you that position."

"It's funny that you put it that way," said Abbey as they walked out of the kitchen.

"What do you mean?" Aliyah asked, raising her eyebrow.

"Andre and I didn't *just* cook together," Abbey disclosed. "But even if I needed a job, I don't know if it's the right, um, *position* for me."

Aliyah stopped and glanced back toward the kitchen where Andre was intensely cooking. "Would the, *um, position* really be that bad?" She grinned at Abbey and nudged her playfully with her elbow. "Andre is very sexy … and I love his accent." They both gazed across the busy kitchen at the chef.

"Scuse me," said a server, swerving around them with a tray full of entrees.

Abbey noticed that three of the plates were the Pump House's signature shrimp and grits, infused with Andre's own vision, avocado hummus. He was an artist.

"Oops, sorry," said Abbey to the server.

"We better get back to our table," said Aliyah with a laugh at the near miss.

"I'll meet you there. I'm going to clean off my dress in the ladies' room," said Abbey.

When Abbey got back to the dining room, Chalie was sitting alone, sleep deprivation catching up with him, almost dozing in his chair. He brightened up instantly when she walked to the table.

"Hey, you," he said, standing up. "The girls went up to check out the terrace on the fifth floor. I told them I'd wait for you."

"You look exhausted," she said. "But I don't mean that in a bad way."

"I don't think I realized how tired I was. I fell asleep, and my face almost landed in my soup."

"You work so hard. How do you do it?" she asked.

"The alarm goes off, and I get up, and I don't stop until it's over," he said. "But I love it. That's the good thing."

Abbey picked up a cloth napkin and dabbed at a bit of Andre's kitchen still on her dress.

"I'm a mess," she said. "I got some flour on my dress."

"You are stunning, as always," he said, then cleared his throat. "Should we join the others?"

As they stood, Abbey's high heel caught the chair's leg. She stumbled, twisting her ankle and falling forward into Chalie's arms.

"Ouch," she said. Her ankle throbbed. "I'm so sorry." She straightened up and took a step but winced from the pain.

"You should sit," said Chalie.

She sat down, and he took her ankle in his hands, while removing the strap of her high heel gently. He firmly but softly pressed the bones of her ankle, then moved his hands upward to her calf, palpating the muscle, making sure there was no injury. She swallowed hard. Her ankle hurt, but she forgot about the pain when he moved his hands upward toward her knee.

He gave her calf a slow, affectionate squeeze and lowered her foot to the ground. "We should get some ice on this ankle," he said.

Rachael and Chalie were married on a gorgeous morning in early June. Their wedding had been at the amphitheater on the Catawba River. Abbey was the maid of honor, and she remembered thinking it was the most beautiful place on earth, with the breeze rustling through the shagbark hickory trees on the bank of the Catawba, under the blue Carolina sky.

CHAPTER 22

S&S MILL

Some residents and local politicians described the old S&S Mill as an "eyesore." The windows on the century-old edifice were boarded, and the perimeter was surrounded by an eight-foot-tall chain-link fence. Perhaps it was an eyesore, but it was not crumbling. On the contrary, the building itself was sound and strong and was used in city planning as an emergency storm shelter.

Abbey had to pay for security from off-duty Rock Hill police officers around the clock; otherwise, the property would have become a den for drug dealers and teenagers looking to get into trouble on Saturday nights. She made sure the grounds were clean and the landscaping, what little there was, was kept trimmed and neat. The cost of security alone was overwhelming and bled the estate's assets down to empty.

It was the last of its kind though. The last castle built by Stewart and Sherrill. The world around it changed, but it was stuck in another era. Rock Hill grew up around it, and Aliyah recognized the value of the property. She also knew that financially, Abbey and Olivia needed to sell, but they also needed to keep the old mill, and its name, on the map. It was an important connection with their past.

Aliyah knew that there were important lessons and meaningful emotions in the past, but she also believed that in business, an overemphasis on the past could interfere with being present. Success had to happen in the here and now. The same thing applied to her life in general. For her, the past was the past. She liked to keep her mind and energy open to new ideas. Her mind was like an iceberg, with a fixed amount of space, and her thoughts were like penguins. If a new penguin was going to get on the iceberg, an old one would have to get off.

Aliyah's vision for Abbey's downtown restaurant was well executed. The restaurant was doing well—great actually—so Aliyah was moving ahead with her next idea, the development of the S&S Mill.

She worked for months to build her proposal. She had investors, buyers, and blueprints. Abbey and Olivia would sell 75 percent of the property outright to a retail investment group, but they would retain 25 percent of the property. The historic buildings would be repaired and repurposed and would include the Stewart and Sherrill Museum of the Carolinas. She was meeting the sisters on Saturday to discuss the proposal.

After the breakfast rush, the three women sat together at a table near the front window. They watched families milling about at the Saturday morning farmers' market across the street and chatted happily for a half hour until Aliyah opened her laptop and turned the screen to face Abbey and Olivia. On the screen was the first slide of her business proposal, "The S&S Mill."

"It's time to talk business," she said. She took a quick sip of coffee to bolster her nerves, then tapped the keyboard, advancing to the next slide. "If you don't do something meaningful with the mill, you're going to lose it, and then it's just going to be wasted. It will get passed off to another generation, who will bulldoze it and turn it into self-storage units or an apartment complex."

She handed them each a copy of her proposal containing every slide of her presentation, printed and bound with a full-color, lifelike sketch portraying her plan for the new S&S Millworks, Rock Hill's Historic Shop and Stay Center.

Tap. On the next slide, Aliyah reviewed the current financials. She discussed what they all knew: The current financial state of the mill was unsustainable.

Tap. Then she reviewed commitments from investors. There would be high-end, name-brand, and independent retail stores.

Tap. There would be beautiful restaurants, office space, and high-end condominiums.

Abbey and Olivia watched without questioning. When Aliyah finished, she drew in a big breath, then sat quietly.

"Who is the buyer?" asked Olivia.

Aliyah knew this would be an awkward moment. "Well, that would be me," she said.

She had misgivings about entering into this proposal because it involved two people she loved. It's not as if they had not conducted business together before. For that matter, she had been intricately involved and invaluable in Abbey's restaurant and Olivia's stage production.

This was different. This time, Aliyah was using the advantage of friendship to profit personally. But they needed her help. No, that was not completely factual. They could easily sell their property to any one of the developers who wanted the mill site. But Aliyah's proposal preserved S&S Mill, made them all a lot of money, and would create something beautiful and lasting for people to enjoy.

Although sales seemed to come naturally to Aliyah, selling is a skill. Like any skill, it takes work to refine and perfect. She was aware that not every human interaction could be viewed through the lens of sales, because while a salesperson learns about the buyer, it's unidirectional, contrived, and purposeful; it's about selling a product. Friendships, on the other hand, are reciprocal, sharing, trusting, and giving. Friendships are about love. Aliyah truly believed this deal on the S&S Mill was good, but Abbey had to believe it, or it was a no-go.

"Do you remember Crazy Curt?" Aliyah asked Abbey. They both began to laugh at the memory.

When they were just out of high school, Abbey had wanted to buy her own car. She needed something reliable but wanted something pretty. Aliyah offered to help; she loved going to car dealerships and watching the salespeople. They had fun together, shopping the Rock Hill-area dealers and checking out cars online. When Abbey found the right car, a baby blue VW Beetle, she and Aliyah went to the dealership. That's when they met Curt.

He was in his early forties and had a handlebar mustache, almost like a caricature of a used-car salesman, right down to his plaid sports coat. He knew Abbey wanted the car, but it was not exactly at her price point. Abbey was going to trade in her old car. He asked for her car keys in order to have her car appraised. They took the new Punch Buggy for a test drive.

Curt was sweet as Smoky Mountain maple syrup as he put together his pitch. He told them about his family, his wife and two children, as if they were friends. He asked about their plans for the future and offered advice. Everything seemed to be going nicely until Abbey told him that she was going to wait on the purchase.

He said he would walk her to her car, which was parked near the service center.

"So do you like the car?"

"Well, yes—"

"Do you want the car?"

"Yes, but—"

"Are you satisfied that I've done everything I can to get this car for you?"

"Yes—"

"Then what can I do to get you into your new car today?"

"I just want to think about it another day."

Then Curt seemed to change, like someone putting on or taking off a mask.

"So what the hell?" he said, raising his voice. "I spent all this time with you, and you're not going to buy the car?"

Abbey was shocked and a little frightened. Aliyah narrowed her eyes.

"This is bullshit," he said, almost screaming. "I've got two sick little kids at home, and if I don't sell another car this week, I'm going to lose my job."

"We will be leaving," Aliyah said directly. She did not allow people to disrespect her. She turned to leave and realized Curt had Abbey's car keys.

"Give us our fucking keys," she said.

133

"Here's your keys," he said. He reached into his front pocket and took out Abbey's keys. As she reached for the keys, he pulled his arm back, threw the keys on the roof, and walked away.

The two women stood there, both astounded, staring at the ceiling with their mouths open. Abbey was about to call her sister and ask her to bring the spare set of keys from home, and Aliyah was thinking they should make a police report, when a man rushed up to them.

"Hello," he stammered, "I'm Curt's manager."

Abbey was still speechless but pointed her finger toward the roof.

"I know. I saw what happened. I am *so* sorry," he said. "It's unbelievable. Curt is an idiot, and he's fired. I told him to clean out his desk and never come back."

He asked them to wait right there, then he left for a moment and came back carrying a ladder. He climbed onto the roof, nearly slipping, and retrieved Abbey's keys.

Aliyah watched the manager's behavior like a research scientist and said nothing. She noticed he didn't toss down Abbey's keys but kept them in his hand as he climbed back down the ladder.

Once back firmly on the ground, he looked a bit frazzled but held out his right hand for a handshake.

"Listen," he said, apologetically, "I know you want that VW Beetle, and I want to help. Under the circumstance, I will knock off another $500 because of crazy Curt and your inconvenience."

For Abbey, like most people, buying a car is the second-largest lifetime purchase, and it is an emotional decision.

People think with their hearts. This car was "perfect" for her, the perfect color, with heated seats …

For Aliyah, a purchase was not particularly emotional. Even as a young woman, she had a sharp acumen for business as well as bullshit. She had done her homework and knew what the car was worth.

"I'll take it," said Abbey.

When they walked back inside together, there was already a bill of sale on the manager's desk, ready to sign.

"You know, that whole thing with Curt was out of hand," said Aliyah, feeling like they had been taken for a ride. "It was a load of shit."

"Maybe so, but I got what I came for," said Abbey.

She seemed happy with her purchase, which Aliyah could see was the overarching goal.

They drove home together in Abbey's new Beetle.

Aliyah was intrigued by the experience, but she had a suspicion. She waited a few weeks, giving the sales crew enough time to forget her face, then returned to the dealership. Sure enough, there was Curt, right back on the sales floor. He had not been fired. She watched from a distance as he worked the customer. He was an expert at his craft and extremely proficient. Experts make their jobs look easy, whether it's a butcher, a baker, or a candlestick maker.

"Crazy Curt," she learned, would pour his heart and soul into a sale. His first hook was getting you to give him your keys to have your car appraised. Each time he got a customer to say yes was part of closing the sale. "Can I get you a bottle of water?" *Yes.* "Take it for a test drive." *Okay.* "Let's go to my office." *Sure.* If the deal was going south, Curt pulled out all the stops with his keys-on-the-roof gambit. He was aided and abetted by "the manager" who would close the sale and split the commission.

"Abbey," said Aliyah, back in the moment. "Our friendship is much more important to me than any sale. This is me, and I'm no Crazy Curt."

Abbey looked at Aliyah and smiled. She had to admit that she liked what she saw. Right now, the old mill was empty and lifeless. If they didn't do something, the mill would have to be sold to the highest bidder, and the last remnant of the Stewart and Sherrill empire would disappear.

"I know," said Abbey. She scanned through the proposal and wondered why she felt attached to something that wasn't really there anymore. With the money from this sale, she and Olivia could pay off their debts and invest in their future.

"I think we should do it," Olivia said, putting her copy of the proposal down in front of her and turning to her sister.

Abbey stared at the picture of the new mill proposal. "Can I think about it overnight?"

Aliyah reached out her hand. "Of course," she smiled. "I'm not going to throw your keys on the roof."

CHAPTER 23

HERE AND NOW

It was Abbey's thirty-first birthday, and she was meeting Rachael for an afternoon run. They had been running partners for the past year, meeting every other day at Glencairn Gardens, a beautiful gem of a park landscaped with cascading streams and fountains.

Rachael had missed their workouts for the past week because she and Olivia were putting in so much time on *Mill Town Girl*.

Abbey found a soft place to sit and warm up under a dogwood tree.

"Oh, I forgot something in my car," said Rachael. She hopped up and returned with Abbey's birthday card, which she had made herself. On the cover were two cheetahs running in full stride. Inside it said, "Happy birthday to my closest friend. I could never catch a better friend than you."

Abbey hugged Rachael. "You're the runner," she said, bending over to tighten her shoelace. "I'm more like a house cat than a cheetah." She leaned back in the cool grass and sighed.

Although Abbey ran every other day, pounding the pavement twenty miles a week, she never thought of herself as "a runner." Runners were fast, sleek, and graceful, like Rachael, who had run cross-country through high school and college.

Rachael began to warm up, so Abbey sat up next to her and began to bend forward, touching her toes. She liked warm-ups and cool-downs. Stretching was so literal—reaching for something. More than that, what she really liked was the time they had to talk. "You're so dedicated. I admire that about you," she added as she worked her calves.

Rachael scoffed. "You've been running for years, so when will you consider yourself a runner?"

"Well, I'm not feeling much like a runner today. I just stopped bleeding this morning. Periods. Why call it a period? Just call it what it is: a bloody week of cramping."

Rachael nodded with a brief smile. She could understand the sentiment, but not completely understand the pain. Her periods were light and mild. In high school and college, they had all but stopped. Still, girls learn to expect the unexpected when they start their periods.

"I wonder where the term *period* originated?" Rachael pondered as she reached toward her right foot, hands forward, in a move so graceful she looked like a ballerina.

"It's a euphemism," said Abbey, standing and moving behind Rachael, pushing down gently on her back to help her stretch farther. She could feel Rachael exhale deeply as she slowly lunged toward her toes. "I think it started in the Victorian era, when it was improper to discuss our evil feminine reproductive cycles or sex."

Rachael laughed. "That's true. My grandmother wouldn't even use the word pregnant. She thought it was rude." She changed directions and began stretching toward her left. Abbey shifted her weight in unison, using her own body to push down and helping Rachael to get the fullest extension.

"*Making love* is another euphemism," snapped Abbey, easing off from their partner stretching. "Really, is that how love is 'made': sex? Maybe it's a part of love, but it's not making it. Sometimes it seems more like taking it."

"Girl," she looked over her shoulder at Abbey with a playful smirk, "you could use a little making love," she teased.

Abbey took a step back and didn't say anything. She thought about the Fourth of July they had spent together, and then she thought about Chalie.

Rachael could see Abbey was a little tense.

"Is something bothering you?" she asked.

Skeletons in my closet and monsters under my bed, Abbey thought.

"I'm sorry," Abbey said. "I'm feeling a little out of it. This is my second period this month."

That caught Rachael's attention, and she stopped stretching. "Really? Is that normal for you?"

"I don't know. It's happened a few times this year I think," Abbey answered.

"Abbey," she said more sternly than she intended. "Why don't you talk to Chalie?"

Chalie was the newest partner at Fort Mill Women's Care. Abbey had a gynecologist who did her annual exams, but Chalie had offered Abbey some simple medical advice in the past. But that was in the past. She could not bring herself to talk to Chalie about anything right now.

"Let's call him," Rachael said.

Abbey shook her head. "No. Let's run. It always makes me feel better."

"So who's the runner now?" Rachael teased, and they set off down the path.

As they wound through canopies of dogwoods and azaleas blooming in white, blue, and pink, Abbey knew she needed to call her doctor. She also knew her tension wasn't just about her irregular periods. She was uncomfortable talking about sex with Rachael, for a couple of reasons.

Her emotional entanglement with Chalie was brief—well, the physical part was brief—and it was over, but it was still a monstrous betrayal of trust. Abbey wore it like a scarlet letter on her conscience. Worse though, was sometimes she still wanted him. She waited endlessly for her emotions to pass, wishing it hadn't happened and thinking time would cover the trespass. They say time heals the heart. How much time does it take?

Isn't love like an addiction? Abbey had smoked cigarettes for about a year when she was eighteen. It was hard for her to quit. Even now, like everyone on the planet, she knew how bad smoking was, but she still sometimes longed for a cigarette. The soft touch on her lips, the feeling of smoke filling her mouth, then dragging it deep inside and holding it until she felt she would burst.

What the hell is it, she wondered, *our penchant for forbidden poison?*

When they were all together, she tried to pretend like nothing ever happened, but it was like living a lie. She felt torn. She loved them both and had physically loved them both. Now, even though she was almost always busy, she spent her alone time all alone, thinking about him. She and Chalie promised they would never reveal it or discuss it, leaving her held captive by the secret and unable to be honest with the people she loved the most.

Abbey went home after their run thoroughly exhausted, just physically and emotionally drained. Did he know that she still loved him? It was a long time ago. It was a mistake. She wondered if he thought about it as much as she did?

Later that evening, Abbey's phone buzzed a text from Chalie: *Please give me a call.* She had been expecting him to call, so the text was a polite way of saying, "If you don't call, I will." She turned her phone off, lay on her bed, and cried.

An hour later, there was a knock on her door. She was wearing a sheer nightgown, which she put on earlier, telling herself it wasn't because she was expecting him. She stood behind the door, unsure if she should even look through the peephole.

"Come on, Abbey. I know you're standing behind the door," he said. He sounded concerned, anxious.

She opened the door slowly.

"Can I come in?" he asked tentatively. He couldn't help his eyes from trailing over her body, which was covered just enough to make him wish he could see more.

She desperately wanted him to come in. She wanted his hands on her, his arms to hold her. Instead, she grabbed a cardigan that was hanging at the door, wrapped it around her shoulders, and then stepped onto the porch, holding the doorknob behind her back.

The cardigan did nothing to hide her beauty, and the cool night air felt good on her skin under his heated gaze. She knew he was tempted, and part of her was glad to see that he was still attracted to her. They stood very close, and she could feel the warmth of his body.

"Why didn't you call me?" he whispered.

"Come on, Chalie." Her heart was beating fast. They hadn't been alone together in so long. She fought the urge to touch his face, to trace his lips with her fingertip, to gently lace her arms around his neck and draw his body tight to hers.

She felt him lean toward her. Then, with a subtle shake of his head, he straightened up and cleared his throat. "Rachael told me what's been going on."

Hearing Rachael's name helped to ground them both. He stepped back, and Abbey pulled her sweater together over her chest, all too conscious of how little she was wearing.

"Yeah, well, thanks for coming, I guess." She looked through him into the night sky, eyes glassy with a tear wash.

He brought her hand up and kissed it. She felt him move in closer again. "Rachael, I'm sorry." He caught his mistake immediately, but not soon enough.

"I'm not Rachael. Remember me? I'm Abbey," she said coldly, pushing him away.

"Shit. I'm an idiot. I'm just tongue-tied."

Abbey's anger bubbled up and over, but it never lasted long before the sadness washed over her.

"I know you love her, Chalie. I love her too. We both love her. You two are not the problem. It's me. I'm the problem."

"That's not true," he said softly. "We both love Rachael, but you are not the problem." He moved toward her again. She took his hand but kept him from hugging her.

They shared a brief silence. She wondered if she should let him in so they could sit and maybe have a drink. There was a time that talking with Chalie made her feel calm, special.

She looked at him and said, "I didn't call because I'm scared, okay?"

She could practically see him shift into doctor mode. "You've been having irregular bleeding?" he asked.

"There's something wrong inside." She began to cry. "Chalie, this is how it started with my mom." He pulled her closer, and she put her head on his shoulder and wept.

He held her as she cried.

"Abbey, just slow down. Most of the time irregular bleeding is hormonal and has nothing to do with anything bad." His embrace felt so calming, but she knew that respite would be brief. She held him tight while she could, wiping her eyes on his shoulder.

"I can make an appointment for you to see one of my partners," he told her as he gently stroked her back.

"No. Really, I've got it covered," she said quietly.

He bent to look into her eyes and brushed the hair from her forehead. He wiped a tear away, and she kissed him on the cheek, but close to his lips, too close for him to resist. He kissed her softly. Then they stood cheek to cheek, wishing they felt differently but knowing they had to say goodbye.

From the corner of her eye, she saw movement, and a sinking feeling hit her chest.

"Abbey?" came Rachael's voice. "What are you ...?" She stopped, unable to complete the sentence.

It was as if time stood still for a moment, all of them frozen, as Rachael stood wide eyed, unable to speak. She looked back and forth between her best friend and her husband. "No, no, no. This isn't happening," she said.

Abbey wanted to say something, but her mind drew a blank. What could she possibly say to make this right anyway?

We never meant for this to happen? But it did happen, and there they stood. Abbey felt helpless and hollow, watching her best friend's heart shatter into pieces.

Rachael's lower lip began to quiver. She turned abruptly, then ran back to her car.

"Rachael, wait!" Chalie shouted. He looked at Abbey, but she nodded toward Rachael.

"Go," she said, and then he ran after her.

At that moment, Abbey no longer cared about ovarian cancer. She no longer cared if she lived or died.

CHAPTER 24

RACHAEL

Rachael didn't know where to go or what to do, so she sat in her car in the well-lit CVS parking lot "listening" to her favorite musical playlist. A lifetime ago, or so it seemed to her now, Rachael researched how the brain processes music for her master's thesis. Her findings supported what her heart had always felt: People needed music. When the melody, pitch, timbre, and rhythm interlaced with words, poetry, rhyme, and prose, it activated the mind in a mesmerizing way. But she wasn't mesmerized tonight. Truthfully, she could barely hear the music over the noise in her own head. Her mind was racing, trying to understand what happened.

Should she go home and throw his things on the front lawn? Take the kids and leave?

The kids, oh God. What will I even say to C.J. and Simon?

The children were accustomed to their father being gone overnight and not seeing him much for days when he was on call. Now though, he might not be coming home. They would need to know what was going on, but how could she tell them when she didn't know herself? The thought of hurting them was more bitter than seeing Abbey and Chalie kissing—and then realizing it wasn't their first kiss.

She shook her head, like a fighter trying to shake off a punch.

This wasn't supposed to happen.

Confusion, emptiness, burning shame.

Why shame?

She felt depersonalized, outside of herself, like she was watching a movie, and the image replayed in her mind.

It made sense in a way. She knew Chalie and Abbey liked each other. But she certainly didn't know they liked each other like *that*.

How had she missed this?

Had she done something wrong?

She should have been more careful.

Guilt? Why guilt?

He was at the hospital so much, and she was so tired when he came home. Sometimes, they could go a week and barely talk, let alone touch. She thought they were going through a rough patch, but that's part of marriage, right?

She wiped her eyes, balled up the tissue as tightly as she could, and threw it angrily on the passenger's seat. When she thought she had her emotions under control, she called home to check on the kids. Her daughter, C.J., answered on the fourth ring, and Rachael started to cry all over again, much to her dismay.

"What's wrong, Mom?" asked C.J.

"I'm sad about something, but it's going to be okay." She reassured her daughter, but not herself. "Grandma is coming over to stay with you and Simon tonight while I take care of some things." She drew in a deep, shuddering breath. Rachael had already texted her mom, who happily agreed to sit with her beloved grandkids without question.

"So you're okay?" C.J. asked. She was just old enough to be left alone for a few hours—also old enough to know when something was wrong.

"Yes, sweetheart. I'll be okay. I promise." She tried to sound convincing. "I'll be home a little later." She heard the doorbell ring over the phone.

"Oh, that's Grandma at the door," said C.J. "See you later, Mom."

"I love you," Rachael whispered softly to the vacant line.

Within seconds, her phone rang. It was Chalie. At first, she thought about not answering, but she didn't want to play games. She wanted him to talk. She needed to know some things.

"What?" she answered angrily. She felt the need to be moving and got out of her car, slamming the door.

"Thank God, Rachael. Please, can we talk?"

She could tell that he was crying himself.

"I don't know if I want to see you right now."

"Please," he pleaded. "It was a mistake, a goodbye kiss,"

"Don't treat me like an idiot!" she yelled. This drew attention from a couple in the parking lot, so she got back into her car and tried to focus.

"I'm sorry," he stammered. "I'm a wreck. It's not exactly how it appears. You have every right to be angry, but please, let's talk."

She felt confused and angry. "Don't come home tonight," she snapped back. She needed a little time and didn't want to have this conversation at home. "I'll meet you at Fountain Park tomorrow at six."

"I can't lose you," he said.

"You should have thought about that before you slept with my best friend."

It was a long night. Rachael tossed and turned in her bed, looking at the spot where Chalie should be. She closed her eyes but could not get comfortable. Hours later, when sleep finally came, she slept hard, but she woke the next morning with an aching, hollow feeling in her chest.

She and Aliyah had planned to meet for breakfast that morning at the diner, but Rachael said she'd prefer breakfast at Denny's instead. That alone was enough to clue in Aliyah that something was off, but it didn't take long for Rachael to tell her what happened.

Her words tumbled from her heart between tears in whispered conversation, as though it were a state secret. Their food came, but they didn't touch it.

Rachael wiped her eyes with her sleeve and took a deep breath. "I thought he loved me." She shook her head, "I trusted them."

They sat in silence for a moment, tangled in thoughts and emotions. Aliyah could see her best friend's devastation and understood how much was on the table. Rachael and Chalie breaking up? It was a stark reminder of how our image of reality changes. How happy things can become sad, beautiful things become common, and precious things are thrown away.

"I know shit happens," Rachael confided, "but all my life, Abbey has been a constant for me, someone who cared about me no matter what."

"Look, I'm not making some lame excuse. What they did was wrong. But it doesn't have to mean that she doesn't care."

"What? Really?" Rachael raised her voice. "Look, I know we've all been friends a long time," she looked into Aliyah's eyes, "but I need you to be *my* friend right now."

"I'm so sorry, Rachael," she said, pushing her coffee aside. "Sometimes my brain is hyperfocused." They were seated in a booth, facing each other. She got up, moved next to Rachael, and put her arm around her. "I will always be your friend."

Rachael hugged her tightly. "So what am I supposed to do?"

Aliyah was a problem solver and had ideas and solutions for just about every problem that she faced. But this was not a business merger or a sale.

"There are a lot of unknowns in this equation," said Aliyah. She looked at Rachael and rubbed her index finger on Rachael's hand. "But one thing I know for sure is that you are the strongest and most capable person I know."

Rachael forced a smile. "I don't feel very strong."

Aliyah smiled sincerely, "That's just what a strong person would say."

Rachael tilted her head back and stared at the ceiling. "I loved her."

Aliyah sighed audibly. "I love her too." The waitress stopped and refilled their coffee cups. Aliyah waited, then continued, "Everybody loves Abbey. Hell, I had a girl crush on her in the ninth grade."

Rachael softened a little, smiling at Aliyah's openness.

"Abbey and I fooled around once in high school," Rachael said tentatively. "I was in love with her." She had never discussed this with anyone, not even Chalie.

"I thought so." Aliyah said with a smile. "Was it the Fourth of July?"

"Yes ... why didn't you say anything?"

"Why didn't you?" said Aliyah. "I just figured it was your business. I mean, come on, you were a preacher's kid. We were all trying to figure out who we were."

"Maybe, but it wasn't a casual thing for me. I mean, she was the first person to kiss me ... and now the last person to kiss my husband."

Aliyah nodded silently.

"I have another secret," Rachael said. "Remember in twelfth grade when Abbey got arrested for having drugs in her locker?"

"I remember the handcuffs left a bad bruise on her wrists, and her mom grounded her for the whole semester."

"Abbey didn't do it. It was me. She lied to keep me out of trouble. I was so scared. They would have kicked me off the track team, and I would have lost my scholarship."

"Damn, girl. Okay, but Abbey's not perfect."

"Yeah, no shit."

"Okay then, we agree. She fucked up."

"But why with my husband?"

"Okay, can we try something I learned in therapy?"

Rachael shifted, a little uneasy.

"Let's try to keep the extreme emotion out of it for just a minute."

"I'll try."

"Have you ever thought about having sex with someone else?" she asked. Rachael said nothing, but the silence was telling.

"Okay," she admitted, "but I didn't do it."

"That's not the point," Aliyah said gently. "The point is," she wanted to proceed with caution, "who wouldn't want to have sex with Chalie? Or with you? Or Abbey? You're all beautiful and desirable. It's biology."

"It's more than biology," Rachael protested.

"I know it is, but we are looking at it scientifically, remember?"

"Okay," Rachael said reluctantly, shifting back a little, creating some distance between them. Aliyah could see the fire return to Rachael's eyes.

"Rachael, I'm on your side. I'm making no excuse for their behavior," she said reassuringly.

"I'm not feeling very open-minded about their feelings," Rachael said.

"No. I wouldn't be either," Aliyah felt angry with them too. She rubbed the furrow between her eyes, then continued. "All I'm saying is, sex is a physical act. It doesn't mean Chalie or Abbey doesn't love you."

"Where does that leave me?"

"Is it over between them?" Aliyah asked.

"I think so," said Rachael.

"Then it's up to you."

She loved talking to Aliyah when she felt confused, and she knew she was right. She had to put her emotions aside for a moment in order to see clearly.

Rachael took out her wallet to pay for a breakfast that they hadn't eaten. Of course, now that her crying was over, she felt a little pang of hunger.

They walked out together and said goodbye, but Rachael was deep in thought. What Aliyah said was true. She was complicating her emotions with irrational thoughts that colored her emotional palette.

She tried to use logic. If A equals B, and A equals C, then B equals C. Rachael loves Chalie, and Rachael loves Abbey, so Chalie loves Abbey. No, that isn't right.

How about a word problem? If two people left Rock Hill traveling north with hearts full of love, and they stopped overnight for an extramarital affair, how much love would be left?

She never liked algebra.

When she got to her car, Rachael sat down behind the wheel and looked at her phone. Before she changed her mind, she dialed Abbey.

"Rachael," Abbey said desperately, "I've been trying to reach you."

"I know," she said coldly.

They both knew where this conversation had to go. It was like a bad dream or a sad movie. You see it happening and want it to stop, but it has to play itself out to find the ending.

"I don't know if I will ever be able to forgive you, Abbey."

Those words hurt both of them. There was a long beat of silence.

There was so much Abbey wanted to say, but every thought in her head sounded wrong and like a poor excuse. *I didn't mean to hurt you.* Really? *I just feel like dying.* Yes, really.

"I'm sorry," she said.

"I don't know what to do with your apology," Rachael replied. Her voice was broken, and her throat scratchy from a night of crying. "I just can't accept that right now."

Abbey was quiet as Rachael's words sank in. "This is all my fault," she said after the uncomfortable silence. "I think you and Chalie need to work this out. You have something special." She meant the words, but before they were even out of her mouth, she knew she never should have said them.

"Stop it, Abbey," Rachael said angrily. "You don't get to do that. You can't fix this because you're the one who broke it! Maybe Chalie and I had something special, I don't know anymore … but what you did?! I can't even put it into words …." She began to cry again.

Abbey remained silent, but tears were coursing down her face as well.

"I've gotta go, but I want you to promise me one thing."

"Anything," Abbey said, holding in a sob.

"Promise me you will go see the doctor."

"I will," Abbey said.

There was nothing else to say.

The rest of Rachael's day came and passed in a dissociated sort of haze. She picked up the kids after school and helped with homework, and then her mom and dad came over. They brought dinner. Rachael had not told them what was going on yet, only that she had to meet Chalie to talk, and with that, they knew that something was wrong. She appreciated that they did not ask questions. She wasn't ready to talk yet, but it felt good to have them near.

Rachael thought about what to wear and realized she had not given much thought about how she looked in a long time. Was that part of being married, or was it something else? Depression?

She chose tight, weathered jeans and a sleeveless black turtleneck that contrasted nicely with her blond hair.

Fountain Park is in the old town district of Rock Hill on East Main Street. Rachael had always thought the fountain was spectacular. The main jet in the center cascades water 150 feet into the air, and the center water column is surrounded

153

by a circle of 144 water jets that fire their streams, arcing in synchrony with the center. Music flows from overhead speakers, so the water moves in harmony. The entire fountain is illuminated with lights that reflect the seasons.

Chalie was waiting at the fountain when she arrived. He had just come from the hospital and was in jeans with a T-shirt—handsome as always, but his eyes were tired and a little red.

He seemed tentative and worried. He walked up to give her a hug, but she held out her hands to his chest, keeping him at arm's length.

"I was afraid you might not come," he said.

"Well," she said, looking away from his face, holding back a tear. "I'm here."

"You look very pretty," he told her. She wasn't sure she trusted the sentiment, but she was glad he noticed. It's easy to feel unnoticed.

They walked slowly together around the fountain without talking. The water in the fountain began to dance to the rhythm of "Sweet Caroline."

He cleared his throat. "Listen, Rachael, I know you're upset," he said, using his doctor voice.

She knew that he was trying to apologize, but under the circumstances, she found his tone condescending.

"No, you listen, Chalie. I'm a grown-ass woman. Don't tell me what I feel. I don't need your permission to be upset."

His whole body ached with the knowledge that he had done something he could not make right again. Doctors take a vow to do no harm, and he had harmed her. It was like malpractice in marriage.

Part of Rachael still wanted him to make things right, but how? The two people she trusted most in the world, the people she could always turn to when she felt hurt or afraid, had upended her world. It was hard for her to tell what her strongest emotion was, sadness or anger. For that matter, it was hard for her to distinguish between those feelings. She felt walled off, inaccessible.

She thought of a sermon her dad had given about anger. Her parents probably thought she wasn't paying close attention on all of those Sundays, but she was. He said that anger is an emotion and is not intrinsically sinful. The problem is, it has a burning tendency to dominate other emotions, even love, and grow into self-centered thoughts and behaviors or into hate, which is sinful.

In spite of the pain, she knew she didn't hate Chalie or Abbey. For some people, there seemed to be a razor-thin line between love and hate. Rachael viewed love less as a feeling and more as a chosen state of mind.

Another part of her wanted to know the details—what they did and when they did it. Why did she want to know? It was like a voyeuristic desire for self-injury. She had been over it in her mind a hundred times since last night and kept seeing Abbey with him.

"Why?" was all she could ask. When the word came out, it drifted in her memory. It was the same question she had been asking all her life. It was the same question C.J. had asked that morning when Crystal died.

"I," he began, then stopped, as if weighing his response carefully or simply stuttering from his own emotion. "I love her," he said.

It hit her hard, in the deepest part of her heart, like a physical pain. She closed her eyes, took in a deep breath, and realized she knew exactly how he felt.

CHAPTER 25

A BAD TASTE

People cope in different ways. Abigail coped by being Abigail. She opened the diner the next morning, made the best coffee in Rock Hill, cooked breakfast for hungry patrons, and waited for her sister.

Breakfast made by Abbey was not overstated, just very good. Anyone can scramble an egg, but there is art in egg excellence. Eggs can be over-seasoned, overcooked and dense, or undercooked and watery.

Abbey's cooking was part of her identity.

Maybe things are what they are, but in food preparation, fine meals—like people—become what they are.

This morning, she was introducing a new dish, German breakfast pudding with South Carolina peach scones. She noticed that the scones were being left on the plates, most with a single bite eaten.

The front door swung open as Olivia arrived in her usual early morning state of caffeine-craving, beautiful grouch. She sat and watched Abbey, waiting impatiently for her to come with the coffeepot, while Abbey moved from table to table, smiling at the customers.

Girls in the South learn the etiquette of a smile early in life. Olivia was a seasoned, professional smiler and could see that her sister's smile, while pleasant and engaging, was more of a requisite hostess's expression.

Abbey came to her table, placed a scone in front of her, and poured her a cup of coffee. Olivia picked up the scone and took a small bite. Her mouth puckered from the bitterness. She motioned to her sister, holding up the scone, and whispered, "The scones are terrible."

Abbey's eyes widened. She took a nibble from her sister's scone, then abruptly put the scone and coffeepot on the table and walked through the double doors into the kitchen. She carried a garbage can to the bread warmer, threw away all of the scones, and then went into her office and closed the door.

Abbey's office was not the typical cluttered mess that might be expected in a chef's office. Their mother taught them that a person's space is a reflection of who they are. Abbey's office was neat, but not too neat. The week's invoices for produce were stacked to the left of her iMac. A notebook with handwritten recipes was to the right.

She stared at the wall, which was painted a soft yellow that might have been a color found on the Painted Ladies, the Victorian row houses in downtown Charleston, South Carolina.

"Weathered marigold," said Olivia. It was the name of the paint color. She had helped Abbey paint the walls a few months ago.

She sat, and they stared at the wall together. The newspaper picture of the four girls in front of the Civitas statues was hanging behind Abbey's desk.

"Here's some worthless trivia," said Abbey. "The marigold symbolizes life in most cultures, but in Mexico they are emblematic of death."

"Hmm," said Olivia. "I wonder why?"

She could tell that Abbey was upset and kept the conversation going to give her time to talk about whatever was bothering her on her own terms. Olivia was usually very direct, but Abbey sometimes needed time to find the right words.

"I did something terrible," Abbey said.

Whether by nature or nurture, Abbey was not usually given to catastrophic thoughts.

"The scones are no big deal," said Olivia.

"No," said Abbey, shaking her head. "It's not the scones. I wasn't thinking this morning and added too much baking powder." She shook her head side to side slowly. "What I did was actually dreadful."

Olivia was a little worried now. It wasn't like Abbey to be histrionic.

"Wait, what? Everyone knows I'm the broken one," she said, smiling nervously. "You can't take that title from me. Who would I be?"

"I had an affair," said Abbey, her gaze not deviating from the yellow wall, pushing out her words.

Olivia sighed, relieved that this was about something she could understand and help with.

"With Chalie," said Abbey.

Olivia sucked in a breath but said nothing as the weight of Abbey's confession settled in. She knew the implications of the words and the changes in the dynamics of their relationships that would follow. The four girls had been a quartet since childhood.

"Chalie?" Olivia asked, hoping somehow she had misheard.

"Yes," said Abbey, her face blank, except for her eyes, which stared as if into a black hole.

"Shiiiit," stammered Olivia. "Abbey … how?"

Abbey shook her head, like trying to wake from a bad dream. "I don't know. It just happened."

"No," argued Olivia, "things like this don't just happen."

Abbey said nothing but knew her sister was right.

"Does Rachael know?"

Abbey nodded.

"Do you love him?" she asked.

Abbey didn't answer. She was always cautious with her thoughts and used her words deliberately.

"All I can think about is Rachael and how bad I've hurt her."

Olivia persisted. "Do you love him, Abbey?"

"I love them both," she said, almost inaudibly.

They sighed deeply at the same time.

"What are you going to do?" asked Olivia.

"I feel like I should just disappear."

There was a tapping on the door.

"Abbey?" came Estelle's voice. "Orders are backing up."

Estelle and Abbey had become Facebook friends. After Abbey opened the diner, Estelle came in one morning for breakfast. A month later, she moved from Columbia to

Rock Hill and had been waiting tables for Abbey ever since. "Retirement's overrated," Estelle had said, laughing.

Olivia looked at the door, then opened it slightly, telling Estelle they would be out in a second.

"Hey, look, I can cook breakfast this morning," Olivia said.

Abbey had to smile at the thought. Cooking had never been one of her sister's talents.

"Girl, you can't boil water."

Olivia knew she was right, so she came up with another idea.

"Well, I'll fill coffee cups." She walked back to Abbey and laid her head on her shoulder. "I don't know where this is going, but I'll be there with you."

Abbey watched her sister do something she had never done. Olivia took an apron from the linen closet, put it on, picked up the coffeepot, and in her sweetest beauty queen smile, began serving customers.

She came to a table where a young mother and father sat with two children. The youngest child, preschool age, was crying. He didn't want his eggs or grits. His parents seemed a little overwhelmed. Olivia looked across the dining room at Abbey, who had noticed the child's tears and was working her magic in the kitchen. When the child's food came out, it was a pancake, masterfully fashioned in the shape of a dinosaur. The little boy smiled. Abbey could bring out a smile in a child, even when she had no smiles left for herself.

Olivia warmed up the parents' coffee and glanced at their plates; both had scones minus a nibble. She picked up the uneaten scones as the little boy ate his pancake.

CHAPTER 26

FRIENDS IN FLIGHT

Abbey was up before her alarm, and the wood floor chilled her bare feet. She showered and put on her makeup, then was out the door to open the diner. It was hardly a mile from her front door, and in the summer she liked to walk, but this was a cold, dark morning. It was early autumn, and the leaves had just started to fall, but winter decided to bare her teeth early, with a cold front bringing frost early to the Carolinas. Abbey had to sit in her car, waiting for it to warm up. She liked to watch the ice melt from the windshield. The ice crystals broke down into little water droplets, which coalesced then pushed back against the numbing frost.

Sitting alone in the cold, she thought of her mother's illness, her "fight" with cancer. Was it a fight after all? Abbey didn't like to fight. She remembered the first time she saw two children fighting. She had been a child herself, and her blue eyes filled with tears, not able to understand why they would want to hurt each other.

She told herself after her mother died that she would never go through all of that. If she ever had cancer, she would say no to treatments. No surgery, no radiation, no chemo, and let what will be, be. No fighting.

She wondered if Olivia was up.

For her part, Olivia did her best to walk a fine line between supporting both her sister and Rachael. The first time she saw Rachael after finding out about Abbey and Chalie was tense.

"How are you holding up?" Olivia had asked.

Rachael had looked away, trying hard to not think of how much Olivia reminded her of Abbey. "I'm not sure how to answer that," she snapped. "I know how close you and Abbey are."

"Rachael," she said softly, "Please don't be angry with me. I've got to love you both through this, 'cause losing either of you is not an option." She felt shaky and drew in a breath. "Know that I am here for you, as *your* friend, *not* Abbey's sister. When my friend is hurting, I'm hurting. Okay?"

Olivia's direct style of communication helped break the ice. She would make no excuse for Abbey's behavior, and while Rachael didn't question Olivia's devotion to Abbey, she also felt Olivia's devotion to her.

She looked down and shrugged her shoulders. "Chalie's been staying in a hotel. The kids are sad … frightened, I guess. I'm trying to hold it together, but … it's hard."

"Is there anything I can do?" Olivia asked sincerely.

"Can we get back to work?" Rachael answered immediately.

Olivia nodded reassuringly, and Rachael smiled.

As the month passed, Olivia and Rachael poured themselves into the play. Rachael made it clear that she preferred not to discuss or be around Abbey, and Olivia respected her boundaries.

Abbey considered leaving, selling her business, and disappearing. Everything and everybody she loved was here in Rock Hill. Some mistakes are too big; some hurts are too deep. She tried to keep up her outward appearance. She ran at the park, but now she ran alone. She worked every day at the diner without any time off; if she worked hard enough, ran far enough, or filled enough cups of coffee, maybe somehow what happened wouldn't matter.

Since she promised Rachael she would speak with a doctor, Abbey reached out to Dr. Song. They had spent many hours together throughout her mother's diagnosis and treatment. Now it was her turn.

Abbey packed for the flight to Maryland, remembering her first visit to Washington, DC. Her father made sure both girls sat at a window seat on the plane, and their noses were pressed against the glass in excitement as they flew over the Washington monument while he pointed out the US Capitol and White House.

After that, she and Olivia were always excited to travel. They loved staying in hotels. It seemed so luxurious. They would usually stay in a room with double queen beds. The girls would choose the bed they wanted, and their mother would set out their clothes for the next day neatly in the drawer of their choosing. Each meal was a new experience. This was where Abbey's love for food began. She loved the restaurants. She thought food choices were endless. Olivia would usually order the same thing for breakfast, lunch, and dinner, content with her favorite choices, whereas Abbey wanted to try everything.

The Charlotte airport was ideal the morning she left, not too much traffic and good parking options. Airport terminals usually buzzed with excitement, but today felt different. Abbey was in an emotional haze.

She found her window seat and stowed her carry-on above her head and her computer beneath the seat in front of her. She was traveling alone and felt guilty that Olivia didn't know about her trip or doctor's appointment. *It's going to be quick, just overnight*, she thought, and persuaded herself not to bother her sister.

The flight was only ninety minutes. She gladly accepted a bottle of cold water from the flight attendant but passed on the peanuts. The man seated next to her watched the flight attendants pass, then nervously shuffled through the in-flight magazine.

"So what brings you to DC?" he asked, then shyly added, "Takeoffs and landings still scare me a little."

"I understand," said Abbey. Although she had never been afraid of flying, she understood fear better than most people. Her first memory of fear was when her father left. She had been too young to completely grasp the concept of war, of people trying to kill one another for reasons that even adults struggle to understand, yet she knew what it was. She knew it because her father was a soldier. She saw images of war on television. Although her mother tried to protect them from fear, she heard fear in her mother's prayers. That childhood fear became reality when her dad died.

Ding ding.

The overhead light flashed a red seatbelt.

"Attention please. This is the captain. I have activated the seatbelt sign because we are expecting some turbulence. Please return to your seats."

Now her unnamed companion did seem frightened. She couldn't help putting her hand over his. He was trembling.

"Everything's going to be okay," she said warmly.

The flight was becoming a little bumpy, and his eyes narrowed as he gripped the armrest.

"I'm embarrassed," he said. "I know what they say— flying is safer than driving a car."

"Especially on the beltway," she joked, trying to relieve the tension. "I look at flying more like being on a boat than in a car. We don't think about it on the ground, but the air has waves, just like water. The bumps are just part of fly—ohhh!"

The airplane dropped suddenly and for longer than Abbey ever remembered happening before. She unconsciously let out a brief scream as the lights flickered and baggage fell from the overhead compartments. The plane leveled off, and she realized she was holding on to her new friend, with her head against his shoulder.

"Are *you* okay?" he asked.

Abbey straightened up and scanned the cabin. Nobody seemed to be injured. The captain came back on the intercom and apologized, and soon they were beginning their descent.

"I'm sorry," she said. "Now I'm embarrassed. My name's Abbey."

"Embarrassed? Hell, I'm terrified," he said, smiling. "I'm Lancaster." He paused before adding, "I know. It sounds like a last name. Call me Lan."

"Flight attendants prepare for landing."

"I'm in town to see a friend," Abbey said. It wasn't true, but cancer was a heavy topic for a first conversation.

"A boyfriend?" asked Lan.

"Flight attendants cross-check."

165

Abbey wondered what that meant. Cross-check? She did a cross-check of her recent past. What was she doing? What was she thinking? She had stolen something precious from someone she adored. Where had that self-destructive streak been hiding? She thought back to her Sunday school classes: coveting.

"No boyfriend," she said. "To be honest, I'm here to see a doctor."

Within minutes they passed over the Washington monument, and then the wheels were on the ground. Lan sighed in relief. "Can I take you to lunch?" he asked.

Abbey's face brightened at the idea, but she felt the weight of disgrace from her recent emotional entanglement.

"Lan, this must sound so cliche, but I just ended a relationship, and it was not good for me. I'm not in the best place right now to start again."

"Well, I'll see your cliche and raise you an overused comeback. We can just be friends," he said, raising an eyebrow. "Come on—we almost just died together on this plane."

He was easy to talk to, like meeting a friend she didn't know she had.

"Okay then, that sounds nice," she said. "But let's make it breakfast. I know the perfect place."

They walked together to baggage claim. Abbey had no checked luggage, but Lan had a medium-sized suitcase and hanging bag. As soon as he retrieved it, they called for an Uber and talked as they rode to the Silver Spring Dining Car.

Lan, as it turned out, was from Lancaster, South Carolina, a town eighteen miles east of Rock Hill. Now he lived in Arlington, Virginia, and was heading home after visiting his family.

"So you're Lancaster from Lancaster," she gave a polite chuckle.

"I know, right. What were my parents thinking?" He shrugged his shoulders and smiled.

"I think it's cute," she grinned.

"Let's just say I had a real need for a nickname."

Their driver turned onto Richmond Highway, and they drove past Arlington National Cemetery. Abbey fell silent. Lan noticed her mood change. "Hey, are you okay?"

She stared at the endless rows of white gravestones. "My dad was a soldier. He died in Afghanistan when I was a child."

They continued on in silence until they were past the cemetery.

"That must have been very hard for a little girl," he said. Abbey just nodded.

"Do you have a picture?" he asked. Abbey scrolled through her phone and found a favorite picture of her and Olivia with their dad. Lan held the phone with a smile. The girls were hard to tell apart. "Which one are you?"

She pointed to herself. "That's me, and that's Olivia. Everyone thought we were twins"

He handed her phone back. "Did you grow up in Rock Hill?"

"Yes. It's always been my home," she said. Thinking of home, she quickly glanced at her messages. There was nothing that couldn't wait. "I went to college at Winthrop. My dad's family owned S&S Mill."

His eyes widened in surprise.

"No way. My grandfather worked at S&S for fifty years."

"That's amazing. Sometimes I forget that the mill was such a big part of the city back then. Olivia and I have been working to redevelop the old cotton mill."

"Olivia? Of course, Olivia Stewart is your sister. I don't know how I missed it. Now that I know, it seems so obvious."

Abbey was not unaccustomed to this reaction. "Yes, she's my heart and soul."

Their Uber driver pulled up to the restaurant, and they exited the car. Lan held the door open for Abbey. "What are the odds?" he said with a smile. "A couple of mill kids meeting like this?"

The Dining Car was just as Abbey remembered it. They sat, ordered pancakes, and then talked over their coffee.

"So what does the daughter of a textile mill magnate do for a living?"

"Well, there's not much magnating happening," she laughed softly. "I own the New York Diner in Rock Hill." She paused, soaking in the reality of owning her own restaurant.

Lan's eyes widened. "I've eaten at your diner. It's really good."

"Thank you," she said. The pleasure from his compliment reflected brightly in her eyes.

"Isn't it hard to start up a new restaurant?"

Abbey nodded, "The first two years were hard," she knocked on the wooden table for luck. "But we're doing pretty well."

Their food came, and Abbey wasn't as hungry as she thought. She ate most of a pancake, but Lan had a healthy appetite and finished his food. They talked about his job as a chemist. He had a degree from the University of South Carolina and worked for an environmental lab that had contracts with governmental agencies.

"I like my job, but working on the political scene in DC can be quite a challenge," he said. "Sometimes I have to step back and get out of the mire of politics to remember what I really do."

"And what do you really do?" Abbey asked.

"The bottom line is, I try to keep our water safe. The name of our company is Sixty Percent. We chose that name because humans are 60 percent water."

Abbey picked up her water and looked through the clear glass. "Here's to Sixty Percent," she said, raising the glass. They clinked their glasses together and laughed.

"So are chefs as crazy as they're portrayed on the cooking shows?" he asked.

Abbey smiled. She knew what he meant. Chefs have a reputation for being self-absorbed and ill-tempered.

"Cooking is an art, and chefs are very passionate about their art. I remember the head chef at the first restaurant I ever worked. He told me that when he could no longer cook, he would be ready to die."

"That's pretty intense."

"He was amazing. For me, it's not only the cooking. There's more to it."

"What do you mean?"

"I love to feed people. And ..." she trailed off mid-sentence.

"What were you saying?" he asked.

Cross-check.

"The thing is, I've done some things recently that I'm not proud of." She hadn't intended for their conversation to be this personal, but Lan was personable and attentive, a good listener. "I haven't been feeling very good about myself. You could say I'm feeling the weight of some bad decisions." She hesitated again, diverting her gaze from his brown eyes. "I guess I don't want you to laugh."

"I won't laugh," he said.

"Well, I'm not really religious." She paused. "But when someone comes into my restaurant hungry, and I feed them, I feel ... a connection to them. I think I understand why Jesus fed those five thousand people."

Lan didn't laugh.

"I can see that," he said.

They sat together quietly for a minute, sipping their coffee. Lan didn't ask about the bad decisions or the doctor's appointment.

"When do you go back to work?" Abbey asked.

"I need a couple of extra days to get back into my nonvacation headspace," he said.

"I can relate," she said, unsure where her own headspace was at the moment. She was sitting with a handsome man she met a couple of hours ago, and her doctor's appointment was in a few hours. She needed to check in to her hotel, get cleaned up, go to the doctor, and be on tomorrow morning's flight home.

"How did I do on my promise for breakfast as friends?" he asked with the slightest blush.

"You did just fine," she said, and he had. Abbey was glad for the distraction, and breakfast had been engaging, but she knew she had to get going.

He looked at the luggage sitting next to their table. "I know this was a chance meeting on a plane, but I'm hoping we might see each other again ...."

"I'm heading back to Rock Hill tomorrow," she said, feeling both relief and disappointment. But she took out her phone. "Can I have your number?" she asked.

Lan chuckled when he saw the airplane emoji she sent him, followed by a smiley face with a wink. He shot her a quick text back, then asked if she wanted to share another

Uber, but her hotel was within walking distance. "You can't blame a guy for trying," he joked.

They shared a polite hug before he got into the car, and she walked in the other direction toward her hotel. He turned and looked at her walking away through the car's rear window. The sun was in his eyes, but she had a lovely silhouette.

She smiled, knowing he was watching her.

CHAPTER 27

THE EXAM

When Abbey walked into the hotel lobby, she took a moment to look around. It was the same hotel she and Olivia had practically lived in while their mother was being treated. It was pretty much the way she remembered it: beautifully decorated but not overstated. The floors were polished marble. No valet, doorman, or bell staff, but a welcoming entryway with warmth from a fire in the guest area.

Olivia was waiting in a high-backed Victorian winged chair next to the fireplace.

Abbey, surprised and relieved, walked up to her sister with a grin.

"How did you know?" she asked.

"Estelle," she said simply. Olivia stood and hugged her sister. "You're not mad, are you?"

Abbey looked at her sister. She was practically a portrait of their mom. A sudden wave of emotion washed over her, and she started to cry. Olivia just hugged her.

"My appointment's in two hours .... I'm scared."

"It's gonna be okay. There's no reason to expect the worst."

"It's not just that."

"Then what are you afraid of?"

"I'm just glad you're here," she said, changing the subject.

Their room was on the second floor. Its walls had been brought down to the original brick, and there were vintage photographs of Silver Spring and Bethesda. The beds were soft and had fluffy white duvets.

Abbey took a quick shower. She was expecting a pelvic exam and wanted to be clean after the morning's airport hustle. She wasn't bleeding; that was good. She used the hotel blow-drier, then dressed quickly in a long-sleeved, cream-colored turtleneck and black jeans with boots. With shaking hands, she put on a little makeup.

"You look nice," said Olivia. "I like those boots. They must be new."

"I got them last week. The heels are a little high for too much walking, but I liked them, so I got them anyway." She turned her right foot so she could see the boots. "You live in high heels. I bet you could run a marathon in heels. Maybe I should change to my sneakers. What do you think?"

Abbey was babbling, nervous. They both knew it.

"No, they're perfect," Olivia said calmly. "Grab your bag, and let's go."

Their taxi driver was a middle-aged man named Yuri. After they got in and gave him the address, they made polite small talk. Yuri spoke English well, but had a rich Slavic accent. Abbey always loved the international aspect of DC.

"Where are you from?" she asked, sitting forward in her seat.

He appeared tentative, but glancing over his shoulder, he saw Abbey's smile. "I am from Russia." He sounded both proud and sad. He looked solid and strong and wore a thick moustache that curved upward at the tips. His beard was full, not long, and trimmed close to his skin. His eyes were warm but the color of blue steel.

Olivia thought immediately about the war in Ukraine, but Abbey deduced from his apprehension that the topic was painful to him.

"What do you miss most about home?" she asked warmly.

"United States is my home now," he said directly. "I have interview for citizenship next month." Then he paused, looking out of the front window as if he were looking across the ocean, and added, "I miss my mother."

Both women nodded. They missed their mother too.

"Also," he said, smiling broadly under his moustache, "I miss the breads, the pastries."

"Oh," Abbey's eyes brightened. "I love to bake pastries." She knew a great Russian bakery in Bethesda, south of Walter Reed. "Have you been to Angeloff's Bakery?" she asked.

"Yes! It is very good. I know the owners! The vatrushka is perfect! Today we should go?"

Abbey thought of the bakery and the cream-filled vatrushka.

"I'm sorry, but not today," Abbey said. They were pulling up at the hospital. It was a massive semicircular, granite building.

"If you need another taxi, this is my number," Yuri said as he handed them a business card. "I think I will go to the bakery today," he added, again showing his pleasant smile.

Olivia smiled at her sister as they entered the hospital. "You make friends everywhere you go," she said.

Abbey just shrugged her shoulders. "He seemed sweet."

She admired Abbey's openness toward people; Olivia was much more guarded. She would have been comfortable sitting in the cab and not talking with the driver.

"Yes, but so do bears," Olivia teased.

"Don't worry, sis, I don't have any illusions about the safety of bears."

They walked into the hospital and checked in at the reception desk. The hospital clinic had a huge, open, mall-like design. On the ground floor, there was a restaurant, coffee vendors, and a piano player next to a wall with a fountain resembling a waterfall. The ob-gyn department was on the third floor.

They arrived with plenty of time for Abbey to fill in her personal information on the hospital's tablet. *Person to call in case of emergency?* She wondered how her mother had answered that question. There was a time when Abbey would have easily been able to put several names on that list. Now there was really only one. She remembered reading a quote that said, "One friend is all anybody really needs." She looked at her sister, who was scrolling through something on her phone. Olivia felt her gaze and looked up.

"Everything okay?" she asked.

"Yes." Abbey wrote Olivia's name in the space.

Waiting rooms are uncomfortable places. It doesn't matter how nice the artwork is or how interesting the magazines are; they are still waiting rooms. Nobody likes to wait.

The ominous door into the inner sanctum of the clinic would open periodically, and a nurse would walk out, call a name, and then disappear with a patient back into the vault of medical secrets and cures.

Abbey had her first gynecological exam when she was eighteen years old. Olivia's first exam was at sixteen because she was afraid that she had an STD. It turned out to be a yeast infection. Their mother had been with them for their first exams. She was conservative in politics and religion, but open minded. She told her daughters what she believed to be the truth about sex, and that they should wait until the time was right. She also made sure they had access to birth control pills and knew how to use a condom.

When Abbey's name was called, Olivia stood up with her.

"Do you want me to come with?" she asked.

"Yes," Abbey answered quickly.

They met the nurse at the door. He was young, wearing the hospital's dark-blue scrubs that looked pressed and starched without a wrinkle. He looked at the sisters, unsure of who the patient was.

"I'm Abbey," she said to identify herself. "I want my sister to come in with me."

"Oh, of course," he said. "The thing is, Dr. Song is still in surgery."

Abbey had traveled four hundred miles to see this doctor.

"My sister came from South Carolina," Olivia said sharply, feeling very protective.

He apologized and explained that one of Dr. Song's partners would see her. They followed him down the hall to the exam room where he took Abbey's height, weight, and blood pressure. There was a hospital gown and paper sheet on the exam table. He handed her a plastic cup and directed her to the bathroom for a urine sample.

"When you get back, please change into the gown. You will need everything off, except your socks." He gave her an extra gown. "You can wear the second gown like a robe. It will cover your back better. Dr. Carson will be in shortly."

Abbey undressed, folded her clothes neatly, and placed them carefully on top of her underwear. She laughed to herself, wondering why she hid her underwear. After all, she was about to have a pelvic exam. Then she sat on the exam table with her legs crossed at the knees.

"How do I look?" she joked.

"Beautiful as always," said Olivia. Her career had depended upon her looking beautiful, but she always admired her sister's ability to be beautiful.

Within moments, the doctor knocked and opened the door slightly. "May I come in?" he asked.

"Yes," said Abbey.

The nurse and a young woman followed him in.

"Good afternoon. I'm Dr. Carson." He stepped in, and the sisters both shook his hand. It was soft, and his fingernails were well manicured. "Dr. Song is in surgery. This is Melanie. She is a medical student. Is it okay if she joins us?"

Dr. Carson was professionally dressed and wore a long white coat with his name embroidered on the left breast pocket. He was about their age and wore a stethoscope around his neck. The medical student was in hospital scrubs and wore a short white coat.

Abbey did not object to the medical student's participation; it just seemed the room was rather crowded.

"Are you Dr. Song's partner?" asked Olivia.

"Not exactly," Dr. Carson said. He sat at the workstation, turning slightly to address them both. "Dr. Song asked me to see to her clinic until she finishes her surgery." He swiped his ID to access the computer. "So Dr. Song is the attending ob-gyn," he said as he typed. "I'm in an oncology fellowship, which means I am an ob-gyn physician now training to focus exclusively on women with specific gynecological problems."

This brought Abbey back to Chalie. She thought about how demanding his residency had been. She remembered Rachael not seeing him for days on end.

"I see in your chart that you've been having irregular bleeding," he said.

"That's right," said Abbey. "It started a few months ago. My periods have always been pretty regular."

He looked through her chart, typing notes while asking questions about her symptoms, when she had her first period, and did she have pain, weight gain, or weight loss. While he talked, he kept eye contact. She felt he cared about all of her answers. Then he asked about her family history and her mother's ovarian cancer.

"I see your mom was BRCA positive and that you are too. Do you have any questions about that?"

"I'm one of those patients who consults Dr. Internet too much," Abbey admitted sheepishly. "I know the genetic mutation carries a 40 percent risk of me developing ovarian cancer and a 70 percent risk of developing breast cancer." She shook her head. "Since learning about BRCA," she added wryly, "the term *mutation* has taken on a personal context."

Dr. Carson smiled. "Access to information is a good thing," he said. "But sometimes too much can be overwhelming. If either of you have any questions during the exam, do not hesitate to ask me."

Then came the inevitable.

"Okay then. Please recline back on the exam table."

He talked to Melanie, the medical student, as he proceeded.

"You see, I refer to the table as an exam table, not a bed," he said as he slid the arms out from the end of the table. They had cute oven mitts covering the metal where the feet rested. "And these are footrests, not stirrups." He smiled at Abbey. "Are you ready?"

"I suppose so," she said.

"All right. Just move down toward the end of the table," he said. He helped position her feet in the footrests, then put on blue nonlatex exam gloves. "Now I am going to uncover you a little." He positioned the paper sheet so that her legs and torso were covered, but her vagina was visible. "You will feel my hand touch your right knee," he said and touched her leg slowly. All of his movements were slow but deliberate. He explained everything he was doing as he proceeded. "You will feel a touch at the vagina," he said, then she felt his fingers moving the skin of her labia as he did a visual exam. He checked for lymph nodes at the top of her legs in the crease of her groin.

Abbey and Olivia listened as he explained to Melanie how important communication was. He chose his words carefully. He did not say, "Spread your legs," but instead, "Please point your knees outward." He did not tell patients to relax, because that never helped a frightened person relax. Instead, he taught patients breathing techniques if they were nervous. He said his communication was intended to be empowering for his patients, to let them realize that they were in control.

"All of the tissue looks healthy," he said. "Now you will feel pressure as I place the speculum."

The speculum. Abbey was always most anxious about this part of the exam. A vaginal speculum is an instrument that allows the doctor to view the tissue inside of the vagina, including the cervix, and to obtain the specimen for a Pap

179

test. Amy had prepared Abbey for her first exam by showing her pictures of a speculum, and teenage Abbey remembered thinking, "They're going to put *that* in *there?*"

Within a minute, it was over. Dr. Carson removed the instrument and handed the speculum to the nurse. Abbey noticed a small amount of blood on the rounded end. She took a deep breath.

"The final part of the exam is a bimanual exam," he said. "I will place two fingers in the vagina, and my other hand will be on your belly. This will allow me to feel your uterus and ovaries. Are you ready?"

"Was I bleeding?" she asked.

"There was just a little blood at the cervix, which can be normal," he said reassuringly.

"Okay. I'm ready," she said.

He again told her every step before he touched her. When he moved his hand to her left, she tensed up.

"Was that painful?" he asked.

She felt a brief wave of nausea.

"Yes," she said.

"I'm sorry about that," he said as he took off his gloves and helped Abbey to a sitting position. "I could feel that your left ovary is mildly enlarged." He saw the concern in Abbey's eyes.

"What is it?" she asked.

"It is probably an ovarian cyst, and it may be completely normal," he said reassuringly. "But we will get an ultrasound done tomorrow morning."

"Okay," she said, swallowing hard although her mouth felt dry. Olivia stood beside her as Dr. Carson wrote orders in the computer.

"Melanie will walk you back to scheduling," he said, standing and extending his hand.

"I guess we'll be staying another day," said Olivia, trying to sound cheerful. She handed Abbey her clothes as the doctor exited.

CHAPTER 28

RACHAEL

Divorce. The word itself sounded so harsh. Was it a bad decision for a good reason? Was it an easy way out or her way of hurting him back? Rachael sat at the traffic light and glanced up at a billboard for a prominent attorney in Rock Hill who advertised Divorce Made Easy. It was the perfect slogan for a gaudy billboard. She imagined it was quite effective. People were stuck in traffic, like they were stuck in marriage, and they look up to see the friendly face of the perfect person, a lawyer, to guide them through a relationship crisis.

Well, it did work. She reluctantly called the number on the billboard and was in tears as she told the attorney about her marriage. Rachael was quite surprised when the attorney recommended couples therapy before considering a legal remedy.

The next step was convincing Chalie, then choosing a therapist. She was worried the initial conversation would end in an argument, but that quarrel never happened. Chalie agreed to go to any therapist she was comfortable with.

Each week, they drove separately to the old-town part of Fort Mill, which consisted of a single, charming street. The office was next to a turn-of-the-century theater that now staged a skateboard shop and a small fitness center.

"Do you love me?" Rachael finally worked up the courage to ask him during their third appointment.

He answered without hesitation. "Yes."

Their therapist listened silently. She wanted them to do the work and considered herself more of a facilitator.

"Out of all the people in the world, why Abbey?" she asked him.

He didn't know how to answer that.

Instead of waiting for a response from Chalie, the therapist looked closely at Rachael. "Rachael," she said, breaking the silence. "I wonder if your feelings about the affair are complicated by your feelings for Abbey."

They had not discussed her feelings for Abbey, and frankly, she didn't want to. "It seems like you're on his side," snapped Rachael. "The problem is *his* feelings for Abbey."

The therapist nodded her head without speaking and scribbled on her yellow legal pad. "I'm trying not to be on anybody's side, or to say it better, to be on both of your sides," she said.

Rachael was lost in thought and despair. "I thought *you* were on my side," she said to Chalie, then she left the room because she didn't want him to see her cry.

A few minutes later, Chalie found her in the ladies' bathroom. He tapped on the bathroom door. "Our time is up," he said when Rachael came out.

She wondered if it was.

CHAPTER 29

DR. SONG

Abbey sat alone in her thoughts. Alone, but surrounded by people in a busy waiting room. She wasn't really thinking about anything specifically but was in more of a blank trance, like everything around her was white noise. Oddly enough, she had been here before. Same room, same trance.

"Stewart?"

No answer.

"Abigail Stewart?"

"Abbey," Olivia touched her hand, breaking the trance, "the nurse called your name."

Abbey gave her sister a smile, and they stood up together. A passerby would hardly be able to tell them apart. They were both wearing blue jeans and loose sweaters with high heels. Olivia wore pumps and Abbey wore clogs. They walked together toward the exam rooms.

"Turn here," the nurse said, as she directed them into the doctor's office.

Abbey felt the weight of that turn. Today was diagnosis day.

Neither sister said much. They knew each other's thoughts. It was enough that they were together. As they entered the room, they saw a chart, presumably Abbey's, in a plastic container hanging next to the door.

The room was decorated with modern furnishings. The paint on the walls was a light, airy gray. There was a medical model of a uterus and ovaries on the shelf, in front of huge textbooks and a large stack of green medical journals.

They sat next to each other on a love seat positioned in front of a desk. The doctor didn't keep them waiting long. Dr. Song was born in Korea. Her features were beautiful, and she wore very little makeup, perhaps some light lipstick. She walked quickly from room to room, like she was on a mission, and carried the seriousness of her profession. Once she entered the room, though, she proceeded to make every patient feel like they were the most important person in the world to her in that moment. She seemed hardly older than Abbey and Olivia. She shook both of their hands firmly, then pulled a chair up next to them so that she wouldn't be impersonally positioned behind her desk.

"Good morning, Abbey, Olivia."

Is it? Abbey wondered, but hospitality was her specialty, so she returned the pleasantry. On any other occasion, this might have been followed by a minute of polite Southern conversation, replete with "How is your family?" and "How about this weather?"

"How are you?" asked Dr. Song slowly, emphasizing each word while looking directly into Abbey's eyes. This was not an overused "Hi, how are you?" greeting or polite chitchat but a deliberate, real question.

"I don't know, Dr. Song. How am I?"

Dr. Song nodded and leaned forward while opening the medical chart. Her manner was kind but direct. "You have a cyst on your left ovary."

She paused so Abbey could process the information.

"What does that mean? Is it cancer?"

Dr. Song was not the kind of doctor who confused incomplete answers for compassion. Abbey's question was the reason she was sitting here, and it was the same as the doctor's own question as a GYN oncologist.

"I cannot answer that question completely. Please let me show you what I am concerned about."

She removed ultrasound pictures from Abbey's chart. "Reproductive-aged women should develop cysts on their ovaries each month as part of the reproductive cycle. This occurs in ovulation. Look."

Dr. Song opened a book from her desk and showed a photo of an ultrasound of a normal ovary. In the midst of the gray echoes, there were several round, dark spaces. "Ultrasound uses sound waves, like radar, to distinguish differences in tissue. It is based on the movement of the sound waves through the body. Fluid spaces give this dark appearance. These are normal ovarian cysts." She pointed to the dark areas on the ultrasound of the normal ovary.

Abbey and Olivia followed the doctor's circling finger and listened to her words carefully.

"Lighter images represent more solid tissue," said Dr. Song. "Now here is your ultrasound."

Her ovary had a larger cyst with a less smooth, mixed appearance.

"This is your ovary. This cyst is complex, not simple and dark. These bright lines represent tissue growing within the cyst."

Abbey was fearful but reassured by Dr. Song's calm, empathic manner and her direct statements. She and Olivia could see why their mother chose her.

Dr. Song closed the chart and looked at the sisters with a warmth that was palpable.

"I have a rather unique perspective. You know, I grew to care for your mother very much. She was a strong, beautiful person."

"She thought a lot of you," said Abbey.

At this, Dr. Song paused. "My mother also died from ovarian cancer," she said softly, solemnly, punctuated by a brief moment of unintended silence.

"Abbey," said Dr. Song. "Your genetic testing was positive, and you have a complex cyst. You need to have surgery."

The words hung in that hollow space between them. Words that hardly needed to be spoken yet absolutely had to be heard. Abbey and Olivia's eyes were focused on the doctor.

"It is the only way to know if you have cancer. The cyst could be a benign process, but it could also be cancer. We have to do surgery to be certain."

Abbey's mouth was dry. She took a deep breath. "Tell me about the surgery."

Dr. Song recommended laparoscopic surgery. She anticipated making three to four small incisions on the abdomen, and using a fiberoptic scope, she would explore Abbey's abdomen and pelvis and address the left ovarian cyst. "This is sometimes referred to as minimally invasive, because small incisions are used." She closed Abbey's chart and continued, "However, in my opinion, there is no such thing as minor surgery."

In Abbey's case, many outcomes were possible. The first question was what to do about the left ovarian cyst. Dr. Song hoped to find a benign process, and Abbey would only need the cyst removed, but she expected that Abbey would wake up with small incisions and without her left ovary.

If, however, she identified cancer during surgery, there were multiple possible surgical outcomes. It was possible Abbey would wake up with a large incision on her abdomen, and without her uterus, ovaries, and fallopian tubes. She could wake with a colostomy bag.

"Why a colostomy bag?" asked Olivia.

"It may be necessary, if the intestines are affected by cancer."

The weight of the answer hit Olivia, and she was speechless.

"Ah, my very own sack of shit," Abbey said, trying to lighten the mood. Inside, she was terrified.

Dr. Song's face remained solemn, but she had compassion in her eyes. "This is a lot to take in," she told them both. Then, directly to Abbey, she said, "Please tell me any questions or concerns that you have."

Sometimes, doctors ask their patients for questions, then seem to rush through the answers. Sometimes, doctors don't ask for questions, because they themselves are afraid of giving an answer. Dr. Song clearly conveyed that Abbey could ask any question, and she would try to give the best answer possible.

For Abbey, only one question loomed in her immediate consciousness. "Am I going to die?"

CHAPTER 30

PRE-OP

Olivia and Abbey had grown up attending a Presbyterian church a block away from their house. They walked to church every Sunday morning in matching dresses. They would play a game, avoiding the cracks on the sidewalk, skipping and jumping their way to the church building, while their mom and dad would greet the neighbors. Olivia's belief in God was not just a Sunday occurrence. She woke most mornings to her mother singing hymns about God's love. She prayed with her dad and Abbey every night. God had seemed very real to her in those days.

Olivia had not been in a church since their father's funeral. After he died, she would think of seeing him again in heaven. Slowly, her hope faded to thoughts, then from thoughts to distant memories. When her mother died, her grief drew a new conclusion. She came away doubting that God existed at all.

Religious people say there are no atheists in foxholes. Olivia didn't think that was true. She could easily envision soldiers hiding in foxholes and having no belief in God but a strong belief in keeping their heads down.

Sometimes late at night she wondered, and sometimes when she was afraid, she hoped.

It had been several years since they met John and the apostles that Easter morning. *John the Baptist*. She smiled at the memory. When John introduced himself, she thought he was quite nice, but a little too heavy on the God stuff. It's not that he was overbearing or that he even once tried to persuade or proselytize. It was his certainty about God that bothered her. It reminded her of her own faith when she was a child. How could he be so naive? He worked with the homeless. He saw the violence. Olivia saw witnesses against God in the form of child abuse and overdose. These witnesses take the stand every day to present their evidence. *So why do I want to see John again?* she wondered. *Well*, she remembered, *he was gorgeous, so there's that.*

The scheduling department called a few hours after Abbey's appointment with Dr. Song to let her know the doctor had a cancellation and would be able to perform the surgery that week. Abbey and Olivia made the necessary arrangements to remain in Washington for Abbey's surgery. Her pre-op with anesthesia had been yesterday.

Pre-op was busy. Olivia sat next to Abbey while she filled out forms. They hardly spoke, wrapped up in the déjà vu of the experience.

Abbey was called into the back, and Olivia went with her.

The phlebotomist was gentle, and Abbey said she hardly felt the pinprick.

Then they waited for the nurse anesthetist, who took Abbey's medical history: no previous surgeries; no known allergies. The anesthetist listened to Abbey's heart and lungs, then looked inside her mouth.

Abbey signed more forms, consents, medical power of attorney, HIPPA, patient rights and responsibilities … the paperwork seemed endless.

Then it was Dr. Song's turn. She checked in with Abbey and reviewed the plan with all the risks. Risks of infection, injury to organs, need for transfusion, and finally, the risk of death.

"At this point, we have discussed so many things," said Dr. Song, with a supportive calm and clarity, "and it seems inevitable that the risks get jumbled together, like alphabet soup."

Abbey nodded, acknowledging her feeling of being overwhelmed. She was out of questions at the moment, so she signed the remaining consent forms, and Dr. Song took her hand.

"I'll see you on Thursday, 6 a.m." She stood slowly and touched Olivia's shoulder warmly.

Wednesday was a frosty morning, the way autumn was supposed to be. Abbey went out for coffee before Olivia woke up, leaving a note saying she was going to a cafe just a few blocks away. She breathed in the cool air. It felt crisp and fresh, like the leaves that crunched beneath her feet.

At the moment, Rock Hill seemed so far away. Her focus had been narrowed by fear. Walking past a pretty townhome, she watched a young woman, about her age, kiss her husband on her way out the door, heading for the metro. She had a pang of emotional pain, thinking of Rachael and Chalie. There are things that can't be walked back, no retakes. Rachael loved her, or had loved her, but now she couldn't say. Still, if not for Rachael's insisting, Abbey would not be having surgery, and the cyst, or whatever it was, would have just kept growing until maybe it killed her. She wished she could tell Rachael how she felt, but there are times when love dictates silence.

Silver Spring was waking up, stores were getting ready to open, and kids were scurrying off to school in small groups. Abbey got to the cafe, bought their two largest lattes, and headed back to the hotel.

When Olivia got out of the shower, she was greeted with the aroma of pumpkin spice.

"Yours is on the table," Abbey told her.

Olivia smiled and stepped out of the bathroom wrapped in a warm terry cloth robe, then picked up her latte and sat on the bed. "I'm feeling nostalgic," she said with a wistful smile. "Being in a hotel and smelling pumpkin spice reminds me of our childhood." Her parents and Abbey had been such a huge part of her own self, an extension of her being, petals on the same flower simply separated by a small space. "I was just thinking," she held her hand out to her sister. "That every part of my life is flavored by you."

Abbey took her hand. "What flavor?" she asked honestly.

"Every flavor."

Abbey sat on the floor next to Olivia's feet, leaning on her legs. "I can't tell you how glad I am that you're here with me," she said. "I don't know how I would have gotten through this without you."

"Hey," Olivia said as she stroked Abbey's hair, "that's what sisters are for."

Abbey kissed her sister's hand.

Olivia took a sip of coffee, then walked to the closet and looked at her clothes. "I was going to go out for a little bit this morning," she said.

"Oh?" said Abbey, a little surprised. "I was thinking about going to Angeloff's, the Russian bakery."

"Can I take a rain check?" asked Olivia.

"Sure," said Abbey, staring out the window at the leaves swirling about in the open-air market across the street. People were setting up their tables, some with fruits and jellies, some with garments and handbags. An artist was setting up easels to display her paintings. The world was going on quietly while she watched.

"So where are you going?" asked Abbey.

She said something about meeting with a digital marketing agency for her play. It was believable.

"In that case, I think I'll go for a run," said Abbey.

She looked in her suitcase for her running shoes. Maybe she was a runner after all.

The Silver Spring Dining Car was just as Olivia remembered it. The morning rush had passed, and the hostess stood behind a large glass case of freshly baked pies, working on balancing the morning's receipts. She was a middle-aged woman with red hair and red reading glasses that had slipped down to the tip of her nose. When Olivia came to the counter, she looked over her glasses and smiled.

"Table for one?" she asked.

"This might sound crazy," Olivia said a bit tentatively, "but I'm looking for John the Baptist."

"Honey," she said, pushing up her glasses and leaning forward. "You're not from around here, are you? You have no idea how *not* crazy that sounds."

Olivia smiled. "Do you know where I can find him?"

"I'm sure he'll be here for breakfast on Sunday," she said, but she could see that was not the answer Olivia was looking for. "I think I have his card around here; let me find it." She walked to the wall near the front door, where a cork bulletin board held hundreds of business cards. "Here it is—Last Chance Attorney at Law," she handed the card to Olivia.

"Last Chance," Olivia repeated thoughtfully as she took her phone from her back pocket.

"You can keep the card," the hostess said.

"That's okay," Olivia said as she took a picture of the card, then handed it back to the hostess. "Thanks for your help." She was going to leave but reconsidered. "May I have a cup of coffee?"

"Why, sure you can. I just made a fresh pot." She seated Olivia at the counter and brought her a steaming mug.

Olivia looked into the coffee cup and took a deep breath. She thought of her first time at the Dining Car and of how much the hostess reminded her of Estelle.

"Do you know Estelle?" asked Olivia. "She worked at the Dining Car for a long time."

The hostess seemed surprised.

"Yes, I do. She was here for twenty-five years." She let out a little sigh. "I'm afraid you missed her. She lives in South Carolina now."

Olivia nodded. "I know. She's the manager of my diner," Olivia said. The words seemed odd, and she realized it was the first time she had thought of it as her diner too.

"Well, I'll be. You seem so young."

"I'm not so young as I look," replied Olivia, who was young by comparison, although sometimes she felt like she had lived a long time. She had already lost her father and her mother. Now she was terrified of losing her sister.

There was a slight pause in their conversation when the door opened and a rush of cold wind blew into the diner.

"Well now, speak of the devil," the hostess said.

"Now June, the devil, really?" His voice was warm.

June smiled a big smile. "John, this young lady has been hoping to see you," she said. "I'm sorry, hon, I didn't catch your name."

"Olivia," said John.

"You remember me?" Olivia said, surprised and flattered.

"Evidently," John replied.

"But ... we only met once. Do you have a photographic memory?"

"Oh no. I forget a lot of things," he said, tapping the pockets on his jacket, then his pants. "Like my phone," he chuckled. "May I join you for breakfast?"

Olivia nodded. "So how do you happen to remember me?" she asked after he situated himself next to her.

"Maybe it's a miracle," said June, setting out silverware and napkins.

From her intonation, Olivia could tell June was not intending sarcasm.

Many people in South Carolina believe in miracles. Evidently, this also applied to Maryland. To Olivia, miracles, if they were real, seemed to be things that happen to other people.

"I'm sure there's another explanation," Olivia said, politely skeptical.

"Just because something can be explained doesn't mean it's not a miracle," said John.

"Maybe so," she said, shrugging her shoulders slightly.

"The truth is, Estelle and I are good friends," he said. "We stay in touch."

Of course, thought Olivia.

"Coffee, John?" asked June.

"Yes indeed." He nodded at Olivia's cup. "Refill?"

"Please. Hot and black," said Olivia.

"Is there any other way?" he said. The lines at his eyes curved up with his smile. "Just bring the whole pot, June …. So Olivia, why are you looking for me?"

Olivia's face, beautiful as always, revealed the fear she had bottled up. "I'm not sure," she said, pressing her lips together, trying to keep her emotions from spilling out.

He just waited.

Before she could stop herself, she told John about her mother's ovarian cancer and her own struggle with addiction. Then she told him about Abbey.

John was an active listener, maintaining eye contact and asking meaningful questions, which helped to clarify her thoughts. It was like she could feel him listening. She didn't intend to, but she started to cry.

"I'm the one who needs a miracle," she said. "I need to believe in something."

John covered her hand with his. It was a strong hand with callouses right along the fingers.

"It sounds like you do believe in something," he said.

June came with their coffee.

"I think I will take one of your pancakes," Olivia said, then turned to him. "I've done a lot of talking. Tell me about you!"

"What would you like to know?"

She knew when she first met him that she found him attractive, but that's not why she was here. Still, she was inquisitive. She saw no wedding ring.

"Are you married?"

"Divorced," he said. "I have a son, Nelson. He's six, and he's my world."

He talked briefly about his divorce and the mistakes he made. "Back then, I was all about me," he said.

His struggle for success was once very self-centered and egocentric. In some ways, maybe it had to be. How else can someone rise above their circumstance? He had to be better than everyone else. He set goals and sacrificed. It's no different in other professions. Athletics, sales, medicine, politics, even ministry—everyone wants to be the best. But then, there you are with your trophies, cars, money, adoring fans, whatever, and you are left with yourself.

Olivia nodded her head in understanding. She had just been crowned Miss America when her cards came tumbling down.

"I've made years of mistakes," she said.

"Someone once told me that the hardest roads lead to the most beautiful places," he said.

"But sometimes, they just lead to the edge of a cliff," she said matter-of-factly.

"I guess there's that possibility too," he admitted.

When her pancake came, she asked him to say a blessing.

He reached across the table and opened his hand. She put her hand in his.

"God, please bless Abbey and Olivia." His words were simple and sincere.

Olivia took a deep breath and, smelling the pancake, realized she was ravenous. She picked up her fork.

"You better bring another pancake," John said to June.

CHAPTER 31

POST-OP

Dr. Song started all of her appointments with an emotional check-in. She wanted to know how her patients were and what their concerns were. She was full of facts about cancer cell types, stages, and treatment. She was always ready to address the big one too, the cancer elephant in the room. The "Am I going to die?" and "How long do I have?" questions. Her art of treating people with deadly diseases was meeting them where they were. To find out where someone is takes empathic listening.

Her patients would start with a problem, like bleeding or an abnormality on an ultrasound. The problem is followed by tests, biopsies, MRI and CAT scans, pathology, surgery, and a diagnosis. Then come chemicals, radiation, nausea, vomiting, bleeding, wound care, hair loss, and wigs. It all stirs together and boils down to this: five-year survival rates. The persons affected—real people—could get lost in that boiling pot. The diagnosis upends their hopes and dreams. How many times had she seen a woman pray she would live to see a child graduate or to hold her new grandbaby? Once, she knew a woman with ovarian cancer who just wanted to live long enough to finish crocheting a Christmas blanket for her daughter. Dr. Song kept that unfinished blanket from her mother draped over her office chair. It was hard for her to not take cancer personally.

Abbey was afraid, but she trusted Dr. Song. She had tried to prepare herself for bad news, but it was difficult to be *truly* prepared. When she woke from anesthesia after the operation, she immediately felt her abdomen, and there were only four small bandages. That was a good sign. She remembered Olivia being there when she woke up but had no memory of Dr. Song coming into the postoperative recovery area to discuss the surgery. Olivia repeated everything the doctor had said. They removed the left ovary with the cyst and did not see any evidence of cancer. Her ovary and cyst were sent to pathology. Dr. Song wanted to keep Abbey overnight.

Later that evening, Dr. Song stopped in to check on Abbey. She tapped on the door before entering, then walked to the bedside and sat next to Olivia.

"Abbey," she said, looking into her eyes for a response, "how are you feeling?"

"I'm a little sore," said Abbey.

She put her hand over Abbey's hand and gave a gentle squeeze. She looked at Abbey's dinner plate to see what had been eaten.

"Have you been able to tolerate any food?" she asked.

"I had a little JELL-O," said Abbey.

"That's perfectly normal for the evening after surgery," she told her. "Have you passed gas?"

"I did," said Abbey.

Dr. Song smiled, happy because Abbey had farted.

These were questions they were accustomed to because of Amy's surgeries.

What the girls didn't know was that before Dr. Song entered the room, she had already reviewed Abbey's vital signs, her fluid intake and urine output, each medication given, and every nursing note.

"May I look at your belly?" she asked.

Abbey raised up her hospital gown, and Dr. Song rubbed her hands together to warm them before touching her skin.

"My hands might be a little cold," she said, first listening to Abbey's stomach with her stethoscope, then gently pressing on her abdomen.

"Everything looks good," said the doctor. "You should be ready for discharge tomorrow. Are you staying at the Fisher House?"

The Fisher House is a nonprofit organization that provides a place to live at no cost for military families needing treatment at military hospitals. There are five Fisher Houses at Walter Reed. Each house provides rooms for multiple families. They are designed to be homelike living spaces, with shared kitchens and living rooms.

"Yes," Olivia said thankfully. The hotel had been nice, but expensive. "How long will we need to stay?"

"It depends," said Dr. Song, turning toward Abbey. "We should have preliminary results by the end of the week."

Abbey was discharged the next morning with a post-op appointment scheduled for that Friday. Olivia had rented a small car. She loaded Abbey up and drove to the Fisher House, a Colonial-style house with six bedrooms. Abbey and Olivia shared one with two twin beds, a chest of drawers, a sitting area, and a small desk. Olivia helped to get Abbey settled in bed, then took the opportunity to call Rachael to work through a few scenes in the play.

While Olivia was talking with Rachael, Abbey stirred, then sat up. Olivia told Rachael she had to go and hung up. "I'm sorry," she said, walking to the bedside. "Did I wake you?"

"No," said Abbey, stifling a yawn. "I feel like I've been asleep for two days." She looked at Olivia's phone.

"That was Rachael," said Olivia.

"You didn't have to stop talking."

"I know."

Olivia was unaccustomed to feeling awkward around her sister.

"Does she know we're here?" asked Abbey.

"No. I haven't told anyone."

They sat silently, disquieted for a moment.

"Please don't let me come between you," said Abbey. "It's important to me that I don't destroy this, your play, your friendship. She needs a friend like you."

Olivia walked to her sister's bed and snuggled in next to her, putting her legs under the warm quilt.

"The play is coming together great, and Rachael and I will be fine," she said. She spoke with confidence but was simultaneously uncertain, like a weather forecast that predicts sunshine even when it's raining.

They sat together in bed and looked out the window at the sunshine. The crisp autumn air would have ordinarily beckoned Abbey, but she needed a day's rest. "You've been with me nonstop," she said. "You should get out of the room today. Get some fresh air."

Olivia had called John last night, after Abbey's surgery, and asked him to pray for her. She had closed her eyes tightly at Abbey's bedside while she was asleep, and he prayed on the phone. Then he asked her out to lunch.

She had not talked with Abbey about John yet, and she wasn't sure why. She was a little cautious because it felt selfish that she had a date while Abbey was recovering from surgery. Also, he was different from other men she had dated.

"Okay then," she pushed back the warm quilt and got out of bed. "I think I'll go out for lunch," she said breezily.

"By yourself?"

Olivia could tell that Abbey knew something was going on, so she decided to lean into it and try to lighten their moods.

"Noooo," she said in a singsong voice.

Abbey narrowed her eyes. "What are you not telling me?"

"You're not even going to believe this," said Olivia, sitting down next to Abbey with an excited bounce. "I have a date ... with John," she added in a tone that suggested Abbey knew who he was.

"John ... from the Silver Spring Diner?"

"That's right," said Olivia.

"So that's who I heard you talking to last night," Abbey said.

"I thought you were asleep," said Olivia. She felt a little embarrassed. "Why didn't you say something?"

"I don't know," said Abbey. Her memory of last night was hazy. She remembered feeling out of her body, like she might be dreaming, or even that she might have died and was watching Olivia from heaven. "I didn't want to change the moment."

Olivia smiled. Then she had a sudden feeling she was unaccustomed to. She was very familiar with getting attention from men, but not accustomed to being worried about it.

"What if he doesn't like me; I mean, the real me?" she asked.

"I simply can't imagine that happening," Abbey reassured her.

She giggled. "I guess, then, I have a date with an apostle."

CHAPTER 32

AWAKENING

She was outside when John arrived. He pulled up in a fully restored classic muscle car. It was a dark red, almost maroon, and looked like it had just rolled off the production line.

"This is pretty nice for an apostle," she said as he stepped out and opened her door.

She thought she saw him blush under his dark skin.

"My donkey is in the shop," he said matter-of-factly.

She wondered if she had hurt his feelings.

"I shouldn't have said that," she said, "It's a beautiful car. A Mustang, right?"

"Yes," he said, seeming surprised. "It's a '69 Mach I. It was my dad's." He looked at the car affectionately, thinking of his father. "I only take it out on special occasions."

She was pleasantly surprised that she had guessed correctly. Although she didn't know very much about automobile makes and models, she noticed the running horse emblem on the front grill. John opened her door and held her hand as she got inside.

It was a cold afternoon. Olivia wore a red denim jacket over her tight sweater dress, with black leggings and warm

UGG boots. John wore a charcoal gray sweater and a black leather jacket. He started the engine, then put on brown leather driving gloves.

"Ready?" he asked.

They went to lunch in Chinatown, then drove out to the National Harbor.

"What is that?" asked Olivia, pointing to a giant sculpture in the sand, near the water.

"It's called the Awakening," he said.

They got out of the car and walked to the sculpture. It was windy, and she had left her coat in his car. John took off his jacket and put it over her shoulders. The jacket was heavy and smelled like him: leather and evergreen. It was warm from his body, and she put her arms into the jacket and zipped it up.

There were five parts to the aluminum sculpture: the face, the right arm, the left hand, part of the bending left leg and knee, and the right foot. The five body parts were positioned in anatomically correct positions, giving the impression that a gigantic man was coming out of the Earth. His face wore a thick beard, and his mouth was open, gasping, as if taking his first breath.

"He looks so desperate," said Olivia as they approached his massive arm, grasping out urgently, almost twenty feet into the air.

"I like to come here on days like today, when it's just him and me," said John. They were the only two people at the waterfront on the chilly afternoon. They walked across the pier to the Capital Wheel, a Ferris wheel twenty stories high, with closed, heated gondola cars.

"Let's ride," said Olivia.

John was hesitant. "I'm not a big fan of carnival rides," he admitted.

His confession—the fact that this big, strong man could so readily admit his anxiety to her—made Olivia feel even more connected to him.

"Come on," she beckoned while taking his hand. "I'll take care of you." She moved a little closer to him, and he smiled.

He bought their tickets, and they hopped into the next car. It was quite luxurious, not at all like a carnival ride. The leather seats were comfortable and inviting.

"This is nicer than my first apartment," he said.

"It's nicer than my *now* apartment," said Olivia, and they laughed.

He kept about two hand widths between them, not because he wanted distance but because he didn't want to presume closeness. When the door closed, she moved in closer to him.

He exhaled more noticeably than he intended.

"Are you nervous because of me or the ride?" she asked.

Her question caught him a little off guard. He relaxed a little, feeling his feet on the floor, but when the gondola car moved, he involuntarily flinched slightly. She put her hand on his arm and smiled her real smile. The wheel carried them two hundred feet above the harbor, and it was nice to see the world he knew from a different perspective. He looked at Olivia. She was so beautiful. He felt amazing, comfortable, and excited. But all too soon, the ride came to an end.

"Do you want to head back to Bethesda?" he asked. He did not want their date to end but was mindful of her sister being back at the Fisher House.

"Let me check on Abbey," she said.

Olivia looked at her phone, and there were no messages, so she texted her sister. *How are you feeling?*

Abbey replied immediately. *Everything is fine here. I showered and feel much better. Stay out as long as you like:) I love you.*

I'll be home by dinner, Olivia wrote. *Why don't we go to the Russian bakery, if you're up for it?* She received an affirmative thumbs-up and a heart.

She turned to John. "I know it's touristy, but can we go to the National Mall?"

"It's one of my favorite places," he said.

Olivia remembered when her father had taken them there. At first, she and Abbey had expected to see a shopping mall, but they were soon excited when they saw the Lincoln Memorial and the Washington Monument. As a child, the white marble and granite seemed to reach forever into the sky.

She and John walked up the steps to the memorial and looked out across the mall, where the reflection ponds captured the blue autumn sky. She imagined Dr. Martin Luther King standing there and delivering his "I Have a Dream" speech.

After descending the steps, they walked to the left, along a path leading to the Vietnam memorial. The wall was so long and dark, with so many names, it was visually sobering. John seemed to know exactly where he was going and stopped about three quarters of the way down the wall. He kneeled down and touched his fingers gently to name on the wall: John H. Marshal.

"My grandfather," he said solemnly.

Olivia knelt beside him and placed her fingers over his fingers.

"My dad was a child when grandpa died," he said sadly. "Dad didn't like to talk about it." They stood together, gazing at their reflections in the highly polished black granite.

She felt a poignant connection, and for the first time in a long time, she wanted to know someone, and she wanted him to know her.

"My dad was killed in Afghanistan," she said, "and my life has never really felt the same."

He thought about her words. "The same as what?"

"Safe," she said.

John stood and offered her his hand, which she accepted. As she rose, she found herself close to his body.

"You know," she said, "I didn't even know your last name, John Marshal."

He could smell her perfume.

"John Henry Marshal," he said smiling, then added, "the third."

"Olivia Stewart," she held her hand up like a Southern belle, "the first."

He kissed her hand, and she stood on her tiptoes and kissed him softly on the lips.

CHAPTER 33

ANGELOFF'S

When Olivia got back to the Fisher House, Abbey was dressed and ready to go in a cute rust-colored turtleneck dress and boots. She was already tired of feeling like a patient. She had no pain, just soreness at the incisions.

"You look great," Olivia told her, happy to see her sister looking more like herself.

Abbey spun around, then stopped, a little dizzy.

"Whew, too much," she said, laughing at her silliness. "But I'm not taking any hard-core pain drugs, just ibuprofen," she said.

Olivia freshened up her makeup, and then they went out to dinner.

Angeloff's had a bakery in the front but a nice casual dining area in the back that served dinner until 9 p.m. Getting a table without reservations usually meant a long wait, but Abbey had called her favorite Russian taxi driver, Yuri, who turned out to be the cousin of the owner. He pulled up to Fisher House with a big smile under his tremendous mustache.

On the drive to the restaurant, snow began to fall. Yuri told them with excitement how he loved the first winter's snowfall. The girls once again found him easy to talk to. Since he was picking them up at the Fisher House outside Walter Reed, he politely asked if everything was okay.

Abbey mentioned her operation and recovery, although not her risk of cancer. The girls were both amazed to find out that Yuri himself was a physician and had practiced pathology in Ukraine before coming to America. He drove a taxi to help support himself while he worked on obtaining his US medical license. He also worked in the research department at the Armed Forces Institute of Pathology in Silver Spring.

When they arrived at Angeloff's, Yuri pulled up to the front, then hopped out to open their door.

"I will stay and bring you home after you finish dinner," he told Abbey and Olivia.

"Then why don't you join us?" asked Abbey, and Olivia agreed.

The burly Russian looked at his watch. He was good-looking and dignified, but not overstated. Abbey noticed he was not wearing a wedding band. She wondered why, with everything happening in her life, she would notice such things.

"Yes," he said. "I like this idea."

He parked his taxi, then joined them at a table.

Abbey asked if he would get in trouble for parking the taxi while on duty.

"No," he said frankly, pointing to himself. "My business is my own."

The women were taken aback by his abrupt reply.

"I didn't mean to be intrusive," said Abbey.

Yuri realized his words had not been translated as he intended.

"Please, I apologize," he said sincerely. "It is my English. I meant to say it is my own business."

The women were still confused.

"No, I am saying not to worry, because look," he took a business card out, identical to the one he had previously given Abbey. "Yuri's Taxi, see? It is my business. I am Russian doctor, but I own the taxi."

Now they understood and began to laugh.

A waitress brought glasses of water, a bottle of vodka, and blini, Russian crepes.

"Ah, now something special for you," he said. The waitress came back with black caviar.

They laughed and all loved the caviar.

Yuri raised a glass to his new friends.

When Abbey asked Yuri where the menus were, he explained that there were none. Rather, the chef prepared a different traditional meal every night. Abbey was intrigued by this idea and impressed by how very busy the restaurant was. Abbey told Yuri about her diner and their home in Rock Hill. He told them about his home in Russia and the richness of the culture. He began his college education in St. Petersburg as a mathematician.

"Have you visited St. Petersburg?" he asked.

The girls said they had not. He was passionate, telling them about the beauty of his beloved city, with its art, architecture, and waterways that filled the city and extended to the Baltic. They could feel the yearning he felt for home. They, too, understood the love of home.

"So you studied mathematics before medicine?" asked Olivia. She would have placed his age in the mid-thirties, but it could have been early forties. "You seem so young."

"Yes. I think my first love was mathematics," he said, putting his hand over his heart. "I began university at sixteen."

"Abbey loves math," said Olivia, teasing her sister into flirting. Abbey deserved to have a nice time, after everything with Rachael and Chalie and then her surgery.

As children, Abbey and Olivia both made good grades, but Abbey struggled with math. Sometimes her homework would take hours, and Olivia would wait patiently for her to finish so they could have some playtime before bed.

Abbey politely kicked her sister's shin under the table. Although she'd had a hard time as a child, she excelled in math in college.

Olivia smiled mischievously.

"In truth," said Yuri, "I remember my father scolding me for grades as a child. Then I came to be comforted by the exactness of math."

Abbey understood his meaning.

"I loved the concepts of equivalents," said Abbey. "If and only if."

"Yes, yes," Yuri nodded his head vigorously. He was delightfully animated. "Proof and logic seem so exact."

"It's not just science," said Olivia. She had put a lot of time and energy into calculus in high school herself. "Music and art can also be understood mathematically."

"Not everything is so exact though," said Abbey, who felt the weighty complexity of her life.

All three were silent for a moment.

"You are surely correct," said Yuri. He took a coin from his pocket, a silver ruble, with the image of Nicholas II on the head side. "There is more to see than what is seen." He put the coin into his right palm, then passed his left hand over his right, and the coin disappeared.

The ladies smiled at his magic.

"It's easy," he said, "to see the beauty in the colors and the images, or to understand the meaning in the words. What about the beauty in the empty spaces and between the words?"

"Like when you can't seem to solve for x," said Abbey, "being comfortable with the inexactness."

Yuri looked across the table and reflected, "Sometimes, things in life are not so logical."

They all seemed to sigh together, then realizing their simultaneous sigh, broke out in laughter.

Then the food came, and it was fabulous. Pelmeni meat pies with light, flaky crust and a delicious lamb filling. There was a soup made with cabbage and sausages and a gelatinized meat dish.

After dinner, they had coffee and waited expectantly for dessert.

Yuri looked at both women. "You both laugh and shine like sprites in the forest," he said, "but something bothers you." He looked at Abbey, locking their eyes together.

Abbey felt like he saw her almost intimately, and she swallowed hard. Not wanting to cry, she simply nodded.

Then a loud noise interrupted them, and someone cried for help just outside the front door.

Yuri rose quickly and rushed to the front of the restaurant. Outside was a porch covered by an awning, with several benches for customers who were waiting for tables. A woman lay unconscious on the ground. Pregnant, she looked to be in her third trimester. A crowd gathered around her.

"Step back!" Yuri bellowed with authority, and everyone moved, allowing him to kneel at her right side.

He pointed to a frightened man standing next to her. "You are the husband?"

"Yes," he said, almost paralyzed with fear.

"Call 9-1-1!" Yuri said very clearly.

Abbey and Olivia were at his side. Olivia also called 911 on her phone.

Yuri looked at the motionless young woman, and he couldn't tell if she was breathing. He tried to unbutton her top button, then grabbed her blouse in both hands and ripped it open, the buttons popping. He put his fingers on her pulse and watched intently for the rise of her chest, to see if she was breathing.

"She has a pulse," he said, then he saw her breathe.

She began to open her eyes. Yuri took off his own flannel shirt and draped it over her.

Yuri asked her name. She had no bleeding or pain. She had not eaten since breakfast and, while standing in line, felt her vision turn black.

"She fainted," he said. "Let's get her inside where it is warm."

Her husband helped Yuri, and they gently stood her up and walked into the restaurant.

A few minutes later, an ambulance arrived. Although she was feeling better, the pregnant woman was loaded onto the stretcher, then rolled into the ambulance, still covered with Yuri's red flannel shirt.

"She is going to be fine," Yuri announced loudly to everyone in the restaurant. The small crowd began to clap.

Olivia looked at Abbey, who was watching Yuri.

"You like him," she said.

"Of course," admitted Abbey. "It's hard not to. But so do you."

Olivia shook her head with a smile.

"I already met an apostle today," she said, smiling at the thought of her day with John.

Abbey had enjoyed their evening, and she thought Yuri was wonderful, but she hesitated.

"I don't need a boyfriend right now," she said. "Or maybe ever."

"Abbey," she heard Yuri call. "Come! Come meet the chef and see the kitchen."

She had hoped all evening for a chance at this.

She closed her eyes and took a breath, feeling attracted to him all the more because he thought of her and knew what she was hoping for.

"Well, why not see what's cooking in that kitchen, sis," said Olivia playfully.

After Yuri brought them back to the Fisher House, he and Abbey talked for an hour in the living room. She found out he was thirty-eight years old and had practiced pathology for five years in Ukraine before coming to the United States. His mother and father were still in Ukraine. He had tried to get them to come to the United States but had not been successful thus far. He worried about them every day.

THE GUARDIANS OF ROCK HILL

"They are Russian, like me, and stubborn," he said with a sad smile. "But also, they are Ukrainian and love their home. Like I am American and love my home."

Abbey was definitely attracted to him—he was both strong and vulnerable—but like Lan, they lived four hundred miles apart.

"That's a long cab fare," she joked when it came up in conversation.

"I would walk four hundred miles to see you again," he said sweetly.

"But you hardly know me," she said. She wanted to tell him about her brokenness and that she was not what she seemed.

"Getting to know you is the idea," he said.

 215

CHAPTER 34

FOLLOW-UP

Abbey's follow-up with Dr. Song was at nine o'clock the next morning. Neither sister was hungry, their nerves getting the best of them; instead, they each got a cup of coffee from the coffee shop in the lobby of Walter Reed, then sat in the waiting room, hypnotically watching cable news until the doctor called them in.

In the medical profession, there is a lot of "hurry up and wait," characterized by the sense of absolute urgency in getting something done immediately coexisting with the understanding that the endless "wait and see" is part of the process.

The path to a cancer diagnosis begins with a question. Sometimes questions lead to answers, and sometimes they only seem to lead to more questions. When the answer comes, it might be good news—a reprieve, a stay of execution—or it might not be. Abbey had watched her mother walk this path, begging God for more time, then being led down hospital hallways with shiny waxed floors, cold and scared, with her private parts exposed through the back of her hospital gown.

Dr. Song was courteous and empathic as always, but after the appointment, Abbey could really only remember hearing a few things: results inconclusive, borderline tumor, stage I, 90 percent survival. The rest of the words all washed together and came out the same color.

Olivia's mind felt congested. Of course, she had been hoping to hear the word "benign." That word was not used, but almost everything Dr. Song told them had an underpinning of hope and optimism. Almost. What is the saying? *The devil is in the details*. She could understand the sentiment.

Abbey's thoughts were different. She felt distant and vacant. Yuri said there was beauty in the empty spaces, but she couldn't see that now. All she felt was the emptiness. It could also be said that *the devil is in the empty spaces*. The unknown.

She asked Olivia not to tell anyone. "I don't want to be a victim," she explained. "What is it that makes everyone want to slow down to see the accident victim, anyway?"

Olivia shifted her gaze nervously. "I don't know," she said. She couldn't see Abbey as being an accident victim. "I'd rather just close my eyes."

Surgery was over, and she had an inconclusive diagnosis. Maybe she should have felt optimism, but that eluded her. Abbey needed to keep busy. When her dad died, she buried herself in schoolwork. When her mom died, Olivia's psychiatric illness had saved Abbey; her sister gave her something to live for. Now it was her diner. She had to get back to work.

They were on an afternoon flight back to Rock Hill. Abbey planned to go straight from the airport to the diner, determined to start settling into the empty spaces.

When Yuri called her that afternoon, she told him that she was gone.

"Gone?" he asked.

"Olivia and I came back to Rock Hill. I have to get to work," she said curtly.

A brief silence followed.

"Abbey, are you okay?" he asked.

"Yes." Her coldness was so out of character, but she couldn't bring herself to talk about her diagnosis or how she was feeling.

Why am I acting this way? She felt outside of her own self, like she was watching herself in a movie. *I met the perfect person at the most imperfect of times, and I can't get attached.*

Yuri felt her response was like a caution light. He wanted to be careful with her feelings but also to be sure she understood his intentions.

"May I call you again?" he asked.

Another brief silence.

"Why don't you let me call you?" she said.

That signal was crystal clear. "Oh, okay. I understand what it means: Don't call me; I'll call you," he said. What he didn't understand was why, after such a lovely evening, she would not want to see him again.

"I like you, Abbey," he said softly. "I hope you call me when it is right for you."

She liked him too, but wondered if it would ever be right for her again.

Just then, she remembered something Dr. Song had said: "I have found there are many things in life that contain simultaneously sharp contrasts, like when there is good news and bad news in the same information, from the same tissue, at the same time."

CHAPTER 35

HOME AGAIN

It was late Friday afternoon by the time Abbey made it to the diner. The front door was locked, which was unusual. She walked around the corner to the alley behind the restaurant to use the back door. The dumpster area was clean as always.

Cleanliness was next to restaurant godliness in Abbey's business philosophy, and that extended from the front entrance to the back alley. Pallets and boxes were neatly stacked, and she had a separate area for recycling. The garbage containers were always covered, and she paid extra to have them emptied frequently.

She personally cleaned the sidewalk and street, with her employees picking up trash, down to the cigarette butts that gathered on the curb. This wasn't just about her view of social responsibility; it was also her love for Rock Hill, the place and the people.

Sights and smells had to be beautiful. Fancy and beautiful are not the same thing. Simple things can be the most beautiful. A welcoming atmosphere is simple. A clean space, a smiling face, simple. Azaleas in Glencairn Gardens, simple. Talking with Rachael, simple. But Abbey's life was no longer simple.

She opened the back door, and it was dark. The diner was almost never closed, yet the front door was locked, and the lights were off? This sent a warning message to her brain. Something was not right. She stopped, backing away and closing the door. Safety had been imprinted on her by her father when she was a child. Keep your senses engaged, be aware of your surroundings. As she stepped away from the back door, it opened, and she was greeted by a surprise from Estelle and the staff.

"Welcome home!" said Estelle as she took her hand and led her inside. Abbey was confused until Estelle pointed to the wall. There was a banner, "World's Greatest Chef," and a beautiful cake. Estelle handed her an envelope with a get-well-soon card signed by all the diner's staff.

The dining room was crowded. Olivia and Aliyah were there with the mayor and Winthrop's president, along with many of Abbey's regular customers.

Olivia walked up, ignoring a covert angry glance from her sister. "Come look at this, Abbey." She led Abbey to the center table, where there was an award from the Southern Restaurant Association. Abbey picked up the trophy, tracing the engraved words with her fingertips. "The New York Diner" she read aloud, "was named the Most Up-and-Coming Restaurant in the Carolinas." Abbey was thrilled. Finally, some good news. Happy tears began to fall as she looked around the room at the cheering crowd.

"How did you get here before me?" Abbey asked Olivia.

"I drove a little fast," Olivia said, laughing.

"We found out about the award last week," said Aliyah, giving Abbey a hug. "Then Olivia told us the good news from the operation, so we had to celebrate!"

"The operation …" Abbey said flatly, and just like that, her mood changed. She looked sideways at Olivia. She had specifically asked her sister not to discuss the appointment with Dr. Song. She felt herself deflating, drowning, exhausted. She rubbed her temples wearily with her fingers, then looked around the dining room. Of course, she did not see Rachael. She hadn't expected to, but hope dies hard.

Abbey had come to the diner that night to try and forget about everything, her diagnosis as well as her disastrous personal life. Her kitchen was going to be her safe place. She felt a wave of emotion and turned quickly, walking through the double swinging doors, through the kitchen, and into the women's bathroom, where no one would see her crying.

Olivia put on her Miss America smile and graciously thanked everyone for coming but explained that Abbey was overwhelmed. Olivia hurried to the back to find her.

She knocked on the bathroom door. "Abbey," she whispered, "please let me in."

"It's unlocked."

"I had to tell them something," Olivia said. "Aliyah and Rach—" She stopped. "Aliyah and Estelle are our family."

Abbey was sitting on the tile floor with her back to the wall. She looked up at her sister.

"You can say her name," said Abbey. "Did she call?"

Olivia shook her head, looking nervously at Abbey with a tear forming in her eye. She put her back against the wall and slid down to sit next to Abbey. She was scared and hurting too. Scared of cancer and scared of how fragile everything seemed.

"What did you tell Aliyah and Estelle?" Abbey asked.

"I lied," she said. "I told them everything was fine."

Abbey dried her eyes and took a deep breath. "How do I look?" she asked.

"Like you always look," said Olivia. "Beautiful."

Abbey walked back to the party, mingled for a few minutes, and thanked each guest personally. When all the guests were gone a short time later, the restaurant employees began to set up for dinner. Abbey changed into her white chef's jacket and began helping with the prep work. She took a bag of Vidalia onions and began to peel them. She sliced them multiple times, vertically and horizontally, chopped them, and then put them in a deep plastic bowl and added dry white wine.

Olivia watched her for a while. "It always amazes me that you have all your fingers," she said as Abbey's chef's knife moved flawlessly.

Abbey felt comfortable again. In her zone. In control. She sliced the last onion in half.

"Ouch, damn it," she said, putting her knife down on the cutting board.

They both looked at her finger. There was a thin red line, which formed into a thick drop of blood. She stepped away from the prep station, applying pressure to her finger.

"I'm sorry," said Olivia. "I jinxed you."

They walked to Abbey's office where she kept the first aid kit. Olivia put an antiseptic on Abbey's finger.

"It's not bad," Abbey said. "It's just part of working with sharp instruments. I should have been more careful."

Abbey was the most careful person Olivia knew. She put an adhesive bandage strip on Abbey's finger, then kissed it, just like their mom used to do when they were kids.

"I love you, sis," she said.

"I love you too," said Abbey. "I better get back to the kitchen."

"I know. I've got to get going too," Olivia said.

Her production team was meeting that night, and things were beginning to move along quickly. She had officially shortened the name of her play, which would open as *Mill Town Girl*.

She and Rachael worked well together. Rachael had remained devoted and professional, although it was awkward at times because the story and the songs were filled with Abbey. She was their inspiration, and they both knew it, but Rachael wouldn't, couldn't talk about it. That cut may have stopped bleeding, but it had not healed.

CHAPTER 36

STRENGTH OF A CHILD

When they were children, the girls liked to ride their bikes on the Tech Park Trail, on the south side of Dave Lyle Boulevard and Gateway, where the four Civitas statues held their positions at the corners of the intersection. It was a time when their world was defined by the places they could pedal on their bicycles.

One afternoon, they met after school in Glencairn Gardens and set off for the trail, which was a few blocks away. Olivia and Aliyah had ridden ahead and already crossed Dave Lyle, as Abbey and Rachael peddled hard to catch up.

Abbey and Rachael entered the intersection safely, while the light was green in their direction. Abbey checked before entering the street and saw a big pickup truck, but it seemed to be slowing for the light, and they had ample time to cross.

After crossing, Abbey pulled to a stop under her favorite Civita, the one who held the stars over her head. Rachael was in the middle of the street when her shoelaces got tangled in her pedals and she fell on top of her bicycle.

The traffic light changed, and the man driving the pickup, now a block away, accelerated. Apparently, he was texting on his phone, watching the traffic light but not watching the street. He didn't see Rachael lying in the road.

Rachael tried desperately to free herself but could not.

Abbey watched in horror from the corner.

"Take off your shoes!" Abbey screamed to Rachael.

She ran into the street, facing the oncoming pickup truck, frantically waving her arms, trying to get the driver's attention. Then she put her hands forward with outstretched arms, bracing herself for impact. She expected in that moment that she was going to die.

Olivia and Aliyah saw Rachael fall and saw the truck. They began to race feverishly toward the intersection on their bikes. Their movement toward the road caught the attention of the truck driver's peripheral vision, and he instinctively moved his foot to the brake. Now looking forward at the road, he saw Abbey standing with her hands in front of her, as if she were a child superhero ready to stop the truck. He slammed on his brakes and swerved to the right. His phone dropped to the floor at his feet as the truck came to a stop three feet from Abbey.

Traffic came to a complete halt in both directions.

The truck driver jumped out, leaving his door open.

"Oh my God!" he said, terrified. "Are you hurt?"

Abbey didn't move. She felt outside of her own self, as if watching from above.

Aliyah ran to Rachael and helped her get her shoes off. They pushed her bicycle off the road.

Olivia walked up to her sister. "Come on, Abbey," she said, touching her right arm and breaking her trance.

The driver offered to call their parents, or put their bicycles in his pickup and take them home, or call an ambulance.

"But," said Abbey, still in a haze, "we're not hurt." Then she turned to Rachael and saw she was bleeding from a mild abrasion on her knee. It was a minor injury and not hospital worthy.

"Are you okay?" she asked Rachael.

Rachael just nodded.

The four girls got back on their bikes, and nobody talked the whole way home. Rachael kept replaying the image of Abbey in her mind, standing in front of her, willing the truck to stop, saving her life.

CHAPTER 37

ALIYAH

The New York Diner closed after brunch on Sundays. Abbey used the time to clean the kitchen, work on new dishes, and once each month, have a business meeting with Aliyah and Olivia. This month, Olivia was wrapped up in preparation for the opening of *Mill Town Girl*, but Abbey and Aliyah agreed to meet at 4 p.m.

Usually when Aliyah arrived, Abbey was in the middle of cleaning. Today, she was surprised to find Abbey sitting in the center of the dining room at a table set for two.

"What's going on?" asked Aliyah.

Abbey smiled nervously and pulled out a chair for her. "I wanted to cook something special …. I wouldn't have the New York Diner without you."

She had made Aliyah's favorite meal: she-crab soup, fire- roasted oysters, and pulled pork.

"Time out," Aliyah made a *T* by pointing her fingers into her opposite palm. "We need to chat?"

Abbey nodded affirmation and whispered, "Yes." She knew this was coming. It was the real reason she had cooked and set the table.

Aliyah sat down across from Abbey with her arms crossed and asked point blankly, "What's going on with you?"

Abbey felt pressure in her chest and a hollow fear, but she knew she had to talk.

"You have every right to hate me," she began, rubbing her temples. "I've tried to figure out how I let this happen." She slowly shook her head. "But ... it hasn't helped."

She wanted to communicate without crying but was having difficulty getting her words out. "That night, when I kissed Chalie—" She stopped, closed her eyes tightly as if trying to both remember and forget.

"Abbey," Aliyah said impatiently. She unfolded her arms and leaned forward. "Look at you. You can have just about any man you want. Why your best friend's husband?"

Abbey covered her quivering lips with her hand. "It wasn't like that." She felt her eyes burning as tears formed.

"Then what," Aliyah said pointedly, "was it exactly like?"

"We were friends," Abbey blurted out. "I loved him ... like a friend." She took a shuddering breath. "And then, I loved him too much. I tried to keep my distance, then one night, I didn't."

She couldn't bear to look at Aliyah, so she covered her face in her hands, "We swore it would never happen again, and it never did."

"None of that makes it okay," Aliyah said flatly.

"I know." Abbey sobbed.

Aliyah sat with her back straight. "Rachael is devastated."

Abbey looked up now; tear tracks stained her face. "Is there anything I can do?" she pleaded.

Aliyah could see that Abbey was also devastated. "No, Abbey," she said softly. "You've done too much, and not enough, at the same time."

Eventually Abbey stopped crying and nodded. "I understand if neither of you wants to ever speak to me again."

"Actually, Rachael wants me to be your friend," she moved closer to Abbey. "What you and Chalie did was fucked up, but I love you like a sister."

Abbey had come to appreciate Aliyah's communication style, no bullshit and no excuses. Aliyah reached out, and Abbey met her midway.

Abbey felt the simple warmth in her friend's touch. She stood, wiped her eyes with her napkin, and then walked into the kitchen and returned with the food. She quietly served Aliyah, cutting a wedge of black-skillet cornbread with pecan butter she had churned that morning.

Aliyah watched Abbey delicately plate her dinner. She knew that food was a way Abbey expressed her love. "My momma used to tell me there's only two kinds of cornbread," she said as she took her first bite, "good and better." The cornbread melted in her mouth. "This one is definitely better."

Abbey poured them each a glass of Chardonnay, then sat down next to her. "Thank you, Aliyah. So how have you been?"

Aliyah thought about her answer. She had something she wanted to say but was waiting for the right moment. "It's been hard, not seeing you," she said honestly.

Abbey sank into her chair, as if her whole body ached. "You know how you can rewind something on TV, or skip a scene on a Blu-ray?"

Aliyah nodded. "Oh yes. We used to rewind the songs on the *Lion King* VCR tape over and over when we were kids."

"I think we wore that tape out," said Abbey with a chuckle, but her smile passed. "Life doesn't work that way .... Grown-up Abbey has had to acknowledge that the repercussions ... have been cataclysmic," she told Aliyah. Twisting her napkin with a sigh, she added, "But inner Abbey wants her friends to remember that she's not a terrible person, despite having done a really terrible thing." She shook her head. She didn't want to talk about herself anymore. She asked about Aliyah's family and her construction on the S&S Mill. "And how is Avery, or Jonas rather?"

"He is," she hesitated with a playful, telegraphing smile, "actually pretty great."

"Really?" Abbey said inquisitively.

"Yes. His gallery just had a show, and he sold a few paintings ...." Aliyah paused.

Abbey grinned at Aliyah's playful secrecy and reached for her wine. She glanced at Aliyah's wine glass. Chardonnay was her favorite, and she hadn't taken a sip.

Aliyah saw the question forming in Abbey's eyes. She smiled a beautiful smile while reaching into her purse. "We haven't told anyone," she said, handing her phone to Abbey. On the screen was a photo, no more than a speck of gray, shaped like a bean against a black background.

CHAPTER 38

RACHAEL AND CHALIE

Before Chalie, Rachael felt like she was moving through life on the sidelines, more as an observer and less like an active participant. That is not to say that she needed him to define her, any more than anyone needs anybody. Who is the real self? Is it the woman as she sees herself, or as she is seen by others? As she is seen by her husband? Her children? Her colleagues? Her friends? Is the real self an amalgam of all those images?

Chalie's affair with Abbey left Rachael with a lot of questions, but it also gave her some answers. She didn't need Chalie like oxygen. She didn't have to consume him to live. She was able to make her own energy, like an emotional autotroph. Yes, she did have needs. That's supposed to be part of a marriage, the reciprocity of giving and taking. Having something to give and needing someone to have. It's right there in the vow, *to have and to hold from this day forward*.

But people don't really have people. That's part of the rip in the fabric of matrimony. She wanted to have someone, and she wanted to be needed, to know that someone needed to have her. She felt that distinctly when she became a mother. It felt special to be needed so much. But the goal of motherhood is to foster independence. To grow. So having someone is an illusion.

She thought of Abbey, standing in front of that pickup truck, ready to die for her. For a long time, she felt like they had each other.

What now?

She was not talking with Abbey, and Chalie was moving out, sort of. Rachael said she needed the separation. She was back to needing.

A relationship crisis can have phases. They had done all the talking they could collectively. Listening is a different thing altogether. Rachael was determined not to become blaming and condemning each time they spoke, but sometimes her feelings just spilled out that way. Objectivity is lost in anger, and then it can be hard to see things as they really are.

Her children were confused and scared. This hurt her more than almost anything else. Intellectually, she knew that children make it through divorce, but she would be fooling herself to think there was no cost to them. She asked Chalie to meet her at the house when the kids were at school. She put his suitcase on their bed. It sat there alone like a silent metaphor.

"So ... um," he hesitated. "You don't want me to take all my things?" He was questioning, searching for optimism.

She did not. She was not at that point, although it loomed overhead and seemed at the same time abhorrent and desirable. *Divorce.*

"No. I mean, I don't know. I just need some time alone," she said. "Don't you?"

Part of her wanted him to say, "No, I just need you," and hold her like he would never let her go. She knew that if he asked, she would let him stay.

Chalie sat on the edge of the bed, elbows on his thighs, and head in his hand.

"I know I hurt you," he looked up directly at Rachael. "And I'm so sorry."

"Hurt?" she said, not with anger, but with honest questioning. She sat next to him on their bed. "We've hurt each other before, Chalie. I don't think what you did can be summarized that easily."

"I fucked up, okay, Rachael," he said, pleading with his hands. "I'm not trying to minimize it, but I can't undo it. We have both made mistakes."

She felt her anger rising, like a burning in her chest. She stood again.

"I never cheated on you."

"I know," he said.

At least not with my body, she thought. Rachael thought of her father's sermons about adultery and how fidelity wasn't just about the genitals; it was also about the heart.

"Are we going to turn your infidelity into my shortcomings now?" she asked. "I know I'm not perfect."

"I didn't mean that," he said. "I love you, Rachael."

"I believe you," she said. "But something is broken, fractured."

He understood fractures. Sometimes they need casting, sometimes an operation. They always needed rest.

"If it's broken, we can fix it," he said.

"Do you know what I've lost?" she asked. "You are my husband, and she was my best friend. My goddamned best friend," she said.

He had never known her to use that word before. There was nothing he could say.

It was a pivotal moment in time, and it just passed by. He picked up his suitcase and closed the door quietly behind him.

CHAPTER 39

A SOCCER GAME

Life can't be placed on pause. It doesn't have that function; it just keeps moving and will pass by, noticed or unnoticed.

C.J. and Simon had to see Chalie. He was a good dad, if often absent. They unquestionably adored him.

Rachael tried not to speak negatively about Chalie; for that matter, her feelings about him were not overwhelmingly negative. Her explanations to the children were simple, with no details of things done wrong but an acknowledgment that they were having a difficult time in their relationship.

They were just finishing breakfast, and Simon had gone to the living room to play a new video game. C.J. was finishing her toasted frozen waffle, about to get ready for her soccer game.

"Where has Abbey been?" asked C.J.

Rachael wasn't sure how to answer her. She had overlooked that the kids were used to seeing Abbey frequently, often daily. She would come by the house, or they would go to the diner or to her house. She was a part of their family.

C.J. was intuitive and inquisitive. Rachael could see the gears in her mind turning, trying to fit the circumstances together. Why would there be a simultaneous absence of her father and Abbey?

Rachael could think of nothing to say. She simply stared straight ahead, looking right through C.J.

"Are you okay, Mom?"

She shook off her cloud.

Am I okay? she thought.

"I will be, sweetheart," she told C.J., brushing the back of her daughter's hair with her hand, then kissing her on the cheek. "Go get your shin guards, then we have to get out of here."

Rachael had grown up playing sports and went to college on an athletic scholarship, so she was a firm believer in protective equipment. She walked to the counter where her phone was charging. There was a message from Olivia, saying that she would be at the game and that they could work on the play that evening if Rachael was free. Nothing about Abbey, and nothing from Abbey. That was the boundary she set. Shin guards for love.

Feeling heavy, Rachael sat back down and opened her photos, scrolling back to a picture of the four of them from ten years ago. They were inseparable and unstoppable. She thought about the first time Abbey kissed her and replayed in her mind how she saw her kissing Chalie. They were so tender. Kisses aren't supposed to hurt.

C.J. had asked her mom and dad to sign her up for soccer three years ago, because a boy in her class that she liked was on the team. She spent most of her first season trying to watch the cute boy while nervously trying to stay away from the ball, but then something changed. She attended soccer camp and was amazed at how the older kids could handle the ball, side to side, foot to foot, and how they could maneuver and make their opponents miss.

Chalie put a net in the backyard, and C.J. practiced dribbling and shooting every afternoon. She worked her cleats to the ground all year, and today she was starting the game for the first time at center forward. It was a championship game between Rock Hill and Lancaster. She was going to be the striker, and Rachael knew she was beyond excited.

Rachael remembered just a few years ago, when the kids on the soccer field looked like schools of fish, moving together toward a piece of bread thrown into the water. Now they knew their positions and played as a team.

That was a unique thing she noticed about soccer. It was extraordinarily individual and also unquestionably team centered. Rachael had been a state champion on a track scholarship, but that was so singular. Yes, she was part of a team, but with the exception of relays, each event was a solitary runner against other runners, although for Rachael, she really ran against herself. She was her own hardest opponent.

She got C.J.'s team's snacks together—orange slices, seedless grapes, and trail mix—then called for Simon, who brought along some dinosaurs and his handheld game console. C.J. bounced out of the car when they got to the soccer field.

Chalie arrived soon after they did. Simon saw him and ran up to his dad, who picked him up and swung him around, then slung him up on his shoulders as they walked over to Rachael.

"Hi, Rachael," he said, swinging Simon to the ground.

She smiled at her son, then turned to Chalie. "Hi. How was your week?" she asked.

Chalie bent forward to plant a brief kiss on Rachael's cheek. At first, she started to turn away, but then allowed it.

He sighed. "It feels strange, asking how each other's week was. We used to ask how the day was," said Chalie.

That was true, she agreed.

"I had a tough case last night, a bad hemorrhage. I was afraid I might lose her," he said.

"Is she okay?" asked Rachael.

He nodded.

Sometimes she forgot how hard his job could be.

"Are *you* okay?" she asked.

He shrugged, then smiled, looking into her eyes. "I am now."

Rachael's mom and dad arrived, and then Aliyah and Jonas pulled up. They all talked for a minute. Rachael pointed toward C.J., who was warming up with the team. Then they walked together to the side of the field, lugging folding chairs and blankets. C.J. had her personal cheering section.

The opposing team was warming up on the other side of their field, and their families had gathered around a set of aluminum bleachers. Sitting unnoticed in the middle of the bleachers was a beautiful young woman, dressed inconspicuously in a baggy sweatshirt and old jeans, with her long hair pulled up under a baseball cap. Abbey blended in with the crowd so that nobody saw or recognized her. Like the others, she came to watch C.J.'s big game, but she couldn't help watching Rachael and Chalie. She made sure not to stare too long, because people can feel a stare. She felt guilty, as if she were being deceitful by watching them, but the regulation soccer field could have just as easily been an ocean of separation. The best thing she could do for Rachael and Chalie was to stay on the opponent's side, hidden in the bleachers.

Olivia arrived, fashionably late as usual, and joined Rachael and Aliyah. Abbey couldn't hide from Olivia, and she felt her eyes almost immediately. They locked gazes across the field. Olivia understood Abbey's need to remain incognito, and nodded once, then diverted her gaze, so nobody noticed.

Just before the kickoff, someone two rows above Abbey made his way toward her, excusing himself as he stepped over a bleacher row.

"Abbey?" he asked, and she turned. "Is that you?"

"Lan," she said with a smile. "What are you doing here?"

"My nephew plays for Lancaster, and my company sponsors his team."

Abbey glanced nervously across the field. She did not want to draw any attention to herself.

"My best friend's daughter …" She was momentarily lost in thought, not knowing if Rachael would ever be her friend again.

"Your best friend's daughter what?" he asked gently. He could tell that something had upset her.

"She plays for the Rock Hill team," she said, pointing toward the field. "That's C.J."

Her pointing toward C.J. drew Rachael's attention from across the soccer field, and she recognized Abbey. She hadn't seen Abbey since that night she saw the kiss. Unwillingly, she felt a brief pang of excitement, then a pang of anger with Chalie, who was sitting next to her.

Rachael stood, feeling crowded, and walked toward a tree in an open area away from the crowd.

The game had started, and people were cheering on the sidelines.

Chalie got up and followed her. "What's wrong?" he asked.

"I just needed some space," she said.

"Did I do something?"

She looked at him crooked and said, "*Really?* Did you do something?"

"Rachael, come on, I know I *did something*." He added, "I meant now. Did I do something wrong just now?"

She softened a little. "No. It's just that we're sitting there like nothing ever happened," she said.

"Is that so bad?" he asked.

Now she was angry again. She thought of Abbey hiding in the visitor's bleachers.

"Do you hear yourself? Do you listen to me?" she asked.

"I'm trying," he said, now frustrated.

She turned away from him, and then they heard cheering. On the field, C.J. was running toward her teammates with her arms above her head. She had scored her first goal.

Rachael closed her eyes and took a deep breath.

Chalie moved toward her in excitement over C.J.'s goal. Rachael put her hands out in front of him, and he stopped.

They walked back to the sidelines with an arm's length between them, but it might as well have been a soccer field.

"I'm sorry," he told her.

"Please stop apologizing," she said.

He misinterpreted, thinking she was accepting his apology, but in her mind, they were only words.

Chalie looked at Rachael, wanting to be optimistic and to believe everything was going to be okay in the end.

Everywhere else in the world, that would be called denial.

CHAPTER 40

LANCASTER

After the soccer game, Lan asked Abbey out to lunch. She said she couldn't because she had already missed Saturday morning at the diner and needed to work through brunch.

"Fair enough," said Lan. "How about after brunch?"

She *did* want to see him.

"Sure," she found herself saying. "Pick me up at the diner at two o'clock." Then she slipped away from the field.

When she arrived at the diner, it was packed. She washed up and looked over the dining room and kitchen to decide where she would be needed most. Her sous chef was running the line expertly. There were tables that needed bussing, so she cleaned them, filled coffee cups, and then joined the food line. Her staff was always glad to see her. She had an intense but calming presence in the kitchen.

A large black-and-white clock hung on the wall above the bread warmer, but she could usually tell the time based on customer flow. Twelve came and went, and the pace slowed.

She stepped off the line and told the sous chef and Estelle that she was popping out for a bit.

"Good," said Estelle. "You need to get away from the diner more."

"I'll be back by 4 p.m. to set up for dinner," said Abbey.

Estelle shook her head.

"Honey," said Estelle, "listen to someone who has done this for a long time. It's why you hired me, isn't it? You've worked seventy hours this week. Just take the night off. The diner will be fine."

The diner would be fine for one night, but she might not be. She tried to keep her private things private, but surgery, infidelity, and betrayal clouded her consciousness. Right now, the diner was the one place Abbey could go to get away from herself. She gave Estelle a smile and a hug, then went to her office to change and put on a little makeup.

Lan arrived promptly and stood nervously at the hostess station, looking around the restaurant for Abbey.

"Table for one?" Estelle asked. He was young and quite good looking. His hair looked wind tossed, and he combed it neatly with his fingers.

"Actually," he said, "I'm waiting for Abbey ...."

"Ah," Estelle said. "She's just finishing up. Why don't you have seat?"

She showed him to a seat and brought him a cup of coffee and dessert without asking. It was an enormous apple strudel.

He took a sip of coffee, then a bite of the pastry, and his eyes opened wide.

"That's just about the best thing I've ever tasted," he said, looking at the strudel, wondering how something could taste that good.

"That's Abbey's magic," said Estelle. "She's why I'm here."

Estelle adored Abbey and thought Abbey was very much like the pastries she created: sweet with a touch of savory; buttery but light; rich in flavor and hard not to love.

Abbey walked out into the dining room and looked around. It was a good afternoon with a steady flow of customers who all seemed to be enjoying their food and their company. She greeted half a dozen diners, giving each her full attention, as she crossed over to Lan and Estelle.

"Abbey," said Lan, "your diner is so refreshing. It's like walking into a happy memory."

Abbey gave him a genuine smile.

"What a beautiful compliment. Thank you," she said. "So what did you have in mind for our afternoon?"

"Have you been to King's Mountain?" he asked.

King's Mountain is the site of one of the most important battles in the American Revolution. The National Historic Battlefield lies about thirty miles north of Rock Hill.

"I haven't been since I was a little girl," said Abbey. It was a lovely day outside. "That sounds very nice."

"Where did you park?" she asked as they walked out the front door.

"Right across the street," he said.

She looked across the street, in front of the bank, and there was only one car parked: a dark-blue BMW.

"That's a nice car," she said.

"It sure is," he said. "But it's not mine." He smiled and pointed behind the car. "That's mine."

It was a dark-red motorcycle. Abbey noticed two helmets strapped to the seat. Lan walked to the bike and took two pairs of leather gloves from the saddlebag, then turned to

Abbey, searching her face for any sign of reluctance, but he saw her smile instead.

Admittedly, this was not what she was expecting, but this added to the adventure and mystery of the moment. She had never actually been on a motorcycle, but the idea was exciting. She was glad she wore long jeans and boots rather than the dress and high heels she was originally considering.

"If you prefer, we can take your car," he offered.

"Absolutely not," she chimed. "Which helmet is mine?"

He gave her the smaller helmet and a pair of small leather gloves that fit perfectly. She put the helmet on, and her long blond hair fell out from beneath.

"Let me get on first," he said, swinging his leg over and starting the motorcycle with a loud, crackling rumble. She climbed on behind him.

She was startled at the sudden jolt of propulsion from the powerful bike. Their helmets bumped, and she grabbed Lan's waist with both hands. She couldn't see it, but he smiled under his helmet at her touch. She took a deep breath, taking in the aroma of his leather jacket. It felt so good to feel somebody. She put her arms around him to hold on for the rest of the ride.

They avoided the interstate and took back roads through the Carolina countryside. They passed the road to the cabin on Lake Wylie, and she thought of her last summer there and Rachael.

The air in her face brought her back into the moment.

The Carolina countryside was picturesque, with acres of rolling hills, farms, and forests. Abbey pointed to a farmer's market ahead, and they pulled in for a smoothie. Lan held the motorcycle steady as she dismounted. She took off her helmet and shook her hair.

"You are so beautiful," he said, unintentionally staring. He looked away and was quiet for a moment, hoping he didn't sound like a lovestruck schoolboy.

She smoothed down her hair and smiled with Southern grace.

They went inside and ended up buying peach smoothies.

"When did you learn to ride?" she asked as they walked around outside.

"I started riding when I was a kid," he said. "But when I moved to DC, I decided to leave my bike at my parent's house. I can hardly wait to get on it when I come home."

She looked at him and held his gaze with wide, playful eyes.

"Teach me," she said.

There was a large empty field next to the market.

"Let's do it," Lan said.

They rode to the field, and Lan rode around the perimeter. The ground was dry and firm, good for a first lesson.

He began by explaining the operation mechanics. She had never used a standard transmission, so he taught her the basics about using the clutch and shifting the gears with her left foot.

Lan had never taught anyone how to ride before, but Abbey was a fast learner. She had excellent balance from riding a bicycle since she was five years old. But an important part of learning to ride is being able to stay in the friction zone. This is the area where the clutch is not fully disengaged, and the motorcycle can move slowly from the friction of the gears just as they are barely engaging. Abbey was finding it difficult to remain in the friction zone. Being on the bike was easy when the clutch was pressed and the gears weren't engaged. It was also easy when the bike had forward motion, with the gears fully engaged. The friction zone and getting started was the most difficult. That was when the engine was likely to die.

Soon enough, Abbey gained confidence, and to Lan's surprise, she pulled away and began to drive around the field.

"Go into second gear!" he shouted.

She shifted and the engine purred as she drove a few times around the field, then came to a stop next to him.

"I don't remember how to turn it off," she said.

He reached forward and cut the engine with the switch on the right handgrip.

He put down the kickstand for her, and she came off the motorcycle, bouncing with a rush of adrenaline. She jumped forward to give him a hug.

"That was so much fun!" she said. "Thank you! You're a good teacher."

"You're a natural," he told her, looking into her eyes, impressed by her adventurous spirit.

They were still standing very close, and she moved slightly toward him. He leaned forward to kiss her. She kissed him too but held back, not with her lips as much as with her heart.

While she was on the motorcycle, she was very in the moment, feeling the engine, her heart rolling with the throttle. Now she was back, standing in the field with somebody new, somebody she wanted to kiss back, but then she had the feeling it was all like playing make-believe. She felt like she was in one of life's friction zones.

Two people can only share one first kiss, and this was theirs, next to a motorcycle on a beautiful Carolina day. His lips were soft and a little salty.

"You taste like vanilla and cinnamon," he said, starry-eyed.

She smiled shyly. "So ... King's Mountain?"

"Oh yeah, right," he said.

They put their riding gear back on and rode to King's Mountain. Abbey kept her hands on his abdomen, but her mind was somewhere else, wondering what she was doing and where she was going. She knew she needed to talk with Lan before they rode too far together.

The battle of King's Mountain marked the first major victory over Cornwallis following the British capture of Charleston, demonstrating the determination of the patriots in the Carolinas and the capability of the fledgling Continental Army to unify and overcome the British.

The park is beautiful, with a winding road through an old-growth forest, leaving the visitor with an impression of the Carolina frontier as it was 250 years ago. They passed a wild turkey, then a few whitetail deer grazing together in a green meadow, before pulling into the parking area. After taking off their helmets, they both drank a bottle of spring water, then walked to the visitor's center.

The National Battlefield is encircled by a 1.5-mile walking trail. They walked on the trail, feeling the solemn quiet of the mountainside where their forefathers fought for independence. Lan reached for Abbey's hand, and they continued on, hand in hand.

"It's hard to imagine charging up this mountain into gunfire," said Lan.

"Or feeling isolated and surrounded on the hilltop," replied Abbey.

On King's Mountain, the British forces held the high ground of the mountain while the bands of frontier patriots cut off any chance of escape at the base. Battles are often portrayed with clear lines of good versus bad, but both armies on the mountainside fought for what they believed in. There were men on opposing sides of this battlefield from the same families.

At the end of the trail, they sat in the cool grass under a shady hickory tree. Since childhood, Abbey liked to lay under trees and look up through the branches. She liked to find different ways of viewing the world. Her mother taught her that. The sky was peeking through the branches and leaves like a three-dimensional tapestry.

Lan lay next to her and looked through the branches, following her eyes.

A red squirrel scampered nimbly across the branches, as if unaffected by gravity, and seemed unaware of the tree-gazing couple.

"Cute squirrel," said Lan. "It must be nice to be so carefree."

The squirrel stopped, as if hearing Lan, and sat on a limb looking at them.

The oak trees back at Winthrop University were home to hundreds of squirrels, and Abbey always enjoyed watching them, especially in the autumn when they were busy gathering acorns and in the spring when they chased each other in circles around the trunks of the oaks. Although the little animals seemed carefree, that is a misconception. Their world is filled with hawks and owls, foxes and coyotes. There are fleas, diseases, and cold Carolina winters. Yet, in spite of the ever-present dangers, they spend half of their time playing in the trees.

"I remember a momma squirrel that lived in the tree in front of our house," said Abbey, "Mom called her One Eye because, well, she only had one eye."

"Aptly named," said Lan with a chuckle.

"One Halloween, Dad helped Olivia and me carve our jack-o'-lanterns. Mine had a cat's face; Olivia's was a pirate. We put them on the porch the night before Halloween, and when we woke up in the morning, we found two pumpkins with big holes where the faces had been. Old One Eye ate both of the faces off."

"Squirrels eat pumpkin?" said Lan, smiling.

"Evidently," she said. "When Olivia and I started to cry, Dad said we should be proud because he couldn't imagine a better use for our jack-o'-lanterns."

Lan turned toward Abbey, intoxicated by her, the fresh air, and the mountain forest. He wanted to know everything he could about her. "Remember our plane ride?" he asked.

"Of course. I thought we were going to die," she said, then reflected on her fear of dying in that moment.

"I wonder," said Lan playfully, "if you believe in love at first flight?"

Abbey kissed him.

She was loving every minute they spent together. In another place or time, this might have been a perfect beginning, but there was something she wasn't telling him—something she hadn't told anyone.

"I think I should be getting back to the diner," she said, sitting up.

His confusion was not unexpected. "Did I do something wrong?" he asked carefully, shading his eyes as he looked up at her.

"I just think this is a bad idea," she snapped, purposefully sharp. She wanted to stop their relationship now, before it really started. Perhaps she could just pretend she didn't like him, make him not like her, and drive him away.

"Abbey," he said, sitting up and reaching for her hand, "tell me what's going on. Please."

Abbey wasn't good at being superficial, and it was too late for that. He needed to know some things about her.

She pulled away from him. "Lan," she began, then she let out a deep breath. She combed her fingers through her hair and looked at the sky, trying to piece her thoughts together, but she began to cry. "I can't be in a relationship with you," she said.

He waited for her to continue, and when she didn't, he asked, "Are you married?" He looked lost.

"No," she said, smiling through a sniffle, "I'm scared."

He moved closer and took her hand again. "Whatever it is, it's going to be okay," he said.

She nodded her head, but she had strong doubts that those words were true.

"When we met on the plane, I was on my way to Walter Reed," she said.

Lan looked at her intently. "The hospital?"

She nodded again.

Lan said nothing, seeing the weight upon Abbey, and he was hanging on for every word.

"I have cancer, just like my mom," she said.

He was bewildered and unsure of what to say. "Are you sure?" was all he could manage.

Abbey bit her lip. "They are going to remove my breasts and my ovaries," she said. Then she bent over in the grass, buried her face in her arms, her long blond hair mingling with strands of pine straw, and cried.

CHAPTER 41

ABIGAIL

The ride back to Rock hill was completely different. They rode on the same roads, but it was a different path. There was no excitement. They didn't feel like lovers, more like distant brother and sister.

Lan rode like he was alone on the bike, keeping his eyes straight ahead, deep in thought. Abbey had been as clear with him as possible. She did not want to start a relationship. He understood why and felt guilty because, although he liked her, he was afraid and didn't know what to say or how to proceed.

Abbey knew it wasn't fair to lay all of this on him. They had shared a few precious moments, but she could not obligate him to the weight of her present world.

She had plenty of time to think about how to say goodbye, and she decided not to. When the motorcycle stopped in front of the diner, she quickly took off her helmet and hopped off the bike, leaving the helmet on the seat as she ran inside without looking back.

When Abbey hurried through the door, Estelle knew something was wrong. It was late afternoon, and the dinner rush had not started, but Abbey didn't want anyone to see her crying. She didn't want to talk, to answer any questions, and she especially didn't want to think about the disfiguring surgery that would take her breasts and leave her barren but, hopefully, save her life.

Aside from talking with Dr. Song, telling Lan about her surgery was the first time she had said it out loud. She had not even spoken to Olivia about it.

That's not to say that her sister didn't know something was wrong, but Abbey had tried to keep her distant, feeling like she had to carry this alone, a penance for her sin.

Olivia knew about the stage I tumor, but not the rest. They had been together that day at Walter Reed when Dr. Song gave Abbey the initial pathology report. She had been very specific in explaining that the report was preliminary. Abbey was alone the next week when Dr. Song's office called to request a virtual appointment the following day. Phone calls like that don't usually end with good news.

"The pathologist is concerned that the tumor cells may not be borderline, so we're sending your case to the Armed Forces Institute of Pathology," Dr. Song had explained. "Your diagnosis could be upgraded to epithelial carcinoma."

Until then, Abbey had thought of upgrades as positive things—like being upgraded to first class—but there was no champagne, cushy seat, or extra leg room with this upgrade.

"So what's the bottom line here?" asked Abbey, trying not to sound as anxious and afraid as she really was.

"If these cells are determined to be ovarian carcinoma, the treatment recommendations will change considerably," said Dr. Song.

Abbey had been given a number of options, and none of them were appealing. One, she could choose to do nothing, in which case she would die. Two, since the affected organ, her left ovary, had already been removed, she could have ultrasounds of her right ovary every six months through her child-bearing years, then have her right ovary removed. At that point, she would be "castrated," or in menopause, as a young woman. She would have to be on hormone replacement therapy or develop brittle bones and grow a mustache like her great grandmother. Three, she could undergo ovarian stimulation and harvest her eggs, which would be cryogenically preserved, and then remove the right ovary. Or four, she could just be done with it and remove her right ovary now.

Although she didn't talk about it much, she always wanted to have a child, maybe two. This was something that had been a part of her earliest memories. Now she was unsure. For starters, she had proven herself an abysmal failure in relationships. While this was not entirely true, it was part of the dark place where she often found herself lately. On top of that, she would never want to pass this awful gene, this genetic fingerprint of cancer, to her child.

Cancer treatment recommendations are individualized and not absolute. She was told how fortunate she was. Her cancer was detected early. Still, she did not feel particularly fortunate.

Then behind door number two were her breasts. Dr Song explained that her risk of developing breast cancer was very high, as high as 70 percent. She could choose to be screened often with MRIs, mammographies, and physical exams, or consider a prophylactic mastectomy. The thought of a bilateral mastectomy, removing both of her breasts, was overwhelming. In some ways, this thought was more painful than losing her ovaries, perhaps because her ovaries were hidden inside, while her breasts were right out there. She thought her breasts were attractive and quietly enjoyed the attention she received because of them. She tried to tell herself that breasts were just adipose tissue and glands, but that didn't help. They were part of her.

When Estelle came to her office, Abbey was dressed in her chef coat and ready for work.

"Are you okay, hon?" she asked. "I thought you were going to take the night off." Abbey still had pine straw in her hair. Estelle came closer and pulled it out.

Abbey looked at Estelle and was so grateful that she had agreed to move to Rock Hill to manage the diner, but it was more than that. She had become a good friend.

"My date didn't work out the way I hoped," she said.

Estelle looked genuinely confused. "That's a shame. He seemed crazy about you," she said, but she didn't push Abbey to explain. "You can still take the night off," she added.

"I don't think so. This is where I need to be," said Abbey, ignoring the worried look on Estelle's face.

CHAPTER 42

INTUITION

For Olivia, writing *Mill Town Girl* was like writing a story she knew very well, because her story was about what she loved most in the world. Taking the story from the page to the stage was hard work. At first, she thought about directing the play herself. Being playwright and director can be both fulfilling and risky. An objective eye is important, because the writer knows the narrative in their heart, but it's unknown, a new story, to the audience. Directors bring their own art to a production.

Olivia had been working hard day and night to get ready for the show's opening. She was at the theater when her phone buzzed. It was on silent because she was working, and the actors were rehearsing. She saw Estelle's name, got up quietly, and walked to the back of the theater and into the lobby.

"Estelle," she said, "is everything okay?" It was unusual for Estelle to be calling on a busy Friday night at the diner.

"Hello, Olivia," she said. "I'm sorry to bother you, but I'm worried about Abbey."

She had been concerned about her sister too, sick with worry until they got the results back from Dr. Song. But the tumor was at an early stage, and Abbey was going to be fine ... *unless she's she not telling me something?* Olivia did feel a bit like Abbey was avoiding her. It was subtle—not returning a text, not spending as much time together.

"What is it? What's wrong?" she asked hurriedly.

"I'm not sure. Perhaps it's nothing," said Estelle. "But she is working so much ... and so hard."

Olivia relaxed a little. Abbey was one of the most dedicated people she knew, and working hard was characteristic behavior.

"You know Abbey," said Olivia. "Nobody works harder than she does, unless it's you, Estelle."

"That's not all," said Estelle. "She had a date last week with a nice young man named Lan. Something must have gone wrong. She won't talk to me about it, and if she's not working herself to death, she's in her office crying."

This caught Olivia's attention. Although she had not met Lan, Abbey had told her all about him, how they met on the plane and went to the Dining Car. Why wouldn't she have mentioned a date, and how could it have gone so badly? That was very un-Abbey like.

"Thank you for calling, Estelle," said Olivia. "I'll call her now."

"I'd wait until after the dinner rush," she said. "She's in her zone right now, and I think her phone is in the office."

"Okay, then I'll call after rehearsal wraps up," said Olivia.

There was a brief silence.

"Olivia, you know, you girls are much more than business owners to me. You're like my family."

256

It was true. Estelle didn't move to Rock Hill for the money. She did it because she had a good feeling about the girls.

"I know, Estelle," said Olivia. "And we feel the same way about you."

They both hung up, and Olivia got back to work, but her mind was on her sister. She walked back into the theater, and Rachael was working with the director on the musical finale, which ends with the opening of the New York Diner. The director had suggested they change the name of the play to *New York Diner*, but Olivia held her position.

For her part, Rachael had poured herself into the play that centered on Abbey, but she had not spoken with her friend in months. As she tried to work through her broken heart, Rachael had established a firm boundary with Olivia about the "Abbey situation." They would not discuss it, to make sure it would not have a negative impact on their friendship.

Abbey insisted that Olivia understand that Rachael was the person most innocent and most injured by the entire affair. Olivia understood, but she knew Abbey was carrying a burden of guilt, shame, and ultimately, loss. She felt helpless as her sister suffered silently. Practically everyone she knew, herself more than anyone, had placed Abbey on a pedestal, but she was as human as anybody. *How can you stop a falling star?* Olivia reflected on that thought, realizing Abbey must have wondered the same thing about her after her fall from Miss America. They were even more alike than she thought possible.

After rehearsal, Olivia tried to call Abbey, to no avail. She sat and stared at her phone, then tried the number again. Still no answer. She stood and paced for a moment, then sat again.

It was obvious that Olivia was distracted. "Is something wrong?" Rachael asked.

Olivia hesitated, trying to adhere to the boundary.

"I don't know," Olivia said tentatively. "It's Abbey."

Rachael's eyes fell to the ground and her head bowed slightly as she tried to find her center.

"Oh," she said. "I, um … guess I better be getting home." Boundaries only work if they are respected. Although she desperately wanted to know more, she could never be a disinterested party or a friend on the sidelines with Abbey. Some people can sit on the side of a pool, content to dangle their feet in the water. She was either all in or all out.

How had everything gone so wrong?

At this point, she didn't know if she was more distraught about losing Abbey or losing Chalie. Their therapist had told her it was not a contest. Wasn't it though? She felt like they were all contestants striving to win some sort of prize. Love and affection, or perfection?

Rachael gathered up her music and copy of the script and walked out of the theater. Olivia watched sadly as Rachael walked away. She could hardly believe they were opening tomorrow. She walked to the stage and discussed the last scene with the director, then tried Abbey's number again.

"Hey, sis," came Abbey's voice. "Sorry I missed your call. It was a busy night."

Her voice sounded okay, but subtly off. Like when you check the expiration date because you can't be sure if the milk is starting to sour. It could just be that she was tired.

"I thought as much. My week has been kind of crazy too. I was just finishing rehearsal," said Olivia. "Anyway, Estelle called me earlier. She was worried."

"About what?" said Abbey, feigning ignorance. Her voice sounded cheerful but contrived, even to her own ears. She knew she couldn't conceal her pain from Olivia, not even over the telephone, but she tried to keep the facade for a bit longer. She knew Olivia wanted to be let in, but if Abbey told her … it became real.

"Abigail, what is wrong?" Olivia demanded. Even with the turmoil of the past few months, Abbey had been Abbey. Now Olivia was picking up on something new. Abbey never acted like this with her, closed and evasive. Throughout their lives, they stood together against the storms.

"I'm just tired. How are your rehearsals going?"

Any other time, Olivia might have enjoyed discussing the progress of her rehearsals.

"Don't change the subject! And please don't shut me out," said Olivia.

"Today wasn't my best day," said Abbey, hesitating as she searched for a believable lie. "It was a slow morning, and I closed early after lunch."

"Oh?" said Olivia, surprised. Closing early was not characteristic of her sister.

"Then, last week with Lan, I wasn't myself I guess," she paused as her mind flooded with thoughts from that afternoon, exactly what she wanted to avoid. "I was worried about the diner—I don't know, but I was tired and not too into the date or whatever. So he brought me home, and I guess I had a little pity party."

Olivia wasn't buying it. Abbey's story didn't fit. "So you closed because it was slow?" she asked.

"Yes," snapped Abbey.

"And you were rude because you were tired?"

The phone line was silent.

"Abbey, why are you lying to me?"

Still no answer.

"I'm coming over," she said.

"Wait," said Abbey finally. "Please ... look, I'm okay. Can we just talk tomorrow morning?"

Olivia hesitated. "Well, okay. I'll see you in the morning," she said reluctantly, now certain that Abbey was hiding something.

CHAPTER 43

OPENING DAY

It was Saturday morning, and *Mill Town Girl* was opening that night. Opening night is traditionally when a play is presented to critics and the press, but it's not the first presentation. That takes place in preview performances, which are full-on paid performances that are discounted, but they are not rehearsals. Olivia was excited with nervous anticipation. She was not unaccustomed to crowds and theaters, but this felt different.

Mill Town Girl was marketed as Olivia's life story, and in a way it was. Really, it was the story of her life through the eyes of her sister. It was a story of Abbey and Olivia, but Rachael and Aliyah were costars.

Although Abbey's character was the central character in the plotline, Abbey had remained distant and excluded herself from every aspect of the production. She stayed away because it was the only thing she could do for Rachael.

Olivia pulled into her parking spot at the diner, then sat at a table like she had done hundreds of times. She looked around for her sister, but Abbey didn't come to fill her cup. Estelle did.

"Good morning," the older woman said, turning over her cup. "Coffee?"

She nodded. "Where's Abbey?" Olivia asked, a touch too brusquely.

"She called in sick," Estelle said, her eyes fraught with worry.

In all her life, Olivia could not remember Abbey ever calling in sick.

"I'll wait on the coffee," said Olivia, standing.

Estelle looked relieved as Olivia rushed out the door.

It was a cold spring morning, and she shivered as she got back into her car.

Springtime in Rock Hill is blanketed in yellow pollen on the car windshields. The yellow floats on top of puddles after the rain, leaving pollen rings on the street curbs. The temperature can be warm as summer or, like that morning, cold as January. Rain can fall in a light mist or with sheets of water and hail, as if angry clouds were opening to pour out torrents of tears from heaven.

The house on Oakland was just a few blocks away, and she was there in minutes. To her relief, Abbey's car was in the driveway, but to her surprise, there was a For Sale by Owner sign in the front yard. Olivia's relief gave way to conflicted emotions. It was unsettling to see the sale sign. Abbey hadn't talked about selling. She realized Abbey hadn't been talking about a lot of things.

The front door was unlocked. Walking into the house always brought a wave of emotion. It smelled like home: coffee and old wood, smoke and lavender. The door made the same sound it always had upon opening, and the light came through the windows with the same golden sparkle. So many things were the same, but something was also different.

"Abbey?"

Her sister already had a cup of coffee waiting for her.

"I knew you would come," said Abbey. She sat at the table, lovely as ever, but looking somehow, for the first time, frail.

"You weren't at the diner on a Saturday morning," said Olivia.

"I'm tired," she said. "I was planning to go in by ten, and of course, I am taking tonight off." She took a sip of coffee. "It's opening night, if you recall."

Olivia smiled, then remembered the sale sign.

"You're selling the house?"

Abbey gave her a crooked smile, then shrugged her shoulders. "I just put the sign out this morning .... We'll see what happens."

"But why?" asked Olivia. The house was a connection between them and between a past they both cherished.

"Do you want it?" asked Abbey. "Do you want the house?"

Olivia had never thought the house would leave their possession. It was like a known thing that didn't need to be spoken about.

"Well, yes," said Olivia. "This house is a part of me."

"Okay," said Abbey. And that was that.

Olivia was both frightened and irritated by Abbey's artificial indifference. "Why did you lie to me last night?"

Abbey knew she had to talk with her sister, but it was opening night. The timing was awful. She sighed. *Is there ever a good time for bad news?*

"My diagnosis was upgraded," she said. "Remember how Dr. Song told us the results were preliminary. Yeah, well, so much for that."

"What does that mean?"

"Ovarian cancer," she said flatly. "Dr. Song said the cancer was an early stage and that I'll be okay." Abbey did not tell her about the additional surgery. The thought of losing her other ovary and her breasts overwhelmed her, and this was a big night for Olivia. Abbey wanted her to be happy.

"So what's next?" asked Olivia.

"I have a follow-up in two weeks," she said.

"I'm coming with you," Olivia said firmly, not intending to be dissuaded.

"No. Your play will be closing. You need to be here," said Abbey.

This was not the first time Olivia had to be in two places at once. She was on a stage when their mom died.

"No. I'll be there with you."

Abbey knew the cancer would claim parts of her she didn't want to lose, but she didn't want it to take anything else away from her sister.

"Let's talk about it tomorrow," said Abbey. "Right now, you should focus on tonight …. Are you nervous?"

Olivia was nervous, not so much about the opening, because she had seen all the rehearsals and was confident it was going to be well received by the audience. Her anxiety was about her sister.

"I guess I'm a little bit nervous," Olivia admitted.

"Me too," said Abbey. "I also haven't seen Rachael in forever. I wonder if she'll acknowledge me."

Abbey refilled her coffee cup, and Olivia noticed the slightest tremble in her hand.

"John will be there," Olivia said, changing the subject.

Abbey's mood lightened at the thought of John coming to see Olivia. "When is he coming?"

"Not until curtain time," said Olivia matter-of-factly. "You will be sitting together, with Aliyah and Jonas." She and Rachael would be backstage.

"Oh my God," Abbey said, pointing an accusing finger at Olivia. "You're in love."

Olivia rolled her eyes and feigned indifference, but she knew Abbey was on target. "I have to get going," was all she said.

Abbey nodded knowingly. "I have to go too." She knew that Olivia needed time for her emotions to age. As they walked out together, Olivia pulled the For Sale sign out of the ground, and Abbey tossed it into the garbage can.

CHAPTER 44

CURTAIN TIME

Olivia was, in spite of her denial, nervous after all. It wasn't Broadway, but there was genuine interest in her play, and Olivia still had pretty good name recognition. Plus, courtesy of Aliyah, online influencers, theater critics, and other movers and shakers would be in the audience. Aliyah knew how to market. The buildup in the Charlotte metro through radio, TV, and online advertising had been done with precision.

Olivia used the dressing room to change into her new dress, which was black, strapless, and could have worked for a night at the opera or an iconic New York nightclub.

John arrived dressed in a stylish black tux. His eyes visibly widened when he saw her, and she was glad he noticed.

"Olivia! Damn, you look stunning," he said. He didn't want to gush, but to him it wasn't flattery; it was just true.

She chided playfully at his choice of words.

"Strong language for an apostle," she said with a smile.

He smiled back. "There's a time for everything and a season for every activity under heaven."

"Every activity?"

"Yes, every activity," he said, then kissed her.

He held up a Starbucks coffee in one hand—hot and black—and a bottle of sparkling grape juice in the other. "For before and after," he said.

This time, she kissed him, then grabbed the coffee.

Rachael arrived with Aliyah and Jonas, and Olivia introduced them to John.

"So this is John the Baptist," said Aliyah. "You know, we have known about you for years." She told him how Abbey had recounted their first meeting.

"The infamous Last Supper breakfast at the Dining Car," said John, chuckling as he shook hands with Jonas. "Nice to meet you."

"I honestly never thought I would see John again," said Olivia, who looked to the door every time it opened.

"Where is Abbey?" John asked.

There was an awkward silence, and Rachael looked away. Olivia had not talked with John about Abbey's affair or her upgraded diagnosis, but it was obvious from the silence that something wasn't right, so he moved on.

"You both look beautiful," he said to Rachael and Aliyah. "For that matter, so do you, Jonas."

They all laughed, except Olivia. She was distracted. The cast and orchestra had arrived and were warming up. Soon, people began filling the room, but Abbey still wasn't there.

Olivia and Aliyah began to meet and greet while Rachael walked with John and Jonas to their seats. The two men talked about college basketball, while Rachael sat staring at the empty stage. Aliyah returned and asked Jonas to meet their investors, leaving John and Rachael sitting alone. At first John sat quietly, but he could tell something was out of place for the occasion.

"Are you okay?" he asked.

"I apologize," Rachael said. She liked his direct manner and the warmth of his smile. He seemed concerned. "I'm dealing with some personal issues … ghosts, you might say."

He thought for a moment at her reaction to Abbey's name.

"Ghosts?" he asked.

"Not real ghosts," she said with a slight smile.

John nodded and turned his body toward her. "I understand your meaning. I'm not sure I've ever met someone *not* haunted by something in their past."

Rachael was trying not to get emotional. She tried to focus on the fact that she had her makeup on and didn't want her mascara to run. But she was at the premier of a musical featuring her music. Music she had written about Abbey. While some songwriters begin with the musical score, or the sound of the notes strung together in harmony, Rachael always started with words—written from her heart.

"I used to think that love could change things, but …" her voice lowered to a whisper as she tried to swallow down her heartache, "love can't change the past."

"That's true," he acknowledged, "but it can change the future."

She excused herself politely and walked to the ladies' restroom.

It was almost curtain time, but Abbey's seat was empty. Olivia was having a difficult time focusing on anything else. She stood up and walked toward the side aisle. John followed her silently as the overhead lights dimmed and her play opened for the first showing. John reached out and stopped her when they entered the lobby.

"What's going on?" asked John.

"Abbey's in trouble," she said.

"What kind of trouble?"

"I don't know," she said, "but I have to leave."

"All right then, let's go."

"No, wait," she said. "I have to see Abbey alone."

He looked at her, worried. "Call me as soon as you can."

She walked to the big theater doors.

"Wait," he said, running to her. "It's cold out there." Once again, he found himself taking off his jacket and draping it over her shoulders.

She thanked him with a quick hug and walked quickly to her car, inhaling the smell of him from his jacket.

All the lights were off when Olivia pulled into the drive. Quietness hung in the air like when you're alone in a dark forest. The front door was unlocked and slightly ajar. She was afraid but opened it wide.

"Abbey?" she said loudly.

It was dark as a cave and cold inside the house. She shivered as she reached for a light in the foyer. She somehow knew Abbey was not in the kitchen, nor in her bedroom. She walked to the dark staircase that led to the turret.

The heavy door was closed, and she pushed against it hard to open it. Inside, light from a waning crescent moon revealed her sister's shadow in the corner.

"Abigail?" she said softly, but the shadow didn't move.

The windows in the turret were all open, and the night air was frigid.

"My God, Abbey, what are you doing?" She walked up to her sister and touched her shoulder. Her sister's skin was so cold.

"You shouldn't be here," Abbey said from the darkness. "It's your opening night."

The flatness in her sister's voice was as chilling as the wind outside. Olivia turned and closed the window nearest them.

"Let's not worry about that, sis," she said. "You know what they say, the show must go on."

Abbey just sat, trying to push back against a wall of her emptiness. "I heard about this forest in Japan," she said, not bothering to wipe away her tears, "where people go to die."

She was sitting on the damp wood with her arms hugging her knees, shivering in the night air. Olivia took off John's coat and wrapped it around her, then sat down at her side.

"What if it's my time?" asked Abbey.

"No!" Olivia cried. "Why—" She choked back a sob. "Why does it have to be your time?"

"I don't know. Dad died, and the world didn't seem to pause," Abbey said, wiping her nose on the back of her hand. "Then Mom, and ..." she swallowed hard. "I just don't think I have it in me to fight this thing."

At first, Olivia couldn't find words. Her insides began to tremble, not from cold, but from fear. "I've lost everyone else," she said, "I can't lose you."

Neither said another word for a few minutes. Then Olivia looked out the window at the porch. "Remember when that soldier came to the door?"

Abbey nodded. She remembered with such clarity and emotion. She could feel the hollow weight in her stomach.

Hear the sound of her mother's cry and the sound of the silence that followed.

Olivia reached out and laced her fingers around hers, just like she did that afternoon.

"I dreamed about Mom last night," said Abbey. "It's like she was alive, and she was so pretty. She didn't have cancer or depression."

Olivia's eyes welled up with tears again. She fought them back and stood up. "Come on, let's get out of here and take a walk." She helped Abbey to her feet.

They walked along the path they knew so well, silently winding their way through the neighborhood, along College Lake, through the fairway on Winthrop's golf course, until they came to the Civitas statues.

Pain makes its own pathways in the mind. With enough repetition, it becomes a well-worn path that's hard to leave.

They sat together under the Lightning Civita as a misty rain started to fall, holding each other for comfort and to stay warm. Abbey looked up at her Civita and saw in her face a strength but also a sadness she hadn't noticed before. Yes, all those years ago, even after the girls had fought and petitioned, the city had sanded down the statue's nipples. Still, she stood there, facing the city, offering her gift. Sad, but still strong, still beautiful.

"I feel disconnected, almost vacant. I don't know what to do," said Abbey, leaning her head on Olivia's shoulder, looking up at the statue.

"About cancer?" asked Olivia.

"About anything," said Abbey. "It's hard enough being who I am. I can't be who I'm not …. I'm just lost."

A car passed on Dave Lyle, briefly shining light in their eyes.

Olivia nudged her sister. "Remember what Dad used to tell us about getting lost in the woods?" she asked.

Abbey nodded.

"Anyone can get a little lost," said Olivia. "The important thing is, when you get off track, stay calm."

Abbey started to tremble from the cold and from her fear. Olivia moved closer, wrapping John's coat around them both.

"Why are there so many ways to die, but only one way to live?" asked Abbey.

They sat silently under the guardians.

Then Rachael and Aliyah came running up the trail.

www.ingramcontent.com/pod-product-compliance
Lightning Source LLC
Chambersburg PA
CBHW031939010726
47493CB00007B/1988